KICKSTART
my heart

LACEY BLACK

BURGERS & BREW Crue

Lacey Black

Kickstart My Heart

Burgers and Brew Crüe, book 1

Lacey Black

Walker

At exactly eleven o'clock, I slip a quarter into the old jukebox on the back wall. The bar is silent as they await tonight's selection. My bar, my choice, and tonight, I'm feeling a little rowdy. The opening melody of "Dr. Feelgood" blasts through the speakers, resulting in a loud cheer from tonight's patrons. As I make my way back behind the bar, I get a few high fives from the guys and even more phone numbers slipped into my palm from the ladies. I wish I could confirm they're all single, but the truth is they're not.

Just a typical Saturday night at Burgers and Brew, the place I co-own with my three best friends. We all have our forte within the business, and mine's behind the bar. Mixing drinks and slinging beers. That's my life, and damn, what a life it is.

I slap Jasper on the back as I slide under the bar and jump right back in to filling drink orders. Everyone's singing along, word for word to the ol' 80's hair band tune, as part of our weekend ritual. It's an ode, a salute to our college days and the band we all grew up listening to. We built this business, taking an old brick building in downtown Stewart Grove and turning it into a staple.

Jasper's the man in the kitchen, the one who comes up with the mouthwatering burger creations we're known for. Isaac is the numbers guy, the man who keeps us in the black and our taxes completed on time. Jameson's the muscle because he's big and tattooed. But he's more than that. Jameson is talented as fuck with a guitar and serves as our house musician Friday and Saturday nights. Then there's me. Walker Meyer, bartender extraordinaire, who keeps the beer flowing, the panties melting, and the tips rolling in.

We're the Brew Crüe, and damn proud of it.

"Dance, dance, dance, dance," the crowd starts to chant, encouraging me to do what I do every weekend when we play Mötley Crüe.

Dance.

When I glance over at Jasper, he's already shaking his head, but there's no missing his wide grin. He knows what's coming. Placing my hands on the bar top, I jump, hoisting myself up on the aged oak. Patrons erupt into cheers as I grin down at them. Mostly, at the ladies. The single ones and even the not-so-single ones. No, I'm not taking any of them home, but that doesn't mean I can't give them one hell of a show.

I twist my ballcap around so it's on backward and start to swing my hips. Mama blessed me with moves, which helps almost double my tips every night. Women go crazy for a man who can dance. That's evident by the number of panties that'll be thrown behind the bar in a matter of moments.

Swaying my hips, I do a little dip and grind, popping my ass out and sending the ladies in the front row into cardiac arrest. They scream and reach for my pant legs, digging their nails into the denim. Instead of shaking them off, I wink and carefully walk a few steps away. Then, when we get to the refrain in the song, I throw my arms out to the side and belt out the words, everyone singing along with me.

It's like karaoke.

But better.

As the song winds down, I steal the drink in Jasper's hand and hold it up over my head. Everyone in the bar does the same. We sing. I dance and drink. The panties start flying.

When an old Hank Williams' song starts up on the jukebox, I throw the crowd a wave and a grin and hop off the top of my bar. Drink orders come flying, and it's all we can do to keep up with them. By the time I holler last call, we're exhausted. Jameson starts to shoo everyone out, including the tall blonde who has been throwing me those fuck-me eyes for the last thirty minutes. Oh yeah, she was ready to go home with me, but little does she know, I don't fuck where I eat.

I don't sleep with employees or patrons, no matter how much they try.

Period.

And they *do* try.

A lot.

Kallie, one of the bartenders, heads out to start cleaning tables, while Jameson follows behind, picking up the chairs and placing them on top of the tables. Jasper plays some ZZ Top, relaxing a bit after working all night in the kitchen.

"Hey, Jameson, grab a case of Ultra," I holler to my friend, who helps me stock the coolers for tomorrow once the chairs are off the floor.

"What else do you need?" Jameson asks before entering the walk-in cooler.

"Two Bud Lights, a Busch Light, and probably two Coors Lights," I reply after a quick scan of the case.

He throws me a salute and vanishes through the heavy door.

"Where's Numbers?" I ask, as Jasper returns to the bar. I'm referring to Isaac, our number-loving friend.

"Where do you think?" Jasper asks, twisting the cap off a bottle of water and tossing it in the trash. Once he takes a healthy pull from the bottle, he starts gathering up trash bags from the receptacles behind the counter. "Newton's always in his office."

Newton, as in Isaac Newton. The *other* nickname for Numbers. Fitting, isn't it?

Jameson slides cases of beer out the door, so I head over to help carry them behind the bar. When Jameson returns with the rest, we get to work filling back up the coolers. Kallie restocks bottles of liquor, making note of the ones getting low or that sold really well throughout the weekend. It helps make my Mondays a little easier when I inventory and order.

"How'd we do tonight, boys?" Numbers asks, making his grand entrance.

I glance at my watch. "It's twelve thirty. What the hell have you been doing up there?" I ask, washing the rest of the dirty glasses and placing them in the rack to dry.

"Working, just like you," he retorts dryly. Isaac moves to the cash register and starts to close it out. He's not always here when we close, but everyone tries to stay on Saturday nights, our busiest night of the week.

Grinning, I occupy myself with cleaning everything up. By one, floors are swept and mopped and everything is stocked and shut down. Kallie signs out on the iPad and Jameson walks her to her car, as he does every weekend. Finally, it's just me and my three partners left in the now-empty building.

"It was a good night," Numbers says, as he finishes off his bottle of water.

"No issues, which always means a good night," Jameson adds, referring to the occasional fight that breaks out in the bar. It doesn't happen too often, mostly because the locals know not to start shit inside this place. Jameson's scary on a good day, but when he's here, he takes his job very seriously. Yet, throw in a little booze and any situation can go from zero to holy shit in less than five seconds flat.

"We sold out of the meatloaf burger tonight, so no complaints from me," Jasper adds.

Burgers and Brew is divided into two large sections, the bar side and the restaurant. Our specialty is gourmet burgers, an idea Jasper had one night in college when we couldn't find a good burger joint anywhere near the campus. He vowed when he opened his own place, it would have the best burgers in town. He's more than accomplished his dream, serving food seven days a week.

I stick my third of the tips into my pocket and throw Jameson his cut. Kallie took hers before she left. "Thank you," he grumbles in that gruff voice.

"Let's get out of here, boys," I holler, shutting off the lights above the mirrors. There's one strip left, lighting the way to the back door.

The night air is cool for late August in Ohio, but I think it's fucking perfect. This is the type of season I'd take all year long. Leaving the windows open at night is the best sleeping weather ever. The only thing that would make it better is to have a naked woman beside me. But that's not gonna happen. When I have someone over, they don't spend the night. I don't snuggle or cook breakfast in the morning. I want none of the bullshit that resembles a relationship.

Period.

"See you tomorrow," Jameson hollers, heading over to his vintage Harley Davidson. He has a Nova in the garage but prefers the bike when he can ride it.

"Later," I reply with a wave, heading for my 1986 Jeep CJ-7.

I wait in the lot until Isaac and Jasper are both in their own vehicles before I pull out onto the main artery through town. The streets are deserted as I drive home, a welcomed reprieve from the heavier traffic of going into work mid-afternoon.

By the time I pull into my driveway and open my garage, I'm more than ready to be home. A hot shower is calling my name. I throw my Jeep keys on the counter and head straight for the bathroom. As the water heats up, I move to my bedroom, tossing my wallet and phone on my dresser and stripping out of tonight's clothes. Dark jeans and a black Burgers and Brew sleeveless T-shirt are pretty much my standard wardrobe, and I don't see that changing anytime soon.

The moment I step under the shower spray, I feel my body finally relax. This is my second favorite way to unwind after a long night. Sure, I could have easily found someone to come home with me, but I really try not to take a bar patron home. Last time I did, I thought she was gonna boil my bunny. Even though I was very clear that our time together was just sex, she didn't like being asked to leave. It took forever before she finally left, but then she showed up the next morning with bagels, wearing a thong bikini.

It was March.

Five days of madness and one restraining order later, I vowed to never bring home one of those numbers I'm given most nights at work.

How do I meet women, you ask?

Easy.

The grocery store. True story. Do you know how many horny, single women are buying food on a random Tuesday night? My favorite is when I find them in the frozen section buying ice cream. There's only one reason a woman buys three pints of ice cream in the middle of the week, and that's because the douche she was dating fucked up. That's when I get fucked. Because they're not looking for forever. They're looking to numb the pain.

I can handle that.

Of course, I don't find all my lady friends in the grocery store. I've met plenty running through the park or even at the movie theatre. All I'm saying is there are a number of options available if you know where to look.

And I'm an expert on looking.

After my shower, I slip my phone on the charger and settle on a playlist. Nirvana starts to play through my Bluetooth speaker, filling my bedroom with enough noise to ease me into sleep. I don't know why I need music, but I do. Always have. Even as a child, my parents said I had to have the radio on to fall asleep.

As Kurt Cobain sings about smelling like teen spirit, I finally drift off to sleep.

Mondays are busy, but for a different reason than other days of the week. Monday is my "office" day. Inventory, placing orders, and our partner meeting takes up a big chunk of my day. I never schedule myself to work behind the bar on Mondays, and usually have one bartender throughout the week, since it's lighter than the weekend. But I'm always there, so if I'm needed behind the counter, I can jump in at any time.

I'm in the storage room, counting liquor bottles and filling out my weekly order form. Def Leppard spills from the jukebox and echoes down the short hallway. The sound of heavy boots thump over the hair band tune, and I already know who's heading my way before he enters the room.

"Jasper's all pissed off again," Jameson announces as he comes around the corner.

"What's new?" I ask, wondering what our finicky chef is in an uproar about now.

"He's going to have a heart attack before he's forty," my broody friend proclaims.

I snort. "We said the same thing in college. How he made it past twenty-five is beyond me. What's got his panties in a bunch this morning?"

"Another server called in sick. He yelled at Numbers to find him reliable help or he was going to do it himself."

That makes me laugh. Jasper is a hell of a cook, but his people skills are lacking. He's the boss in the kitchen, plain and simple, and can be a little pushy or hard to work with. But really, he just wants everyone to do their job. He knows everyone makes mistakes yet struggles to accept them. We know it and love him for his strong personality, but also have no trouble putting him in his place when needed.

We tend to go through servers quickly. At least those who aren't truly committed to the job. The ones who are make great tips, and if you can deal with a hot-headed boss, then you're golden. If you show up when you're scheduled and do your job, you're going to be just fine.

"Isaac made some calls and had two interviews earlier. He wants to hire both and train them together. This way, if one doesn't work out, we still have the other to fill the hole."

"Day shift?" I ask. For some reason, it's harder to fill that shift than the night one. Nights are covered by those who attend the nearby community college mostly. The tips are slightly better, since we're usually busier for dinner than lunch. But don't count our noon crowd out. This place is still plenty busy, and those servers make damn good money too.

"Yep," Jameson confirms, jumping right in and helping me count cases of brew.

Our Server Manager, Gigi, is an older woman with decades of experience. She handles the training and scheduling of our servers, and also works the lunch crowd with two others. She's fun, yet incredibly efficient, and isn't afraid to put Jasper in his place when he starts to get a little out of line. We love her, that's for sure.

We spend the next thirty minutes inventorying, and while I head to my small office to place this week's order, Jameson heads off to tune his guitar on our small corner stage. We don't hire bands, usually, but we don't need to. Jameson is one hell of a musician, and his acoustic sessions on Friday and Saturday nights draw a damn good crowd.

When the orders are placed and my stomach growls, reminding me I haven't eaten lunch yet, I slip out of my small space and head down the hallway. My destination is the kitchen to grab a quick snack before our owners' meeting, but I'm stopped in my tracks. There's a woman walking in the opposite direction, and for some reason, I'm enthralled. Her long, blonde hair hangs down her back in long waves and her black pants form to her ass like a second skin. And her hips—fuck—the sway of her hips has my cock getting hard in no time flat. For some reason, I can't seem to make myself move my feet. I just stand there, watching her go.

Just before she pushes through the door that leads outside, she stops. Slowly, she turns around, and the craziest thing happens. I'm struck by lightning. Not literally, but damn, does it feel like it. My heart is pounding as our eyes meet from about fifteen feet apart. Even through the slightly darkened hallway, I can see the emerald green in her eyes. She has the creamiest white skin, almost too pale in comparison to my darker coloring, and her makeup is subtle, not nearly as smoky and dark as I'm accustomed to seeing here.

She's simply breathtaking, and I want her as mine.

"Hey, man," Isaac says, coming up behind me and slapping me on the back. "Did you meet Mallory Sargant?"

"Mallory?" I ask, my eyes still glued to the beauty before me.

"Yeah, Mallory. She's our new lunch server."

Just like that, I'm doused with a bucket of ice water. My heart drops into my shoes and my shoulders probably visibly sag. She's a server. Of course she is. Mallory is an employee of Burgers and Brew, which can only mean one thing.

She's off-limits.

Mallory

Blue eyes.

That's all I notice. The most unique blue eyes I've ever seen. They're light, yet have a darker navy ring around them. They're magnificent, really, and I can't seem to look away, even though I try.

"Mallory, this is Walker Meyer, one of the owners. You'll see him over on the bar side if you need alcoholic drinks, but Gigi will go through all of it in more depth tomorrow morning," Isaac says.

I finally pull my eyes away from the tall, muscular guy beside him and smile at my new boss. "Great. I look forward to it. Walker, it was a pleasure to meet you," I reply, stepping forward and extending my hand.

Walker places his large hand in mind. When our palms meet, an electric current zips through my fingers and courses through my veins. It's the most shocking and exhilarating sensation I've ever experienced. "Pleasure, Mallory." The way he says my name, it's like that first lick of an ice cream cone on a hot summer day. I just want to...sigh.

And maybe ask him to say it again.

"Well, Mallory, we'll let you go. You'll meet the rest of the team tomorrow morning. See you at ten," Isaac says cheerfully, throwing me a little wave.

"Thank you, Mr. Thompson," I reply, turning back to the doorway.

Isaac chuckles behind me. "Just Isaac, Mallory. Isaac is fine."

"Right. Sorry." I feel a slight blush return to my cheeks as I give him a quick grin and fly out the door. I don't look back at the other eyes, even though I can feel them on me. Instead, I keep my gaze locked forward, as it should be. My motto is don't look back, and I'm trying to stick to it. Lord knows, my past is nothing to look back on willingly.

I hop into my beat-up Ford Escape and head toward my apartment. It's on the edge of town, just a short ten-minute drive to my new place of employment. It's somewhat mild for late August, which I'm grateful for, since the air-conditioning works at fifty percent on a good day. Instead of grumbling about the temperature of air filtering through, I opt to roll down the windows and let the warm breeze blow my hair.

Smiling, I think back to my interview. I was so stinking nervous. I haven't had to do a formal interview in forever. My last two jobs were cashier at our local grocery store and merchandise stocker at the farm supply store. Both positions I was offered without so much as a glance at my application, much less a reference check. See, my hometown of Gibson, Indiana was small enough where everyone knew everyone, and if you didn't know someone, there was always another employee willing to vouch for you. That's what you get with a town of twenty-four hundred.

The best part about today's interview was the position. Day shift server. That never would have happened in Gibson. All the best shifts are taken by the older servers, and all the later shifts are for those with less seniority. Those usually involved less hours. I always fell in the last category.

As I pull into the dinky apartment parking lot, with potholes the size of buckets, I recall the moment my eyes met Walker's. There was definitely something there. Lust. I could see it written all over his handsome face. I'm not oblivious to the look a man gives a woman when he's thinking about getting her naked. Hell, not that long ago, I was used to seeing that look on a man who I thought adored and cherished me.

Boy, was I wrong.

Rolling up the windows, I slip out of my car and make sure it's locked. This apartment is in a somewhat questionable part of town, but I can't beat the price. Rent and utilities for a two-bedroom, one bath, third-floor apartment for only four hundred a month. You just have to ignore the stained carpet, the yellowed linoleum and ceilings from cigarette smoke, and the window air-conditioning unit that sounds like a plane landing in the living room.

It's home.

I'm making the best of this fresh start.

I hit the dollar store and bought carpet cleaner, some scrub brushes, and a few rugs. I can't afford to repaint it yet, but I'm hoping after a few weeks' worth of tips, I'll have some extra cash saved up for those little details. The landlord made it very clear he wasn't worried about splashing some paint on the walls, so instead of complaining about the dinginess of the space, I decided to take it upon myself to help spruce it up.

As I hit the concrete steps, I slip my hand into my purse and pull out my keys. The front door is propped open, the tenants apparently more concerned about airing out the hallways than their own safety if the wrong person snuck in. I push those thoughts out of my head, though, and head up the stairs. When I hit the platform for the second floor, I make my way down the short hallway to the last apartment on the left. Number 205.

I knock loudly over the sounds of *Wheel of Fortune* coming through the old wooden door. "Just a minute!" the deep, older voice hollers.

The moment the door is unlocked and opened, I smile. "Good afternoon, Mrs. Fritz."

She shuffles back, granting me entrance. "Hey, Mallory. How'd the interview go?"

"Really well," I tell her, entering the apartment that's identical to my own. "I got the job. I start tomorrow." I'm all smiles now, anxious to start earning my own paycheck again.

Mrs. Fritz grins, her aging eyes crinkled at the corners. "Oh, I'm glad," she replies, shuffling toward her old rocking chair.

"Mama!" The sweetest sound ever fills the living room as my daughter comes running toward me.

"Hi, Lizzie Lou. Did you have fun with Mrs. Fritz?"

She nods, her big green eyes sparkling and her blonde pigtails bobbing.

"She was an angel, like usual," Mrs. Fritz adds. She's only watched my daughter on two other occasions, but now that I have my job, she'll be helping me out regularly.

"Why don't you go clean up the dollies and then we'll go home, okay?"

Lizzie nods, running off to the second bedroom where Mrs. Fritz set up a small twin-sized bed and some old garage sale toys for the kids she babysits. "She was no trouble?" I ask, taking a seat on the floral couch that's older than me by a good decade.

"None, dear. She's a good girl."

I instantly smile at the compliment. Even though I might be a tad biased, I think Lizzie is a wonderful little girl. Smart, funny, and compassionate, even at the young age of three. "I'm glad to hear it. Are we okay to start tomorrow on a regular basis?"

"Yes, I'm good. Just as long as you remember I have Bingo at the community center on Wednesdays at four thirty. I never miss Bingo."

"That shouldn't be a problem. I get off work at four, and I'll buzz straight here to get her. You'll be sitting in that folding chair by the time the first ball is called," I assure her, praying I'm right. Isaac said it's rare I'd have to stay past my four o'clock quitting time.

"Well, if anything ever happens, I supposed I could drop her off to you."

"We'll call that our backup plan, Mrs. Fritz. I'll do everything in my power to get here by four-fifteen so you can get to Bingo."

The older woman nods. "I appreciate that, dear. Coverall is creeping up again. Last time it got up to six hundred dollars before someone won it."

Wow, six hundred dollars. What I could do with that money. Hell, I wouldn't even complain about half of that amount. Anything to put more food on the table and make sure Lizzie has what she needs. What little savings I had went toward our move. Burgers and Brew was the third place I applied to and the first offer I received. I'd be silly not to take it, at least for now. I can rebuild my savings, and maybe then, if it's not working out, I can find another job. Until then, I'm all-in as a day shift server at the local gourmet burger restaurant.

"I'll run and check on Lizzie and help her clean up her mess," I say to the old woman watching the television.

When I slip inside the small bedroom, I find my daughter throwing the last doll into the basket. I grin as she heads my way, her arms already extended up. "Thank you for picking up. You're such a good girl," I say before kissing her small cheek. She giggles as I use my nose to tickle the side of her neck.

"Mama, stop it!" Her laughter makes me smile and fills my heart with joy. My daughter's happiness is my only goal in this life. To love and protect her, to give her the life she deserves.

The one we're creating here, in Stewart Grove.

"Okay, Mrs. Fritz, I'll see you tomorrow morning at nine forty." I wave at the woman and lock the door behind me as I go.

Even with the open doors downstairs, the second floor is humid and stuffy. I can only imagine what the third floor is going to feel like. As we trudge up the old, dirty steps, Lizzie tells me all about her short time with Mrs. Fritz. I slip my key in the knob and release the lock, grateful to be inside. The air isn't much cooler, but it's better.

After relocking the door and sliding the chain into place, I say, "Let's go see what we have for a snack."

Lizzie grins from ear to ear. "Cheese!"

I chuckle as we head into the tiny kitchen, my foot catching on the corner of the ripped, worn linoleum. There isn't much in the fridge, but there's enough to get us through a few days. I'm hoping the tips start rolling in tomorrow, and we can restock the cabinets and fridge quickly.

Finding a cheddar and Colby jack cheese stick, I remove it from the wrapper, help my daughter hop up on her booster seat on one of the two chairs left by the previous tenant. No, they don't match the table, but I don't care. We have a place to sit and eat, and it didn't cost me anything. I'm hoping I'll be able to paint that too, when money starts to come in.

I cleaned out my checking and savings to move here. Not that I had a lot to begin with, but it was enough to secure this apartment with first and last month's rent, as well as give me the gas money I needed for the trip. We didn't bring much, just whatever I could fit in my car.

Not that I wanted much from my old life anyway.

Shaking off the unpleasantries of what I left behind, I glance down at my daughter. "Would you like some milk?" Lizzie nods eagerly, taking another bite of her cheese. When I pour the small glass, I take the empty seat beside her. "Tomorrow Mommy starts her new job. That means you get to go play with Mrs. Fritz again. Is that okay?"

Light green eyes gaze up at me. She seems to think about my question before nodding her approval.

"Good. And tomorrow, when I get off work, we'll go to Walmart and grab a few more things for your room. Sound good?"

"Yay!" she exclaims, her blonde pigtails bouncing as she gets excited to go shopping.

Smiling, I reach over and swipe a strand of hair off her forehead. "Finish your cheese and milk, and then I'll turn on a movie, okay?" She agrees, and I just sit there and watch as she sips her milk like a big girl from her favorite purple cup and shoves the last of her cheese stick into her mouth.

When she's cleaned up, we head into the living room. I was able to bring the old twenty-seven-inch television from our old place, along with a well-used DVD player. Lizzie goes over and picks out a Care Bears movie, grabs her purple blanket, and curls up on the couch. I know she'll be out in a matter of minutes.

While my daughter takes a nap, I wash dishes in the sink and prepare for dinner. Mac and cheese and hotdogs. Again. But they're cheap and easy, and Lizzie loves them. There's a noticeable pile of dirty clothes on my bedroom floor, but I hate the idea of leaving Lizzie up here unattended, even to just run down to the basement to start a load of laundry, but considering I only have one pair of black pants, I'm definitely going to need to have to bite the bullet. Maybe when she's asleep I can lock her in here and run down to start a load. It won't take very long, as long as I have everything sorted up here and ready to go.

I glance around my bedroom, which consists of two opened boxes of clothes that also serves as my dresser. There were a few wire hangers left in the closet, and after I rebent them into shape, I was able to hang a few shirts to hopefully help with wrinkle control. Mentally, I add hangers to the growing list of merchandise I'm going to need from the store.

Slipping off the black pants and white button-down shirt I wore to my interview, I hang them back up to wear again tomorrow and throw on a pair of legging capris and a fitted T-shirt. I'll have to provide my own pants for work, but Isaac assured me they'll have five polo shirts ready for me when I arrive tomorrow. I'm grateful I don't have to go out and buy clothes to start the job.

The job.

My mind returns to Walker. Those eyes were the most brilliant blue eyes I've ever seen. Like sapphires sparkling under the Caribbean sun. Throw in chiseled arms and hair a woman could get her fingers tangled in, and you have a recipe for trouble.

But I shake it off.

I have no business thinking about him, or any man for that matter. Especially not Walker, who's basically one of my bosses. I just left behind one I thought was a good guy, who ended up being anything but. My heart starts to race as I think about Devon and the trouble he caused. Of the damage he's done. Of the fact I could have very easily lost my daughter.

I blink back tears and leave my empty bedroom. After making sure Lizzie is still sound asleep on the couch, I slip into the bathroom to take a quick shower. Usually I take one before bed, but I could definitely use it right now, especially since I know the tears are coming and there's no way to stop them.

When I'm alone in the small room and the water is hot—or as hot as I can get it— I finally let them fall unchecked from my eyes. I cry for the life I wanted for my daughter. The one I thought we had but was stripped away in a single moment. I cry for the fact I was naïve and dumb and didn't see Devon for who he really was. And I cry for the future and the big question mark it possesses.

Finally, when the tears subside, I wash my face and my body and get out. I grab a towel to dry off, only to put on the clothes I just took off once more. I stare at my reflection in the mirror. My eyes are tired from lack of sleep and worry, but I'm determined. I'll make a good life, a better life, for Lizzie and me. I'll start my new job tomorrow and earn enough to get settled. Lizzie and I will be fine.

I know it.

Walker

"I hired two new servers today," Numbers announces, as he takes the last empty seat at our table of four.

My mind instantly goes back to the beautiful blonde I met in the hallway. The one who's pushed her way to the front and center of my mind no less than three times already, and it's only been an hour.

"Finally. Do they have experience?" Jasper asks, sipping his water before pushing the fourth plate of food over to Isaac.

"Both do, yes. They start tomorrow. Gigi will be ready for them," he says before taking a hearty bite of his burger. "Mmm, what's this?"

"I call it the Morning BJ," Jasper announces with a wicked grin. All of our burgers have an unusual, and somewhat sexually laced innuendo name to them.

Isaac slowly chews, glancing at the ingredients between the bun. "Is that..."

"Jam? It is. Bacon and jam, hence the BJ. It's onion jam, which is slightly sugared and caramelized onions. I played around with it all night last night, until I got it just right," Jasper says, taking his own bite, slowly chewing and clearly critiquing his masterpiece.

"I really like it," I tell him, already halfway through my burger.

"Me too," Jameson mumbles, his mouth full of food. But Jameson likes just about anything.

"I'm thinking of introducing it in this weekend's menu."

"Definitely," Isaac agrees. "I can get my sister to work on a graphic for social media. Maybe even some teaser ones leading up to it Friday night," Isaac adds, already inputting notes into his phone. His sister, Hannah, helps with our social media accounts, constantly posting and keeping our pages fresh. Apparently, that's pretty important, but I couldn't care less. Sure, I have a Facebook page, but I'm barely on it. Most of my posts are tags from one of my friends.

"I'll make up a fresh burger after we finish our meeting so you can photograph it," Jasper replies.

"Sounds good. Now, anything you want to add for this weekend on the bar side?" Isaac asks, his eyes meeting mine.

Clearing my throat, I wipe my mouth, my wheels starting to turn. We rarely offer deals in the bar, mostly because we don't have to. We don't need a sale or special to draw in the customers, but we will offer them on occasion, especially when we debut a new burger special. "Well, since your hamburger is titled Morning BJ, how about the blow job shot?"

This particular shot is popular for girls' nights or bachelorette parties. Even though there are a few different ways to make it, our recipe consists of half an ounce Kahlua, half an ounce of Bailey's Irish Cream, and a dollop of whipped cream on top. The catch to the blow job shot is you're supposed to take the shot without using your hands. So, girls will set the shot glass on the counter, wrap their lips around the glass, and guzzle the booze, usually leaving a small trace of the whipped cream on their lips.

Blow job shot.

"What are those priced at?" Isaac asks.

"Five," I confirm.

"Will a dollar off still cover our expenses?" he asks.

"Definitely. Both liquors are popular enough, I'll probably amend the order I just placed to add another two bottles of each," I add, swiping a fry through mustard and popping it into my mouth.

"Sounds like a plan," Isaac replies, making more notes in his phone. "I'll have Hannah add it to the graphic."

He moves on to music, asking Jameson about his set for Friday night. We usually publicize a few songs from his set to grab potential patrons' attention. But like the rest of the business, we don't have to promote it too much. Jameson draws a crowd all on his own on Fridays, with or without mentioning a few of the songs he'll be performing.

Isaac goes through our numbers for most of August, complete with bar graphs and pie charts. While the bottom line is important to me, as long as it's in the black, I'm good. I focus on the numbers for my side of the business. Summers are a double-edged sword. Everyone is out and about, enjoying the beautiful weather, but then at the same time, there tends to be more activities we're competing with. Fairs and festivals, sporting events, and family vacations can put a damper on our numbers, but by the looks of things, August of this year was better than August of the last five years.

I know because Numbers added a graph for that too.

When the meeting is over, we clean up our mess and prepare for the early dinner rush. We do a lot of take-out orders between four thirty and five thirty, including curbside pickup, which we just started earlier this year. I don't pay too close attention to all the details, but one of the servers gets a small table section and is in charge of managing the curbside pickups, which are scheduled fifteen minutes apart.

Jameson tinkers with his guitar while I pour a few draft beers to some after-work customers. They're complaining about a coworker who does very little work and takes as much credit for the project as possible. I let them bitch about their day and head down to the far end of the bar where my daytime bartender is getting ready to head out.

"Good day today?" I ask, wiping the top of the hardwood.

"Not bad," Jillian replies, clocking out on the iPad.

Jameson appears almost out of nowhere. "Ready to go?" he asks, motioning for the door. He's always made it a habit of walking female employees out to their vehicles, even in the light of day. He's a damn good guy, if you can get past the gruff and ink.

"Yep," she replies, hopping off the stool and heading toward the back door. "See you Thursday, Walker."

I wave and dive into next week's schedule on the electronic device, checking in on the suits down the bar every now and again. My schedule is a hell of a lot easier than the servers and kitchen staff Isaac and Gigi deal with. I have six total bartenders, all part time, who work various shifts and hours. Jillian is my main day girl. She opens for me and stays until midday four days a week.

Then there's Austin, my weekend day guy. He works as a part-time mechanic during the week and most weekends for me. My weekend night crew consists of Kallie, Kellen, and Dalton, and I also have Selma, a twenty-three-year-old college student, who works Wednesday evenings and also fills in where needed. Some of my team members have been with me for years, which makes me grateful as fuck I don't have the turnover Jasper has. I'd go fucking insane.

I find one time-off request from Dalton for the weekend two weeks from now and fill in around it. It takes me less than thirty minutes to get the next pay cycle's schedule set and send it out to the staff, Isaac included. Then I power down the iPad and stick it under the bar to charge.

Monday afternoon rolls into evening, and I'm fairly busy. Some dinner guests stop over for a drink before they hit the restaurant, and a handful of locals hit us up for a few drinks after work.

In between helping with a few customers, I mentally run through my Tuesday schedule. It's one of my two days off. I always schedule myself off Tuesdays and Sundays. Otherwise, I'd work seven days a week, and did for a while in the very beginning. When it's your baby and you're watching every expense, it's easy to get caught up in bad habits and working yourself to death.

By the time ten rolls around and I lock the doors, I have everything stocked for tomorrow and cleaned. It takes me fifteen minutes to close out the register, lock up the bank bag, and head for home.

It's definitely a lot cooler than it was when I arrived for work, but I decide not to take the time to put the top up on the CJ. Having it down is one of the great pleasures of owning a Jeep. Instead, I throw on a hoodie I keep in the back seat just for these kinds of nights and hop behind the wheel. The only problem is, even with the music turned up and the wind chilling my face, my thoughts still return to Mallory.

I don't even know her, yet I can't stop thinking about her.

That definitely won't do.

Tuesdays are my catch-up day. Laundry, yard work, and grocery shopping are completed on Tuesday, since I'm invited to my great aunt's house every Sunday for lunch. She stopped bitching about not seeing me in church years ago, but I don't push it when it comes to Sunday lunches. Aunt Edna will tan my hide in the front yard and then make me sit on it at the table while she tries to stuff me full of food. She's a feisty woman, but I wouldn't have her any other way.

She's also black.

But blood alone doesn't make family.

My mom was adopted as a young child by my grandparents, Alma and Herschel Washington. My mom, Marie, was one of seven children of all different races and origins taken in and raised by the Washingtons. They didn't care what the color of your skin was. They gave you food, clothes, and enough love to fill the holes left by your past.

When my mom was in high school, she found herself pregnant her senior year. My sperm donor wasn't man enough to step up and take care of a child he helped create, begging my mom to get rid of me. When Mom refused, then so did he. He's never provided for me financial or emotionally, and you know what? Fine. Fuck off. We got by just fine. Of course, we had my grandparents, and even my aunt, Edna.

Edna never had kids of her own, so she's very close to all seven of her nieces and nephews. Most of them have moved away over the years, including my grandparents who relocated to Florida, but there are still a few who stayed in Ohio. Every Sunday, we gather at Aunt Edna's for an incredible home-cooked meal. It'll be my mom, Uncle Donald, and just a single cousin, Jamal. Occasionally, a few cousins from Cleveland will come down and join us.

So today is the day I try to catch up on all the housework and maintenance, because I never know what my Sunday will entail, usually a little of the same at Edna's place. After throwing a load of darks in the washer, I spend a bit of time picking up around the house. I bought a decent-sized three-bedroom ranch home on two acres on the outskirts of town. My nearest neighbor is a half mile away, which is good, considering I like my music loud, especially when messing around the house.

Like now.

Def Leppard is loud as I clean the kitchen and bathroom, the worst jobs ever. I'd rather weed eat the yard with a fucking pair of scissors than scrub bathroom floors, but here I am, on my hands and knees like my mom taught me, scrubbing around the base of the toilet with a Clorox wipe. Apparently, boys can be messy.

When both bathrooms and the kitchen are done and I've run through the shower to clean up, I shut off the music, grab my keys, and head for the door. Usually I like to hit the grocery store before I start yard work, especially on hot days. Backing the CJ out of the driveway, I head for the smaller of the two grocery stores in town.

It's fairly busy for a Tuesday, but that's nothing new. The family-owned business offers a senior discount on Tuesdays, and most of the blue hairs in town take advantage of that five percent discount. When I pull in, I head for the back of the lot, preferring to leave the closer spots open for the older shoppers.

As I walk through the automatic door, Bernice, the greeter, is there with a wide smile on her face. "Hey, Walker."

"Well, good morning, Bernice. How are you today?"

"Oh, I'm well," she replies from her perch on top of a stool. "Your Aunt Edna was here earlier today. I think she got chicken for Sunday."

"Mmm," I say, grabbing the closest cart. "Aunt Edna's fried chicken is what dreams are made of, Bernice."

She nods. "You know, you should find a nice, respectable young woman to take with you Sunday. I think it would really brighten her day."

I smell a setup...

"Yeah? I thought her day would already be bright, considering I'm there."

Bernice chuckles. "Oh, silly boy. Your aunt mentioned during Bingo just last week that you never bring friends over. There was that one." She snaps her fingers. "What is his name?"

"Jameson," I reply, completely amused.

"Yes, him. Good-looking boy, if you're into that sort of thing. And if you are, your aunt would still love you."

I can't help it. I bark out a laugh. "Good to know, Bernice, but I'm not gay. I just don't have a lot of time to date."

"Well, you don't have to *date* them. Back in my day, we would go out on Old Town Road and go parking. There's no shame in a little nookie," she informs me.

I blanch and try to keep those images out of my head. "Listen, Bernice, I gotta grab some stuff and get back home."

"You bring someone with you to Edna's soon. I know! The new Sunday school teacher is a cute young thing. I bet you could court her," she hollers as I start to walk away. "And remember the nookie! It does wonders for your mood!"

Four old women in the produce aisle stop and turn in my direction.

Hell.

I grab the first bag of raw spinach, drop five avocados into a produce bag, and snatch some potatoes without even checking them before hightailing it out of there. It doesn't take me long to fill my cart and head for the checkout. I'm lucky, when I get to the front, Bernice is busy chatting with one of the ladies from her church, so I load up my sacks in the cart, pay for my food, and slip out the door, throwing her a wave as I make my escape.

The late morning sun is high in the sky as I head toward home. There are some older worn-down houses on this end of town, nestled behind the water tower and a public park. A large brick structure stands tall at the edge of town. An apartment building that's definitely seen better days. The front steps are sunken and broken, the bushes so overgrown you can barely see the first-floor windows, and trash strewn in the parking lot. Sad, because it used to be a great looking building, if only someone would put a little TLC into it again.

When I get home, I unload my groceries, put them away, and get back to laundry. I have three more loads to do, plus all the outside stuff. Time to crank back up the tunes and get to work.

Mallory

My first shift yesterday at Burgers and Brew was amazing. Sure, I was nervous. I haven't waited tables in a few years, but it all came back to me quickly. Gigi was patient and encouraging as she trained me and Angela. Plus, I went home with thirty dollars in tips, which was my cut of the tables we handled together.

Now, I'm ready for day two. As I slip in the back entrance and turn to the left, I run smack into a wall. No, not a wall, because big arms wrap around my shoulders and keep me from stumbling back. When I glance up, my eyes connect with those exotic blue ones that invaded my dreams the last two nights.

"Mallory."

I shiver.

Why do I react this way when he says my name?

Shaking my head, I mentally chastise myself. This is one of my bosses. Drooling isn't work appropriate. "Walker, I'm sorry. I didn't see you. I'll be more careful."

He slowly grins. It's a panty-melting smile, one I'm sure he has perfected over the years. "You're fine," he assures me.

We stare at each other for a few long seconds, neither of us speaking. I realize his arms are still around my shoulders, my hands gripping the T-shirt at his sides. Clearing my throat, I pull back, releasing my hold on his clothes and feeling sad when his arms fall away from my body.

"Oh, Mallory, you're here," Isaac says, coming down the stairs from his office. He offers me a smile before turning to his friend. "Have you talked to Jasper yet? He wants your opinion on a promotional idea he has."

"I was heading that way when Mallory tried to tackle me," he says, clearly teasing and making me blush three shades of fuchsia.

"It was an accident," I assure Isaac, who doesn't seem to notice my mortification.

"Well, I'll see you both later," Isaac says, turning and heading down the hallway.

"I, uh," I stammer, throwing my thumb over my shoulder and pointing in that direction.

He smiles.

Dammit.

"Okay, I need to clock in. I'll see you around," I finally spit out before basically turning and sprinting toward the back room.

I push through the door and find Gigi and Marla getting ready to start. We're all in matching polos with the company logo on the front. I slip my purse into my assigned locker, tie my apron around my waist, and slip my phone into the pocket. Gigi told us we could hang onto them, as long as we promised not to abuse them. The only person who would be calling me is Mrs. Fritz, and that's as good of a reason as any to keep it close by.

"Angela quit this morning," Gigi informs me as we head out to start our shift.

"Really?"

"Yeah," she replies with a sigh. "Jasper's difficult to work for. I know that. Hell, he knows that. But he's a really good guy, Mallory. I hope you can stick it out." There's something pleading in her aged brown eyes.

"No worries there, Gigi. I have bills to pay," I state, as I help place silverware rolled in a napkin at my tables. Rent will be due at the end of the month, and there's no way I can risk losing this place. My daughter needs a roof over her head and food in her belly. Getting butt-hurt by a jerky boss is the least of my worries.

"Good," she replies, giving me a kind smile. "I think you're going to fit in nicely here."

Gigi hurries off to help set tables and prepare the menus.

"You're gonna have the middle section today, Mallory," Marla informs me as she fills pitchers with ice water.

I nod, recalling which tables were in which section from my first day of training yesterday. I glance around, movement catches my eye through the open double doorway that leads to the bar. Standing there behind the big, gorgeous hardwood is Walker. He's setting out a glass and filling it with what looks like Coke from the fountain. Even from this side of the building, I can see how big and imposing he is. He plops a straw in the glass and takes a long pull. When he does, our eyes meet again.

"That's Walker," Marla says, coming up behind me and hip-bumping me.

I clear my throat and look away. "I met him Monday after my interview."

"He's a nice guy. Wednesdays are usually his only day shifts, so you won't see him much behind the bar when you're here. He usually works evenings," she states, sticking a stack of straws in her apron and handing me a pile for my own.

I glance back over one more time to find him watching me still. His hands are resting on the bar top, and I can feel the heat of those blue eyes all the way over here. Forcing myself to turn away, I try to push Walker and his sparkling baby blues out of my mind and focus on the task at hand.

My first table is an older couple, who orders classic cheeseburgers with waters to drink. I keep their glasses full, a rule Gigi has for serving the customers. Fill their glasses when they hit half-empty.

Our hostess, Stella, seats a small group of four guys in my section next. I can already tell they're going to be a handful. "Welcome, gentlemen. My name's Mallory. Can I get you something to drink?" I ask, handing each one a menu.

"Coors Light," the first one replies.

"Jack and Coke."

"Whatever Summer Ale you have on tap," the third one states, scanning his menu.

"And I'll have a Miller Lite and your phone number, sugar," the fourth guy says, making the other three chuckle.

I give him a polite smile. "Well, I can definitely handle the beer, but I'm all out of numbers," I reply with a shrug. "I'll go get those drinks and give you a minute to look at the menus."

Slightly rattled, I make my way to the counter to get their drinks, only to realize I'm in the wrong place. I need to head over to the bar for alcoholic beverages.

To Walker.

Knowing the longer they have to wait for a beer, the less of tip I receive, I hold my order tablet in my shaky hand and walk through the doorway. The lighting is less bright on this side of the business, but not too dark. Jameson's sitting at one end of the bar, watching a baseball game on the television, while Walker's down at the other end, talking to an older gentleman in a worn flannel and bib overalls. I head for our ordering point in the middle of the bar. Even though he's speaking with the customer, I feel his eyes on me.

The moment I stop at the counter, he pushes off and heads my way. "I need a Jack and Coke, Coors Light, Summer Ale draft, and a Miller Lite, please," I spit out as soon as he stops in front of me. Walker doesn't move to fill my order, and when I glance up, I find his eyes intently watching me. "What?"

"You okay?" he asks, those blue eyes filled with concern.

"Yeah, why?"

He lifts one shoulder. "You're out of breath and all frazzled."

"Oh," I reply with an awkward chuckle. "I'm fine. Just my first set of tables by myself."

Walker gives me the slightest grin. "Don't worry, you'll be fine," he says, reaching down and grabbing a glass. I watch as he makes the mixed drink, pours the draft beer, and grabs the two bottles from the cooler. "Here ya go."

"Thank you," I reply, carefully lifting the tray up off the counter.

"Anytime, Mal."

Again, I feel his eyes on my body like a caress as I walk away, but I push that out of my mind as I head back to my table. He's completely unnerving me. I definitely didn't have this problem yesterday when Jillian was behind the bar.

Once I deliver the four drinks and take their orders, I check on my first table, and find a third table being seated. I'm busy enough that I don't give Walker another thought for a while. Well, not until the table of four unruly guys decides they need another round. As I'm turning to leave their table, the one who asked for my number drags his hand across my ass. It could easily be accidental, but the way all four of them snicker, I know it was anything but.

I head into the bar, and Walker is already waiting for me. "Same. Coors Light, Miller Lite, Summer Ale draft, and Jack and Coke," I reply, but realize it's not necessary. He's already filling the order before I have it all out. "Thank you."

Before I lift the tray, he reaches out a hand and places it on my arm. "Those guys giving you trouble?" There's something in his tone that gives me pause. When I glance up, I see he's watching them and the corners of his mouth are tight.

"Oh, uh, no. I got it."

He gazes back at me. "If you're sure," he says.

Swallowing hard, I confirm, "I'm sure."

Walker nods once and moves his hand, letting me get back into the restaurant. I deliver the drinks, careful to stay away from any wandering hands, and head over to the kitchen to wait for my orders. I don't have to wait long, and my first table's food is ready moments later. I slip their plates on my tray and head for where the couple is waiting.

"Here ya go," I state, setting each plate down on the table. "Would you like any ketchup or anything else?"

"Ketchup would be great, dear," the woman says.

I notice their glasses are right at half-empty, so I return a minute later with a bottle of ketchup and a pitcher of water. And this is how the next thirty minutes goes. I only have to ask Gigi one question while totaling the couple's check, and I'm easily able to manage my lunch tables.

By the time the foursome of guys have had a third drink and their plates are empty, I stop by to collect their empty dishes. "Can I get you guys anything else?" I ask, clearing the table.

"I don't remember seeing your number," the guy I now know as Tommy replies with a grin. It's a decent grin. Straight, white teeth on display with full lips, but it does nothing for me, not even the slightest hitch in my heartbeat. Definitely not after seeing Walker's smile.

"That's because I'm all out, remember?" I reply with my own grin.

As I move over to grab the fourth and final plate, I feel a hand slide up my leg. I jump, the plates clanking together, but not falling. I try to pull my leg away, but his hand holds me firmly. When I glance down and see his hand on my leg, I start to panic. I don't make a move, but my heart starts to hammer in my chest and my breathing comes out a little choppy.

"You sure you don't want to give it to me, baby?" Tommy mutters, trying to sound all smooth and sexy, but falling way short.

"Is there a problem here?"

I know that voice, and I've never heard it so...tough.

"No, no, man, not a problem. I was just waiting for Sweet Thang here to give me her number," Tommy replies, laughing.

"I believe the lady has already told you no," Walker replies, not laughing in the least.

When I glance back at him, I see his big arms crossed over his chest and his hard eyes laser-focused on Tommy. I reach out with one hand, careful not to drop my tray, and rest it on his muscular forearm. "It's okay, Walker. I'm good."

His eyes meet mine and he relaxes just a bit.

"Yeah, *Walker*, she's fine. And she will be even better once she gives me her number," Tommy smarts off, those lines around Walker's mouth returning once more. His eyes narrow down at the cocky jerk sitting in the chair.

Walker bends down and gets a little closer to the half-drunk customer. "Listen, man. You don't touch my employees—*ever*—or I get involved. Got it?"

Tommy swallows hard and leans back, holding up his hands in surrender. "I see, I see. You're fucking her. That's fine. You could have just said that. When you've had your fun, I'll take my turn."

Walker growls right before he moves. Fast. I almost didn't see it coming. I'm able to step back to avoid being knocked down, but barely. Walker grabs Tommy by the shirt and helps him stand. Tommy stumbles, knocking over a half-full beer bottle, and sending the table into disarray. All I can do is watch in shock and horror as the guests are basically escorted right out the front door.

My very angry boss turns to one of the guys and says, "Go pay the check. And don't forget a fucking tip."

Two of them return to where I stand, shellshocked, and stare at me expectantly. I fumble with my order pad and walk back to the servers' station. I can feel all eyes on me as I try to use the touchscreen. My hands are shaking so dang bad, which only causes tears to well in my eyes.

Suddenly, Gigi is there, taking the pad from my hand and keying in the rest of the ticket. "Seventy-five fourteen," she states politely, yet with a touch of authority.

The Jack and Coke guy pulls out his debit card and pays for the entire bill. When he signs his name on the receipt, he gives me a sympathetic look. "I'm sorry about Tommy. He's not usually like that."

Before I can reply, Gigi hands him his copy of the receipt and says, "Have a nice day."

The guys give me one last look and hightail it out of the restaurant like their asses are on fire.

"I'm so sorry," I stammer, as Gigi turns to look at me.

"Don't you dare be sorry, Mallory. That's not your fault. We don't get too many inappropriate customers in the restaurant, but it does happen. I'm so sorry he touched you. The guys, they don't allow that kind of behavior. If it ever happens, make sure you tell someone right away, okay? One of them, Walker or Jameson, will take care of it."

I nod, blinking rapidly to keep the tears at bay. "Okay."

She smiles a gentle grin. "I think your other tables are all right for a few minutes. Why don't you run in back and take a few deep breaths, and then come back out and jump back in. You're doing a great job, Mallory."

Again, I nod, unable to find the words. Truth is, I want to tell her I don't need a few minutes in back, but I know I do. I'm on the verge of tears and the last thing I want is to cry in front of the customers. It's only my second day, dammit.

I slip through the back hall and into the employees' room. The air is a little warmer back here, but it doesn't feel as stifling as the restaurant. I find myself slipping my phone out of my apron and glancing at my wallpaper photo. It's of Lizzie from her third birthday a few months back. She's smiling widely, her lips covered in chocolate icing from the cupcakes we made. It reminds me of a different time, a better one. Before everything around me started to unravel piece by piece.

The door opens behind me, so I quickly slip my phone back into the apron and turn around. I expect to see Gigi or Marla there, not Walker. "You okay?"

"I'm fine," I reply, my throat suddenly very dry. "I'm sorry to cause such a scene in the middle of the lunch rush."

He steps forward, already shaking his head in disagreement. "I don't want to hear you apologize again, Mal. Not for that. You did nothing wrong. That asshole, or any other one for that matter, has no right to put his hands on you. Got it?"

I nod, my eyes wide as I gaze up at him. He's not the tallest guy I've ever seen, but he's definitely big compared to my average five-foot-five height.

"Good," he replies with a slow smile. When it meets his eyes, it's like his whole face lights up with it. I always thought I was an ass woman, but here I am, completely turned upside down by a smile.

"I should get back out there," I state, making no move to step around him.

Walker nods but doesn't step aside either. Instead, he reaches forward and gently tucks a strand of hair behind my ear, the outside of his finger grazing against my cheek. "Knock 'em dead, Mal," he says, letting go of my hair and stepping aside.

I practically bolt from the back room and return to the restaurant, happy to see a new table being seated in my section. The first moment I pass Gigi at the servers' station, she hands me a fifty-dollar bill. When I glance down in shock, she just whispers, "Your tip from earlier."

Smiling, I slip the bill into my apron and get back to work.

Deep breath.

I've got this.

Walker

"What the hell happened earlier?" Jameson asks the moment I return to the end of the bar where he sits, sipping a Sprite.

"Some douchebag was manhandling the new server," I reply, my blood still boiling, even though it happened almost an hour ago.

My friend practically growls. "I hate that bullshit."

"Me too, which is why I escorted them out the front door." Even now, I still see red when I think about that dick's hand wrapping around her leg. I wish I could say it was luck I glanced up at the right moment, but that'd be a lie. I was watching her as she smiled and chatted with the customers, making her job look so damn easy. The way she moved, the gentle curve of her tantalizing hips, it had me looking into the restaurant every five seconds like a damn lunatic.

"Good. Hope they don't come back," Jameson mutters between sips.

I observe him for a few seconds. He's watching the ball game behind me on the television, but I can tell he's not really seeing it. He's spacing out, his mind a million miles away like he used to do in school.

Of all my friends, I've known Jameson the longest. He was the troublemaker, the rebel in high school. We bonded sophomore year over our utmost hatred for all things math and have been friends ever since.

We met Jasper and Numbers during college. Jameson didn't attend, choosing to work full time as an auto mechanic, but he would often come hang out with me on campus. We went to a fraternity party one night and got to talking to Jasper about the shitty rap music they were playing.

Numbers we didn't meet until a year later and that was by coincidence. Jameson, Jasper, and I were hanging out in the bathroom of some dive bar, smoking something we shouldn't have been. Numbers walked in, wouldn't even make eye contact, and went over to do his business. Right when he started to piss, the smoke alarms went off and water started shooting from the ceiling.

We all ran out of there like our asses were on fire, poor Numbers still trying to zip up. It didn't take us long to realize it was our fault the alarm was going off, in light of a little recreational pot smoking in the bathroom. Soaking wet, we made it to Jameson's Nova, one new friend in tow.

So there you have it.

We became friends because we were…

Wait for it…

Smokin' in the boys' room.

I lean forward, placing my elbows on the bar. "Tell me."

Jameson glances my way, his dark eyes assessing. He digs a cigarette out of his shirt pocket and holds it between his fingers. He's tried quitting a dozen times but can't seem to kick the habit. I wait him out, knowing he'll probably use the need to smoke excuse to get out of this conversation and retreat outside. I'm surprised though when he doesn't.

"I have this idea," he starts, exhaling loudly and resting his own elbows on the bar.

"Tell me," I repeat.

Jameson glances my way, a hint of nerves filters through his facial features. "You know how I've been tinkering around with making beer?"

I nod, remembering a few years back when he bought one of those at-home brewing kits. The first few rounds weren't that great, but he slowly perfected his recipe and now makes some damn good brew. "Yeah, sure."

"I've been looking into, I guess tryin' to figure out, what it might take to start up a brewery."

His confession surprises me yet doesn't at the same time. "Yeah?"

He nods. "I've been researchin' it online, and well, the building next door is vacant."

Easily, I fill in the blanks. "That's a phenomenal idea, man. Are you thinking of doing this yourself or maybe expanding Burgers and Brew?" I know which way I'm leaning, but this is his idea, so I keep my opinion to myself. For now.

His eyes meet mine. "Do you think the guys would be interested?"

"Hell yeah," I state bluntly.

He glances back down at his Sprite. "It would be a way for me to contribute a little more around here," he adds with a shrug.

"What the fuck are you talking about? Some days, you have the hardest job of all of us."

"Maybe on Friday or Saturday nights, but the rest of the week? I feel like I'm just taking up space."

"That's bullshit, Jame. You pitch in over here all the damn time, and even though you won't set foot in the main office, you help everywhere. We appreciate the hell out of you," I say, hating that he feels like he's not contributing as much as the rest of us.

"I know," he replies with a sigh. "I guess, well, this might be a way for me to do more. And I've really enjoyed brewing beer at home."

"It's damn good beer," I add.

He gives me a small, crooked smile. "I think so too. I have the recipe pretty much right where I want it." He takes a deep breath. "It won't be easy or cheap."

"When have we ever wanted easy or cheap, man?" Four guys starting a business from the ground up wasn't either.

"Well, last time Amie was in here, I got both," he replies with a cocky grin. Though, he doesn't mean he's paying her. He's just referring to the fact she's a quick, easy lay whenever she comes into the bar, which sometimes, is often.

I snort a laugh. "True. She's always willing to go for a ride, and I don't mean on your Harley."

Jameson turns serious once more. "What do you think Numbers will say?"

"Well, you say you've been doing research? Make him a pitch. I'll help you. We'll make sure we have the answers ready to go for any questions he might have. I think it's a great idea, man, and it fits our business venture. Our own brewery makes complete sense to me, and I think the others will agree."

"Maybe."

I'm already shaking my head. "No maybe about it. Do it."

Before he can reply, we're interrupted by the clearing of a throat. We glance over to see Mallory standing near the middle of the bar with a nervous look on her face. "Sorry to disturb you."

My feet are already carrying me toward her. "You're fine. It's my job to take care of you."

Her eyes widen, and I realize what I said. The crazy part is, I actually like the thought of taking care of her, which is fucking crazy. I don't know her. She could be married or dating someone for all I know, though I'm certain the first is out of the question. She doesn't wear a ring, and I've gotten pretty good at sniffing out the single and taken ones. Even the latter ones who pretend they're not.

"Umm, well, I need a gin and tonic and a white wine," she replies.

While I start to pour her drinks, I see my friend moving from the far end of the bar. "Hey, Mallory. Sorry to hear about what happened earlier. Things like that don't happen too often, but if they do, let us know right away. We don't put up with that shit," Jameson says, towering over her.

If she's nervous by his imposing size, she doesn't let on. "Thank you, Jameson. I will."

He nods before turning and heading toward the back door, most likely to have that cigarette. "Here ya go," I say, as I place the glasses in front of her.

"Thank you," she whispers, taking the drinks and heading back into the restaurant, my eyes following her the entire time.

Kellen arrives just before four, so I clean out the tip jar and make a retreat to my office to get a little paperwork done. First though, I need some food.

"Hey, man," I holler, as I push through the double swinging doors and find Jasper by the grill. He throws me a pointed look, a reminder he doesn't like anyone in his kitchen, but I ignore him, like always.

"Here," he says, sliding a plate across the counter toward me.

"What's this?" I ask, noticing the huge burger and pile of steak fries.

"Up All Night. I was making one for Newton, so I threw one on for you too," Jasper replies, throwing four homemade, freshly pressed patties on the grill.

"I don't like swiss," I grumble.

"I know," he sighs. "I used cheddar for you and threw on extra mushrooms."

I grin, secretly loving when he has to alter his perfectly crafted burger creations for one of us. Mostly because it pisses him off that not everyone likes everything he puts together. I find it amusing when he gets all worked up and tries to argue with us, trying to convince us we like something we don't. "Appreciate it," I holler with a grin as I slip back out of the kitchen with my food. He mumbles something as I go, but I don't pay much attention. Instead, my focus is now on the blonde standing in front of me at the servers' station.

"Afternoon go okay?" I ask, as I slip in behind her, the scent of vanilla filling my senses, which tells me I'm too fucking close to her. Yet, as I grab a bottle of mustard, I can't seem to force my legs to move back.

She gives me a warm smile. "Yeah, it went good."

My heart does this weird double-beat thing when our eyes met.

Mallory looks down at her watch. "Shoot, I have to go," she mumbles, using the computer system to clock out before turning and heading out of the restaurant. "See you later, Walker."

I wave, watching her ass as she goes because it really is a spectacular view. After squirting a generous blob of mustard on my plate and chatting with Gigi about the incident from earlier, I take my food and head to my office. When I reach the hallway, I find Numbers there, talking in hushed tones. As I approach to slip past them, I realize he's talking to Mallory.

Something burns in my chest as I watch them talk, their heads pulled in close, as if they don't want to be overheard.

Mallory notices me first and pulls back, giving me a small smile. Isaac glances to his right but doesn't move right away. "Hey, man."

"Hey," I respond, my feet stuck on the floor. I glance from him to her, this weird tightness settling in my chest. They aren't doing anything wrong, per se, but I don't like the fact they're standing so close in the hallway talking.

What the hell?

Is this...jealousy I feel?

I clear my throat and pass by them, trying to keep my eyes down. Unfortunately, my eyes don't get the memo and they glance up right when I pass by. She looks unaffected as she slings her purse over her shoulder and waves goodbye, slipping out the back door in a rush. She moves so quickly, it only hits me a few long seconds later that no one escorted her outside to her car. I push open the back door just in time to see her getting into her small SUV. Only when I see it back out of the parking spot do I move on.

When I push through my office door, I can tell I'm not alone. "You got a minute?" Isaac asks, following behind me and taking the empty seat across from my workspace.

"Sure, if you don't mind if I eat while we talk. I'm starving," I reply, trying hard to push any thought of Isaac and Mallory together out of my mind. I should be happy for my friend, but I'm not. It pisses me the hell off.

"Go ahead. I just wanted to get your take on what happened earlier."

I swipe a fry through the mustard and pop it into my mouth before I reply. "Group of four guys eating lunch and one got a little handsy with Mal."

He looks up, amusement on his face. "Mal?"

I realize instantly my mistake. "Mallory, the new server."

"Yes, I know who Mallory is," he says with a grin.

"Anyway," I continue, taking a quick bite of my burger. "I saw one guy wrap his hand around her leg and hold her. Her body went rigid, so I reacted."

"Threw them out?"

"Yep, but not before I made one of the them pay the bill. Gigi said he left a fifty for a tip."

"Good," Isaac responds, throwing one leg over his knee as he gets comfortable. When I don't say anything else, he finally says, "Jameson asked for some time to talk. Any idea what that's about?"

I shrug, not really wanting to step on Jameson's toes and say more than he's ready to say. "He has an idea he wants to run by you."

Numbers watches me eat. "You know what it's about?"

"I do," I reply, chewing my food. Once I swallow, I add, "I think it's a solid idea, and we should all be open-minded and listen to what he has to say."

"You mean me, specifically?" he asks, his fist under his chin as he stares across the desk at me.

Again, I shrug. "All of us."

"Okay, I'll do that. Is it something we can talk about Monday during our meeting, or should I schedule something before then?"

"I think Monday is good. Jasper should be in on it too."

He nods and stands. "All right then. I'll let you eat your food. Thank you for taking care of the problem earlier," he says, clearly referring to the incident with Mallory. It bothers me the way he says it, like he appreciates me taking care of *her*.

I sigh and push my plate away. It shouldn't bother me if Isaac wants to date an employee. Fuck knows he rarely steps away from the office long enough to date in general. It seems logical he'd gravitate toward someone he could see almost daily.

Besides, I'm the one with the rule of no dating the employees.

Me.

So why the hell does it burn my gut so much to think about her with him and not me?

Mallory

What a day.

The moment I tuck Lizzie into her bed, her tired little eyes drift closed. I turn on the night-light before flipping off her bedroom light and stopping to watch her. When everything went down in Gibson, I found myself just watching her sleep. Sometimes, it was the only thing that would calm the storm in my mind.

Now, I'm a little more at peace, even though I still look over my shoulder all the time.

I probably always will.

Quietly, I pull the door until it's a few inches from closing and head for my bedroom. Well, what will be my bedroom someday. First, I need things like a bed and a dresser, but both of those will have to wait.

When I left Gibson, it was with only the things I could fit in my Ford Escape. Lizzie's toddler bed, favorite toys, the TV, and clothes took up most of the room. I was able to cram two boxes of clothes and toiletries in the front passenger seat, as well as some bags of food from the cabinets and some basic cleaning supplies on the floorboards. My old car was filled to the roof, especially with a car seat and a little girl inside. But we made it, and so far, it's been a good decision.

A safe one too.

I rotate some of my clothes, tossing the dirty ones into a bag to wash and hanging up a few more things from a box. I was able to get two days out of some of my black pants, which means I really need to wash them tonight. The plan is to slip down to the basement quickly once I know Lizzie is asleep. Then, I can run back down later to flip them into the dryer, if it's working. Mrs. Fritz told me both of the ones in the basement haven't been working properly. I guess if they're not, I'll just bring the clothes upstairs and hang-dry them.

When I make sure Lizzie is out like a light, I grab the bag of dirty clothes and my laundry soap and silently slip out of the apartment, making sure the door is securely locked behind me. I move down three flights of stairs as quickly as I ever have, happy to find one of the washers available. I drop the clothes inside and some detergent, shut the lid, and turn on the machine. It's old, but it'll do. Once the machine starts to fill with water, I head back upstairs.

My heart is racing as I unlock the door, making sure it's fortified tight behind me. First stop is the small second bedroom, where I find Lizzie sleeping in the exact same position she was in earlier. The thought of leaving her unattended, even for five minutes, is enough to send me into a panic attack, but sometimes a single mom has to do what a single mom has to do. Maybe I should look into a cheap baby monitor for future laundry trips.

I use the bathroom sink to wash my bras and hang them over the curtain rod to dry, humming a tune I can't seem to get out of my head. As I'm hanging my final undergarment, I realize where I've heard that particular song. It was playing on the jukebox the last time

I went over to the bar to get drinks. The time when he told me it was his job to take care of me. I don't know why I took it the way I did. He didn't mean personally, other than in the work-sense. He takes care of me as he takes care of *all* the employees at Burgers and Brew.

I'm nothing special.

Yet, that doesn't explain why my heart got all excited and did a pirouette in my chest when he said it.

I've thought of Walker on and off all day. I'm sure I'll never forget the look in his eyes when he saw me talking to Isaac. It was almost predatory, envious even, which is silly because I'm nothing more than an employee to either. The man who hired me stopped me before I could escape to make sure I was okay from the lunchtime incident. The moment he asked, his hazel eyes so full of concern, I almost broke down in tears. The only thing that saved me from doing just that was seeing Walker standing there, watching us.

I can see why women would be attracted to Isaac. His dark hair is styled nicely, and he has high cheekbones that only seem to highlight his handsome face. The problem is, I'm not attracted to him. In fact, the comfort level I feel with him is more like siblings than anything else. After the interview, he asked a few personal questions and offered a few suggestions as far as used furniture stores, the best times to grocery shop, and even which parks have the best and safest playground equipment for Lizzie. He's a great guy, and one I'd happily call my boss and my friend.

Then there's Walker.

Even though I try not to think about him, I do. Too much. From his drop-dead gorgeous face to his muscular build. Plus, those eyes. And that smile. And those big hands. Not to mention the way his jeans hug his hips and form around his ass.

Exhaling, I glance at the clock and realize it's about time to switch the laundry over. Grabbing my keys again, I check on Lizzie before slipping out of the apartment. I make my way down the flights of stairs and to the basement, the scent of mildew and dampness filling the air.

First thing I notice is my bag on the floor. I had left it sitting on top of the washer so someone would know it was in use, but the vibrations of the spin cycle probably sent it flying. When I open the lid, I glance down, stumped.

It's empty.

I close the lid and open it a second time, as if by some voodoo magic, clothes will suddenly reappear. They don't, however, and I'm left staring in shock at the empty basin. I check the second washer, only to find it empty as well. Even though the dryers have an out of order sign taped to the top, I check them too. Both empty.

My clothes are gone.

Mrs. Fritz lets me drop Lizzie off thirty minutes earlier than our agreed upon time so I can run to Walmart and buy some black pants. I'm damn lucky I only lost one of my work shirts. I still have four more, but that doesn't mean I don't need to be more careful. Apparently, you really shouldn't leave clothes unattended in the basement laundry room.

Case in point: my missing clothes.

Worst part is I don't really have many to begin with. When I left Gibson, I was more concerned with making sure Lizzie had everything she needed, and my personal belongings came secondary to hers. So, here I am driving across town to Walmart in hopes they have some. If not, I don't know what I'm going to do today. I won't have time to hit the second-hand stores before I need to start my shift.

I power-walk through the front entrance of the store and head straight to the clothing section. There's a small rack of office-appropriate clothing, and fortunately, they have dress pants. Except, they're pretty picked over. They don't have my size. All I can find in black is a size smaller and two sizes bigger. Quickly, I grab both and head for the dressing room.

The employee is over stocking socks and takes a few minutes to stop what she's doing to unlock the door. As soon as I'm in, I rip off my maroon and gray yoga pants and slip on the first pair. They're the ones that are too big, and clearly, they're just that. Lizzie could probably get in them with me. My last hope relies on a pair of pants that are too small.

Swell.

Oh, these babies are tight. Fortunately for my ass, there's a little stretch to them. Sure, it's difficult to button them, but desperate times, and all that. I rip the pants back off and throw them on the seat and climb back into my yoga pants. Making sure I have my purse, I grab the too-big pants and slip them on the rack and my too-small pants and head for the register.

There's only one register open, and it already has a line, so I quickly make my way to those self-check registers. I touch the screen and scan the tag on my pants, tossing them in a plastic bag.

"Well, those pants will certainly liven up the place a little."

I gasp, realizing the deep voice is very close behind me, yet recognizing it at the same time. Spinning, I find Walker standing directly behind me, his eyes cast downward and taking in my weird pants.

"Are those pineapples?" he asks, the hint of a smile on his full lips.

"Oh, uh, yeah," I stammer, glancing down at the little dancing fruit all over my leggings. "Don't worry, I'm not wearing them to work in. I got new pants." I hold up the bag, like an idiot, as proof.

His smile is completely amused as he asks, "New pants? What happened to your old ones?"

I pull a few bills out of my purse and try to slide them in the machine to pay. "Well, apparently, someone needed them more than me. They were gone when I went down to get them from the washer last night." The machine spits my wrinkled bill back out, so I try again.

Walker senses my growing agitation and steps up beside me, reaching for the crinkled five-dollar bill. When it slides in easily for him, he turns and catches my gaze. "Someone stole your clothes?"

I swallow hard and shrug. "It happens."

His earlier easygoing grin gone now. "It happens? Are you kidding me, Mal? That doesn't happen."

I turn away, mortification creeping up my neck, as I slip the rest of my money into the machine.

"Where? At a laundromat?" Walker pushes, clearly not happy my clothes were stolen.

"At my apartment. I've never used the machines in the basement before, and when I went down to get them from the washer, they were gone."

He seems completely flabbergasted by this. "What else did they take?"

"One of my work shirts, but I have four more. I'll purchase a new one as soon as possible," I add quickly.

"We'll get you a new one," he states, the agitation still very evident in his voice.

"No, please don't. It's my fault. I'll let Isaac know I need to purchase a replacement."

There's a tick in his jaw. "No way, Mal. We have tons of those shirts. You don't need to buy one. That's why we order them in bulk. It's part of your uniform, and we furnish it." As the machine spits out my change, his features finally soften. "Listen, I don't know where you live, but please don't use those machines in the basement anymore. You can use my machine anytime. Or even Isaac's."

I slip the change into my pocket and grab my bag. "Thank you for the offer, but that's not necessary. I can go to a laundromat."

"You can but know the offer stands. Anytime you need it."

I turn and find those heavenly blue eyes zeroed in on me. "Thank you, Walker. I appreciate it." I'll never take him up on his offer, but he doesn't need to know that. He's being helpful and kind, and I truly do value it. It's been a while since someone of the opposite sex has been so caring.

Of course, he's probably just doing it because I'm his employee and my clothes were stolen.

I glance at my watch and realize I'm almost out of time. "I'm sorry to run, but I need to get to work." I start to back away from where he stands.

"Have a good day, Mal."

"Thanks, Walker. You too."

I turn and hurry out of the store with not much time to spare. The drive to work goes quickly, but my mind is still back at Walmart. On Walker. I probably shouldn't have told him about my clothes being stolen, but he caught me off guard in my crazy leggings. I was afraid he thought I was actually going to wear them to serve food to their customers. What a sight that would have been. I'm sure Gigi would send me home in two-seconds flat, and Isaac would probably have my final paycheck in his hand as I walked out the door.

No, there's no way I'd jeopardize this job right now. I need the steady income, and the tips have been a nice little bonus too. It's wonderful to get a portion of my money each day, instead of waiting until payday to get it all. It definitely helps so I can stock up on things I need for Lizzie and the apartment.

There are two workdays left this week. That's two more days of tips. Maybe this weekend we'll be able to get a few more necessities. Like better shoes and maybe a bed. I could really use one of those. That old, worn-down couch isn't the most comfortable thing to sleep on, but I'm not going to complain. I'd endure years of discomfort if it meant Lizzie has what she needs.

My own well-being comes in second to hers.

She's my everything.

Walker

I don't knock on his door, I just push my way in. "Do you know where she lives?"

Numbers looks up from his computer screen. "Well, good morning to you too. What brings you in so early on a Thursday?"

"Mallory. Do you know where she lives?" I'm unable to mask my irritation, and even though I shouldn't be, I'm taking it out on Isaac.

He sits up straight in his seat. "Yeah, why?"

My irritation turns to anger. I'm angry he knows where she lives. I'm angry because I don't. And I'm angry that I'm angry about it. "Her clothes were stolen last night from the washer."

"Seriously? What the hell?"

"I know," I state, plopping down in one of the two chairs in his office. "I saw her this morning at Walmart buying new pants and she spilled the beans. Oh, she needs more shirts too. They got one of those, but maybe we can give her a few more. If she's having to use a laundromat, it might be a little longer between trips. Make sure she has six or seven? Plus, I volunteered the use of your washing machine, if she needs one."

I'm rambling, but I can't seem to stop.

"Why not volunteer your own?"

"I did."

Isaac just grins. "Interesting."

"What is?" I ask, crossing my arms over my chest, because I know whatever he's about to say, I'm not going to like. Or I'm going to like it too much and have to deny the fuck out of it.

"You like her."

Called it.

Deny it is...

"As an employee, she seems great," I reply vaguely.

"And as a woman?" he asks, smirking at me.

"Not mine."

Isaac barks out a laugh. "Because you have rules."

"I do."

He shrugs. "Well, your loss then," he says, grinning, as he turns his attention back to his computer. "I'll make sure she gets a few more shirts."

"Thank you," I reply, standing up and heading for the door.

Just before I cross the threshold, he calls my name. When I turn around, I meet his gaze. "You know, you're usually one of the biggest rulebreakers I know."

"What's your point?" I ask.

Again, he shrugs his shoulders. "Just seems silly not to break your own rules every now and again." Then he gives his full attention back to the computer, basically dismissing me.

That's fine, because I'm stuck on what he actually said as I make my way down the stairs and out the back of the building. I don't work until four, so there's no reason for me to hang around for five hours. Besides, the whole reason I was in Walmart this morning was because Aunt Edna called, complaining her security light outside wasn't working right. Sure, I could wait until Sunday to fix it, but I know that's not what she really wants. If she feels safer with that bright-ass light illuminating her backyard, then I'll replace the bulb in that bright-ass light.

I jump into my Jeep, but don't throw it in gear. Instead, I sit there and think about what Isaac said. If he was interested in her, why would he insinuate I should break my no-dating-employees rule? And why the hell do I want to go back inside, especially knowing she's in there working?

Growling, I throw the Jeep in reverse and pull out of the lot. I've never been so anxious to get away from my business as I am today. The only problem is my confusion over Mallory and the feelings she drums up are riding shotgun alongside me.

It's just after eleven on Sunday morning when I pull into Aunt Edna's driveway. My mom's car is already there, as well as Uncle Donald's, my cousin Jamal's, and even Bernice's old Chevy Cavalier that's only a few years younger than mine. But there's also a fourth car I don't recognize.

I hop out and head for the house. Talking filters from the backyard, so I slip through the small place Edna's called home for four decades and head for the kitchen.

"There he is," my great-aunt says, standing at the stove, stirring something that smells like fried chicken gravy. It's one of my favorites.

"Good morning," I reply, stopping to kiss her cheek before slipping the butter pecan pie into the fridge.

"Whatcha got there?" she asks, glancing around me to sneak a peek in the box.

"Pecan. It's from Jasper. He made a couple last night when he was bored," I state, grabbing a can of Coke from the fridge before I close the door.

Edna shakes her head and chuckles. "That boy. He already cooks better than I do, but now he bakes too?"

I laugh at her indignation. "No one cooks better than you, Aunt E."

She preens like a proud peacock at the compliment.

Jasper is a damn good cook. Sure, we may offer specialty burgers and a few sandwiches on our menu, but the truth is he can make just about anything. And baking is how he de-stresses. Occasionally, we'll offer a dessert special, but that's usually something the kitchen can whip up in a large pan like bread pudding or apple crisp. Sometimes cookies. I know when he's overthinking something because he bakes. Pies, cakes, fancy breads like pineapple zucchini or strawberry banana. Last night, it was pecan pies, which told us he was working through some shit in his head.

"Everyone outside?" I ask, taking a long drink of my Coke.

"Mmhmm," she replies before turning off the head on the stovetop. "Gravy's ready. Why don't you go on back and say hi to your mama. We'll be eating in five minutes," she says, practically pushing me out the door.

I place a quick kiss on her cheek before exiting the kitchen and stepping out onto her small patio. Mom and Uncle Donald are sitting on the swing, talking, and Jamal is on his phone, as always. But then my eyes meet Bernice, and what's probably the real reason my ornery aunt pushed me out the door quickly.

There's a young woman sitting across from the woman at the picnic table. Bernice spies me first, her face lighting up with a grin. "Oh, Walker! I'm so glad you're here," she says, glancing over at the woman with a gleam in her eye.

Sighing, I realize what this is immediately.

A setup.

I head for my mom first, bending down and kissing her cheek. "Morning, Mom."

"Hello, Walker. You look nice today," she says, taking in my jeans and basic gray T-shirt. I put absolutely no effort into my appearance, but I usually don't. I try to make sure I don't dress like I just rolled out of bed. One time I made the mistake of coming over for lunch in joggers. Edna wacked me with a rolling pin and told me Jesus doesn't appreciate my laziness.

"Thanks," I mumble, reaching over and shaking Uncle Donald's hand.

"How was work last night?" he asks like clockwork. He inquires every Sunday morning, always interested in hearing about the business.

"All good. Jameson played last night, so we had a good crowd."

He nods. As much as I'd like to stay and chat, I know I have to continue to make my rounds.

I walk over to Jamal, his legs kicked up on the end of the picnic table from his chair. I knock his feet off with my hand, causing him to stumble in his chair. "Hey."

"Feet off the table," I tell my younger, twenty-four-year-old cousin. "Aunt Edna will tan your hide if she catches you."

He snorts. "I know, but she's so fun to rile up," he says, teasing and smiling.

"Lunch is about ready," I tell my cousin, turning and heading to my last stop before lunch. "Bernice, always lovely to see you," I say, kissing her cheek.

"Oh, Walker, I'm so glad you're finally here. I wanted to introduce you to a friend," the old, meddlesome woman says with an anything but innocent smile. "Walker, this is Suzie Perkins, the new Sunday school teacher I was telling you about."

Of course she is.

I plaster on a quick friendly smile and extend my hand. "Suzie, nice to meet you."

She turns fourteen shades of red as she takes my hand and whispers, "Pleasure to meet you as well."

Bernice claps her hands together. "Well, I'm going to run inside and help Edna finish the food. Why don't you take my seat, Walker, and visit with Suzie?" And then with the agility of a twenty-year-old, she gets up quickly and dances away, leaving me to get to know the woman who was clearly invited here for my benefit.

"Can I get you a drink, Suzie?" I ask, accepting my fate and taking the vacated seat left by Bernice.

"Oh, no thank you. I had a water just a few minutes ago." She gives me a polite, friendly smile, but it doesn't cause any sort of reaction, not in my chest or in my groin.

Not like the one I get when Mallory grins.

I nod and gaze out at the backyard, awkwardness settling in to keep my company. "So, you're a Sunday school teacher?"

She nods. "And preschool during the week. I teach the three-year-old room for the church preschool program. This is my first year."

"That's nice," I reply.

"And I hear you're a business owner?" she asks eagerly, her brown eyes sparkling under the sunlight.

"I am. My friends and I own Burgers and Brew. Have you ever been?" I ask, already sure I know the answer.

She shakes her head. "No, sorry. I've only lived here a little over a year."

Plenty of time to check out a few local businesses, in my opinion, but then again, Suzie doesn't exactly look like the *brew* type. She's more wholesome and probably spends her evenings practicing relaxation breathing techniques and reading her Bible. Nothing wrong with it at all, and I can even see why Bernice and Edna would like her, but I can already tell we're not a good fit.

"Lunch is ready," my aunt hollers from the back door.

"Shall we?" I ask, waving my hand for Suzie to go in front of me. I'm a complete gentleman, never once glance down to check out her ass. Not like Mallory, where my eyes seem to seek it out all on their own.

"Suzie, why don't you take this seat here by Walker," Bernice says, motioning for the empty chair beside my usual spot at the table.

"Thank you," she replies, slipping into the empty seat.

Mom is smiling at me across the table. I roll my eyes, letting her know I'm not amused by today's arrangement, but all she does is laugh.

Lunch is pleasant, though completely predictable. Bernice and Edna do everything they can to engage Suzie and me in conversation. It's so bad, I'm ready for them to get up and go outside to eat to give us alone time. But they don't. Instead, they start conversations centered around me or the woman beside me, their matchmaker wings on full display now.

When Jamal and I get up to collect the plates, Edna stops me. "Walker, why don't you take Suzie outside and get to know each other a little more." The crazy old bat throws me a wink, as if I couldn't pick up on the signals she was throwing.

Resigned, I escort Suzie back the porch. She takes one of the seats under the big oak tree, which I'm grateful for. I was afraid we were about to be sharing the swing. When she glances up at the sun peeking through the tree branches, she says, "Can I tell you something?"

"Sure," I reply, kicking my legs out straight.

"I think we're being set up."

I bark out a laugh. "I think you're right."

She blushes a lighter shade of pink and looks at me through her lashes. "Can I tell you something else?" When I nod, she continues. "I think you're a nice guy, but...well, you're not really my type."

My entire body relaxes. "Suzie, I have to say I agree with you. You seem like a great woman, but I don't really see this going anywhere. I've enjoyed visiting with you this afternoon," I tell her, honestly.

She grins a pretty smile with straight white teeth. "I've enjoyed it as well. Maybe we'll see each other around sometime?"

I nod. "I'm sure we will. Stewart Grove isn't that big of a town."

She giggles. "I'm learning that. Someone told me it's named after two old men who got into a fight?" Her eyes light up with excitement as I tell her the story I've been told since I was a young boy.

"The legend goes, Gerald Stewart and John Grove both claimed the land where the town was built. They worked for the railroad, building the main system across Ohio. When they arrived at the particular building site, both men supposedly purchased the land, claiming the town as theirs. Hence, Stewart Grove. Both men declared the other stole it from him until the day they died. Actually, they passed away two days apart. Grove went first and then Stewart right after. They say he died of a broken heart because he had no one to fight with anymore."

Suzie laughs. "That's a wild story. Did they ever find out who really owned the land?"

I nod. "They both did, legally. The large parcel was divided into two sections, and neither man realized it. A north half and a south half, with the railroad being the divider."

She shakes her head. "That's funny."

"Their descendants are still here and argue over whose land it was."

"Wow, what amazing history. They probably thought they were bitter enemies but were really friends all along. God works in mysterious ways, doesn't he?"

"That He does, Suzie. That He does. Wanna go inside and grab some pecan pie before Bernice swipes it all?"

She jumps up, flattens out her skirt, and says, "I'd love to."

"After you," I reply, leading her back to the house. My feet are a lot lighter now that I know we're on the same page. She isn't any more interested in me than I am of her. Suzie's a nice girl, who will no doubt make someone very happy someday.

That someone just isn't me.

Now I get to deal with my meddling pain in the ass aunt.

Mallory

I swear I just start to doze off when I hear the first door slam. I don't have to wait very long before the arguing starts, easily filtering through the thin walls. Some of the words are clear as day, while others are muffled, but I can tell right away it's going to be a long night.

Quietly, I get up off the couch and go peek in on Lizzie. She's a heavy sleeper and hasn't woken up yet from the noise coming from the apartment next door. When I spy her sleeping soundly in her toddler bed, I carefully pull the door closed to keep the extra sound out.

The shouting grows louder as I make my way into the kitchen for a drink. The man on the other side of the wall appears to be screaming about the remote control, while the woman is denying having lost it. It seems silly, really, to be having an argument over something as trivial as a TV remote, but nothing surprises me anymore. Last night it was because she adjusted the thermostat a single degree warmer.

It reminds me of Devon and how quickly he would fly off the handle there at the end. He wasn't always like that. Not in the beginning and not for the first few years of our relationship. Yet, I can't help but question how well I really knew him, even back then.

The last six months we were together, he seemed to grow increasingly more agitated, his fuse shorter by the day. They tell me drugs will do that to a person, but I wouldn't know. I've never done them.

A door slams, followed by the pounding of a fist and demands to open up. Sighing, I head back to the living room and try to get comfortable on the couch. These are the times I wish I had headphones or something to play music. Instead, I turn the television on low to try to drown out the commotion on the other side of the wall.

The first night it happened, I was afraid. For Lizzie and myself, as well as the woman. But it doesn't sound like it gets physical, just that they like to yell. The fighting doesn't happen every night, but most anyway, and thanks to walls made out of tissue paper, I get to enjoy their spats as if they were happening in the room with me.

I try to focus on the movie, but it's hard to watch *Dora the Explorer* when someone's being called a dumbass on the other side of the paneling. Yet, I leave it on, determined to ignore the dispute and keep my attention on the girl's magic backpack.

After an hour of listening to the fighting, the television already off thanks to the end of the DVD and being too lazy to get up and change it, my eyelids finally grow too heavy to control. It's starting to quiet down next door, and I'm hoping it stays that way so I can get a little sleep before Lizzie wakes up in the morning, demanding my full attention.

Just as I start to drift, I'm startled awake once more. A loud moan echoes through the wall, followed by another. "Really?" I whisper, rolling over and jamming my pillow over my head.

Something starts smacking into the wall in quick rhythm, the moans of pleasure growing increasingly louder. The noise level increases, as does their panting and groaning. I can hear the thrusting and the slapping of skin as if they were having sex right beside me. "Yeah, baby. Do you like that hard cock? You want me to fuck you with this big dick?" I hear him grunt.

"God your dick is huge! Fuck me harder!" she yells.

And he does. The woman is practically screaming in orgasmic bliss as he pounds into her, whatever they're against most likely about to burst through the wall like the Kool-Aid Man.

"Jesus, just get off, will you, so we can all go to sleep?" I whine, holding the pillow tightly against my head.

Finally, he explodes in an eruption of colorful language. The banging stops. The moaning and panting subside. Blissful silence surrounds me as I slip the pillow beneath my head and take a deep breath.

When all is quiet, I get up and check on Lizzie once more. Still sound asleep, curled in the middle of her bed as if nothing was going on a few rooms away. I leave the door cracked open so I can hear her if she wakes and fall back onto the couch. The clock reads almost midnight. My eyes are heavy, and I'm exhausted from the day, but my mind goes ahead and conjures up images of Walker.

Inappropriate images.

Ones of him pounding into me from behind, as he brings me to orgasm twice before taking his own.

Desire swirls in my belly, but I ignore it. No way am I slipping my hand beneath my waistband and touching myself, even though the need is very much there. Instead, I ignore the hum between my legs, close my eyes, and try not to think about him.

It doesn't work.

I've successfully avoided Walker, though not so successfully when I close my eyes. I've only seen him in passing, and he was off yesterday. Six whole days of not having to worry about doing something embarrassing like tripping over my own feet or dropping a tray of drinks. But today is a different story. It's Wednesday, and I know he works the same shift as me.

I slip inside the back room and get ready for the day. I tie on my apron, yawning. I still can't believe, though I'm eternally grateful, Lizzie slept through all of last night's excitement. Me, on the other hand, still struggled to fall sleep long after my neighbors had.

"Gonna be a busy day, ladies. We have our favorite two parties coming in this afternoon," Gigi says as she enters the room in a flurry. She looks at me, the new girl with only a week's experience. "You can handle it." It's not a question, but a statement. She gives me a reassuring smile and leaves just as quickly as she entered.

"Tips are usually pretty decent when these groups come in," Marla says, as we follow behind Gigi. "You and I will take the larger group, with Gi taking the slightly smaller one. Plus, we'll have our regular tables, so you'll be on your toes today."

We busy ourselves with setting up the dining room for lunch service, Marla telling us about the phone call she had last night with her daughter in college. It's easy to relax around these two, especially when they tease Jameson, who often comes in to help. I'm not sure what hours he keeps, but he seems to be here all the time, especially if he works the evenings.

"Good morning, ladies." The voice is familiar but not the one I expected. It's not Jameson, but Walker.

"Hey, Walk!" Marla hollers, rolling silverware and placing them in the tub.

When I turn around, I find Walker's eyes cast downward. Specifically, on my ass. He must feel my own gaze on him, but when he looks up and realizes I busted him, he doesn't seem to be embarrassed. In fact, with the faintest grin he gives me, I'd say he rather enjoyed it.

"Morning, Mal," he says a tad quieter, his voice low and husky.

I shiver.

"Hi," I squeak in an octave two levels higher than my normal voice.

"You heard the Johnson Group and Precision Ag are both coming in today, right?" Gigi asks Walker, as he leans casually against the servers' station.

"Numbers told me," he tells her, his eyes still locked on me. "You ladies need any help in here?"

"Nope, we're good, but thanks," she replies, grabbing pitchers and filling them with ice water.

"All right, I'll let you do your thing. I'll be ready in the bar when you need me," he says, slowly pushing off the wall and leaving the restaurant, the scent of his soap lingering in the air.

"Mmmm, Gi, did you see that?" Marla asks.

"Oh, I definitely did."

"See what?" I ask, glancing over my shoulder to where the two older ladies stand, smiling.

"See that man ogle you as if you were a steak dinner," Marla states, laughing.

"What? He did not!" I argue, though I know it's pointless. He really was staring at me like I were a tall glass of water in the hot, summer desert.

Both ladies laugh, at my expense, of course. "Oh, he was," Gigi confirms. "It was like your butt was stamped with some sort of coded message."

"Yeah, it said 'Property of Walker Meyer.'" This from Marla, who is barely able to get the words out before bursting into fits of laughter.

I can feel the heat in my cheeks as I busy myself and avoid their gazes.

"We all set?" Jasper asks from the doorway of the kitchen. This might actually be the first time I've seen him outside of his domain.

"We are, Jasper," Gigi states.

"And the new girl can handle the extra tables?" he asks. The hairs on my neck stand up. No, I don't think he's trying to be a jerk, but I believe he's too busy to bother learning my name. Especially if they go through servers as quickly as I've heard. But I guess with that warm greeting, I can see why some don't stay.

"Her name is Mallory, and yes, she'll be fine. She's doing great." Gigi gives him a look, letting him know she doesn't appreciate his attitude.

The chef gives her a cheesy grin, before turning his eyes on me. They're dark, like melted chocolate, with a hint of mischief and knowledge. He seems to take in my appearance from head to toe, but not the way Walker does. No, his eyes on me feel like a caress.

When Jasper returns to my face, he smiles widely and winks. "Don't mess up, Mallory," he says before returning to the kitchen.

Gigi sighs. "Ignore him. He's just trying to get under your skin. He thinks it weeds out the weak ones." She rolls her eyes.

I stand up tall. "I can handle him."

Her lips form a wide smile. "Good. Now, we're getting ready to open. Let's make sure we're set."

The lunch rush is steady, and so are the take-out orders. We're moving, but all three of us are able to handle it. Gigi took the smaller of the two groups, a work meeting of twelve. Just as they were wrapping up, the bigger party of twenty-two arrived. Marla works on filling water glasses, while I take drink orders. When I have everyone's written down, she sets out to get soft drinks, and I head to the bar.

"Mal," Walker croons in a voice as soft as silk. "What can I get you?"

I run through the fourteen drink orders, most of them mixed concoctions. When Walker has the first seven done, he says, "Run these to the table and I'll have the other seven done in a minute."

Carefully, I carry the full tray of drinks back to the large party and start distributing them. Once my tray is empty, I return to the bar, where Walker has my next seven on a new tray and ready to go. "All set," he says, plopping an olive into a martini.

"Thank you," I say, grabbing the round tray and heading back.

I make a few more trips to the bar over the next two and a half hours. Apparently, this group eats first and then conducts a meeting of some sort. Marla and I hang around and refill glasses whenever needed, but for the most part, our job is winding down. In fact, our shift is winding down too, and it's nearing four o'clock.

"If you need to leave, I can finish up. I'll bring your half of the tip tomorrow," Marla offers.

"Okay," I reply, grateful she'll allow me to leave when I need to. Though, I do feel bad sticking her with the cleanup. However, it's not like I can stay. Mrs. Fritz needs to leave as soon as she can on Wednesdays, which means I need to head out at four.

I refill the water pitcher when I hear Manda over with Marla. She's one of our replacements for the dinner shift. "I'm not helping, Mar. If she's not here to clean her table, then I'm taking the tip."

"Oh, knock it off. You know that's not how it works," Marla chastises the younger server with purple and black hair.

"Just sayin'," she argues, disappearing into the kitchen.

Well, that settles that. There's no way I'm going to leave at four. Not only will I not risk the tip, but I don't want to seem like the employee who doesn't do her share.

I pull my cell phone out of my pocket and dial Mrs. Fritz. "Hello?"

"Hi, Mrs. Fritz, it's Mallory. I'm stuck at work for a little longer. Can you drop Lizzie off on your way to Bingo?" I ask, hoping the offer still stands.

"Oh, sure, but I can't stay long. I always get there early enough to secure a good Bingo seat."

I smile. "Okay, not a problem. I can meet you at the back door. This way, you won't even have to get out."

"That's perfect, dear. I'll see you in a few minutes."

Signing off, I slip my phone back into my apron, my mind spinning. Now, what am I going to do with my daughter while I finish up my shift?

"Trouble?"

I startle, spinning around to see Isaac standing behind me.

"Oh, uh, yeah. It's Lizzie. My babysitter has somewhere to be, but I'm not finished with my shift yet."

When I interviewed for the server position, I was upfront about my single mother status. While I explained it wouldn't be a problem during the day, I mentioned my sitter often makes plans for the later afternoon and early evening. Isaac assured me he would be flexible and understanding, even going as far as to mention he and his siblings were raised by a single mother himself.

"Will she stay with me if we go up to my office? Then you can finish up down here."

Lizzie went to Mrs. Fritz easy enough, but Isaac? I'm not sure.

"Why don't we try? If that doesn't work, we'll come up with plan B. You go back in the dining room, and I'll holler when they get here."

I nod and sigh in relief. "Thank you, Isaac."

He gives me a polite smile. "No problem, Mallory. I understand. Remember, I grew up in a diner, waiting for my mom to get off work when she had no one to watch me."

I do remember him telling me. He sat in a booth in the far corner more times than not.

I hurry back to the dining room and jump right in refilling water to those requesting it.

"I thought you needed to go? It's after four," Marla says.

"I have a temporary solution to a problem and can stay a little longer," I assure her, collecting empty glasses and cans as I go.

"Can I get the check now?" the man at the head of the table asks.

"Sure thing. Just give me a minute," I tell him, hurrying over to servers' station.

Manda is there, watching my every move. "I thought you were leaving."

I just shrug, typing away on the monitor. "I'll be out of your hair soon enough." When I print the bill, Marla checks it over to make sure we didn't forget anything. I glance at the total again, shocked that one business could spend that much money at a burger joint. But then again, this isn't just any burger place.

Isaac peeks around the corner and waves. "I'll take them the bill," Marla states.

"Okay, I'll be right back."

I hurry off to the back door and smile when I see Lizzie in the back seat of the car, strapped into the old car seat my sitter had from her grandchild. "Thank you, Mrs. Fritz. I'm sorry you had to bring her to me."

"Oh, no problem, child. I'm a step closer to that big BINGO coverall payout!"

"Well, I'll let you go so you can get your spot," I tell her, propping my daughter up on my hip as the car pulls away.

We step inside, and I set her down on her feet, Isaac staying back and out of the way. "Honey, Mommy's not quite done with work yet. Would it be okay if you go upstairs with my friend Isaac and sit in his office?" My daughter's big green eyes look up, taking in the tall man in front of her.

Isaac squats down and smiles. "Hi, Lizzie. I'm Isaac, your mom's friend. I have some popcorn and fruit snacks upstairs. If you want, we can run up and have a snack while your mom finishes up. She'll be up in just a few minutes." Shocked, I look over at my boss, who just grins. "I picked up a few things, just in case she had to come in someday," he replies with a shrug.

My eyes fill with tears. No one has ever been this understanding, this helpful before. I was fired from my grocery store job because Lizzie was sick, and I had to take three days off. "Thank you." Turning to my daughter, I ask, "Will that be okay? Mommy will only be a few minutes."

Lizzie turns those big eyes back to Isaac. He instantly smiles and says, "I have a princess coloring book and brand-new crayons too. Do you want to come color me a picture for my office?"

Suddenly, my daughter lets go of my hand and extends it to Isaac. "Okay," she whispers.

He takes her offered hand, carefully leading her toward the stairs. "We're going to go up here to my office, okay? And you can have some snacks and color while Mommy finishes up."

"I'll be right up, baby," I tell her, watching as they go up the stairs together.

When they're out of sight, I head back into the restaurant. Marla is running the credit card through the machine as the large party starts to head out the door. While she meets with the gentleman to have him sign the receipt, I start collecting what's left of the dirty dishes and glasses. Manda hovers nearby, but never offers to help. I would turn her down anyway. This is my table, my tip, and I've worked hard for it. I want to finish it out.

"You did great," Marla whispers when she joins me.

"Thanks."

"Seriously, I'd work with you any day, honey," Marla states loudly, handing me a fifty. "That's your half."

I stare down at that single bill as if it were about to share the secret to happiness. Combined with what I've received in the last week, I have enough for next month's rent already. "Thank you," I whisper, my throat suddenly dry, my heart trying to beat out of my chest with excitement.

A week's worth of tips was able to cover my rent. That means I should be able to have enough for things around the apartment, like a bed and more towels, very soon. I slip the bill into my apron where the rest of today's tips are stored and finish cleaning up. Fifteen minutes after the party left, my job is done, and I can run upstairs and grab my daughter. Hell, I think I'll take Lizzie to McDonald's for a Happy Meal to celebrate a successful day.

I quickly clock out, stop by my locker to grab my belongings, and head for the stairs with a smile on my face.

I can't wait to see my daughter.

Walker

"I have to run to the kitchen to help Jasp," Numbers says, as he comes out of his office and flies down the stairs. "Go hang out in my office, will you?" He doesn't even give me time to respond, just disappears around the corner.

I was headed up to see if he'd put any more thought into Jameson's idea. He presented it Monday at our meeting, and it was hard to get a read on Isaac. Jameson had some statistics ready and was able to answer most of Isaac's questions, which, in my opinion, went a long way with the sales pitch. I shared my thoughts, mostly being in favor of looking into it more, which everyone was in agreement with. Isaac has been locked in his office for two days now, researching and poring over data. I'd expect nothing less from him.

Shaking my head, I finish climbing the stairs. A part of me wants to go to the kitchen to see what's wrong, but then again, there's always something with Jasper. Since Isaac told me to wait here, I think it's best to do that.

I slip into his office but stop in my tracks.

Sitting at his desk is a little girl, coloring.

I close my eyes and count to five before opening them again. Yep, she's still there. Only this time, she's looking right at me. She's little, with big green eyes and blonde pigtails, and watching me like a hawk. "Uhh, hi," I stammer, my feet stuck in the doorway.

"Hi," she whispers, moving her hand up to her mouth.

Finally, my legs carry me farther into the room. Very slowly, I move to the chairs in front of the desk and slide down on the first one. "What's your name?"

Her wide eyes take me in. "Lizzie."

The corner of my mouth turns upward. "Hi, Lizzie. I'm Walker. Whatcha doing in here?"

She holds up the red crayon.

"Coloring. I see," I say, leaning over the desk and looking at her picture. The colors are all over the place, nowhere near in the lines, which reminds me of when I was younger. I didn't like to color in the lines either. I want to ask why she's here, but I'm not sure I'll get an answer. Lizzie is pretty little, maybe four? I'm shit at guessing ages, so I could be way off base here. "Do you want some help?" I ask, moving my chair closer to the desk so we're sitting directly across from each other.

Lizzie hands me a green crayon and turns the books so I can color the blank page next to her masterpiece.

We don't say anything right away. I just color the crown on my page green, and sneak peeks of her out of the corner of my eye. She's concentrating hard on her art, which makes me smile.

After a few minutes, I switch from a green crayon to a blue. "You're good at coloring," I tell her, earning me the biggest grin. She sticks her tongue out of the side of her mouth and scribbles across the paper with purple. I stop and watch, completely enthralled with this pint-sized little girl. She's fucking adorable and has my heart galloping in my chest.

Lizzie reaches into a small bag on the desk and pulls out two fruit snacks. She slips one in her mouth and holds the second up for me. Unable to stop myself from smiling, I take the offered snack and pop it into my mouth. When was the last time I ate a fruit snack?

I hear footsteps on the stairs and just assume it's Numbers coming back up. I'm a little anxious to hear what he was to say about Lizzie. You know, like who is she?

"Lizzie, are you ready to go?"

That voice. It's soft and feminine—definitely not Isaac's—and the one that has invaded my dreams many nights in the last week.

"Mommy! I color!" Lizzie boasts, grinning up at the woman I feel step up beside me.

I glance up and find her gaze on me. She seems just as surprised to see me sitting here with her daughter than I am to discover she *has* a daughter.

"I see that," she replies softly, turning to face Lizzie. "That's a beautiful picture."

Lizzie goes right back to scribbling across the page, this time with a yellow crayon.

"Where's Isaac?" Mallory asks, standing beside the desk and watching her daughter color.

"Uhh, kitchen emergency. I was coming up the stairs when he was heading down. He asked me to wait in his office. I admit, this wasn't what I was expecting to see when I walked inside." There's a long, pregnant pause as we both watch Lizzie. "So, you have a daughter."

Mallory's lips turn upward. "I do. Lizzie is three."

I lean back in my chair and observe mother and daughter for a few minutes. Mallory compliments the girl on her outstanding coloring skills, even though the page is full of multi-colored scribbles. There's a definite resemblance, and to be honest, I'm surprised I didn't notice it sooner. They have the same hair and eye coloring, though the shape of Lizzie's face is different. She must get that from her father.

Why does that thought not set right in my gut?

"Thank you for hanging out with her for a few minutes," she says, breaking through the silence.

"No problem."

"I promise this won't happen a lot." Mallory rushes on to add, "My sitter had plans today, and I wasn't quite finished with work. Isaac said she could drop her off here for a little bit."

Isaac. Clearly he knew she had a child, and readily agreed to hang out with the little girl while Mal finished up her shift. The thought that my friend knew about Lizzie and I didn't really grates on my nerves.

"It's fine," I reassure her, leaning back in my chair.

Lizzie takes the coloring book and holds it up to her mom. "Done!"

"All done?" Mallory says, her eyes lighting up with love as she takes the coloring book. "Are we taking it home to put on the fridge?" The little girl shakes her head no and points to me. Mal seems shocked as she looks across the desk. "This is for Walker?"

Lizzie nods.

When Mallory rips the paper out of the coloring book, the little girl walks over and hands it to me. "This is for me?"

Again, she nods, sticking her finger in her mouth in a shy manner. "Well, how about we go downstairs and hang it up?"

Lizzie smiles and reaches out her hand. I take it in mine, my hand looking gigantic wrapped around hers, and head for the stairs. We take our time going down, her little legs stopping on each step. Mallory trails behind us until we reach my office.

"Where should we put it?" I ask the little girl, who looks around at my bare walls. Then, she points to the place directly in front of my desk. "Good choice. Then I can see it every day when I'm working."

I lift her up and set her down on my office chair and grab the tape. I put a piece on all four corners and head for the empty wall. "Here?" I ask, making sure it's in the right position. Lizzie nods eagerly and watches as I stick her masterpiece up on my wall. "There. It's perfect," I tell the little cutie.

She agrees with a grin.

"Okay, well, we should get going, Lizzie. Walker has work to do, so we better let him get back to it," Mallory says, walking over to pick up her daughter.

I shove my hands into my pockets and find myself saying, "I'm off work now." Not sure why I volunteered that info, but I did.

"Well, I had a big day today and I thought maybe we could grab a Happy Meal on our way home," Mallory says to her young daughter. The delight that fills the little girl's eyes is enough to make me smile.

"Willy?"

"Yes, really," she says, shoving the small bag of fruit snacks into her purse. "Do you want a cheeseburger or chicken nuggets?" she asks as they head for my office door.

"Nuggies!" Lizzie exclaims.

Mallory and I both laugh. "Well, thank you for watching her for a little bit. Will you tell Isaac thank you too?"

"I will." I step forward, wanting to volunteer my services again, but I'm not sure that's wise. Even though this little girl has already melted through that thick block of ice I call a heart, I know it's not a good idea to position myself in their lives. Not while Mallory works here.

"Bye, Walk!" Lizzie hollers, waving over her mom's back, as they leave my office.

I drop down onto my chair and pull it up to my desk. However, the moment I glance up and see the art on my wall, I find myself grabbing my keys and calling it a day. Locking my office door, I decide to head home. I could use a workout or a run—*anything* to get my mind off Mallory and Lizzie.

The problem is the moment I step outside, I see Mallory's little SUV still in the lot, trying to turn over. I bypass my Jeep completely and head for her car. She startles when I knock on the window and reach to open her door. "Sorry to scare you."

"It's okay," she mumbles, her cheeks a little flushed.

"What's the problem?"

She glances down at the steering wheel. "Won't start."

"Crank it so I can hear," I instruct, listening to the engine's slow attempt to turn over. "Sounds like the battery or the alternator."

Her face falls. "Oh. That sounds expensive," she mumbles.

"We can start with a battery and go from there. If it's not the battery, I can return it and buy the necessary part," I assure her, holding the door open. "Want me to run you home?"

She glances back at Lizzie, considering her options. "We could wait here," she suggests, a strand of hair falling across her forehead.

I shove my hands back into my pockets to keep from reaching for it. "It might take me a little time, and I thought you might want to get Lizzie home."

Mallory sighs and grabs her purse. "Okay, you're probably right." She opens the back door and unbuckles Lizzie from the car seat.

"Nuggies!" Lizzie shouts once more.

Mallory looks on the verge of tears. "No, no nuggies now, sweet girl. Mommy has to fix her car." She reaches into the back of her vehicle and tries to unfasten the child's seat. Considering she's only able to use one hand, it's difficult, and I can tell she's struggling.

Without saying a word, I step up beside her and take Lizzie. The little girl comes to me willingly and places her small hands against my cheeks. When she brushes against my stubble, she giggles the sweetest sound ever. "Nuggies."

Mallory wrestles the car seat out of her vehicle and sets it on the ground. Those green eyes look sad. Defeated. "I knew I shouldn't have said anything," she whispers, almost to herself.

I grab the car seat with my available hand and start to head for my Jeep. Mallory makes sure she has her purse and a small bag and locks her doors. "Should I put up the top?" I ask when we're standing beside the CJ.

"Uhh, I'm not sure. Is it super windy?"

"It can be." I set Lizzie down in the driver's seat, who instantly stands up and grabs the wheel. She starts turning it and making a noise, like she's driving. Laughing, I set the seat on the back bench and pull the seat belt. "Through here?" I ask, trying to figure out how this contraption works.

"Yes, like that," she says, reaching over the roll bar and pointing.

"Okay, I think I got it. Hop in, and I'll get Lou."

"Lou?" Mallory asks, her eyes smiling for the first time since I found her outside with a car that wouldn't start.

Shrugging, I explain, "Lizzie Lou. I don't know where I came up with it, but I just shortened it to Lou."

She fastens her belt while I try to strap the toddler in the seat behind her mom. Fortunately, Lizzie helps me out by sticking her arms through the harness straps and holding the buckle. "Thanks," I tell the little one, bopping her on the tip of her nose and making her giggle.

I jump into the driver's seat and start my old Jeep. "If it's too windy, I'll put the top up."

Mallory nods and slips her sunglasses on her face. I'm not sure why, but she looks sexy as fuck sitting in my CJ, wind already blowing her blonde hair.

I back out of the parking spot and find Jameson heading my way. "Hey, man, you busy?"

"Nope."

"Can you run to the auto parts store and grab a battery for her Escape?"

"Can do," he says. "What year?"

"Oh one, but you don't have to do that. I can get one," Mallory argues.

"I got it, Mallory," Jameson insists, like I knew he would.

"I'm gonna run them home and I'll meet you back here," I tell him, throwing the manual shifter into first gear and driving away once he waves. Pulling out into the street, I head toward the golden arches.

"Oh, Walker, I live the other way," Mallory says, pushing hair that has fallen from her ponytail behind her ear.

"I was heading to get nuggets."

"Umm, that's not necessary."

When I reach a stoplight, I turn and look at her. "I don't mind running over there real quick, even though it's against my religion to get burgers from there."

Something crosses her face. "Well, I have to get a battery now." Her gorgeous face flushes with embarrassment as she casts her eyes downward.

That's when it hits me. The money she was going to use to buy McDonald's is now going toward her car. Realization sets in. Things are tight for Mallory. She clearly has a budget and sticks to it.

The light turns green and I continue on my way, pulling into the parking lot. "Walker," she starts, but I cut her off by placing my hand over hers.

"I got it, Mal."

She swallows hard. "I'll pay you back," she insists.

"I'm not worried about it, Mal. I can surely pay the artist for such a wonderful piece of work now hanging in my office," I state, releasing her hand long enough to downshift. She doesn't seem convinced. "Please. Let me buy her some chicken nuggets."

"Nuggies!" Lizzie hollers from the back seat.

When it's our turn to order, I pull forward and Mallory sighs. She leans over me, her intoxicating scent wrapping around me like a warm blanket, and waits to place her order. "Can I get a four-piece nugget meal with fries, sweet and sour sauce, apple slices, and white milk, please?"

"What do you want?" I ask, as she sits back in her seat.

"I'm not hungry."

I just stare at her. "You didn't eat anything for lunch today."

Her eyebrows pull together in question. "How would you know that?"

Shrugging, I reply, "I'm observant." *Of her.* The truth is, I noticed when she took her quick break today, she only drank a glass of water. She didn't order anything from the kitchen, even though they get a free burger and fries as part of their employment. It makes me wonder if she's taken advantage of it at all during her time with us.

Mallory swallows hard and I can hear her stomach growl. "I'll eat at home," she assures me.

"Is that all today?" the woman in the speaker asks.

"Add a McDouble and large fry too, please?" I reply, pulling my wallet from my pants as she gives me my total and tells me to pull around.

After paying, with food in hand, we head out and toward Mallory's place. She gives me directions, which coincidentally, is the same way I take home. However, I'm a little shocked when she tells me to pull into the old apartment building on the edge of town. The one that's practically falling in and delipidated. "This is where you live?" I ask, pulling into a parking spot and looking up at the building.

"Yes," she says with an edge to her voice. Mallory looks up and takes in the building before us. "I know it's not in the best shape, but it's a roof over our heads."

With my heart hammering in my throat, I pull the keys from the ignition and jump out. "I'll grab Lou. You get the food." Lizzie comes to me easily and wraps around my waist like a spider monkey. She instantly starts chatting about nuggets and dolls, which brings a smile to my face.

We walk up the stairs, all the way up to the third floor. Mallory stops in front of apartment 303 and slips a key into the lock.

She holds the door open for me and promptly locks it after we enter her space. It's old and sparsely decorated, but it's not too bad. You can see she keeps it clean and picked up.

Mal sets the food on the small table and opens the Happy Meal. I set Lizzie down on the booster seat on one of the mismatched chairs. The little girl reaches for a fry and sticks it in her mouth, while her mom opens the little cup of dipping sauce.

"If you give me your keys, I'll bring your car back as soon as it's running," I tell her, sticking out my hand.

Mallory pulls them back out of her purse and hands them over. She also grabs a stack of small bills from her wallet, most likely her recent tips. "Thank you for your help."

I wave off the money and just grab the keys. "We'll settle up later," I tell her. Though, I have no intentions of asking to be reimbursed. I pull on Lizzie's pigtail playfully, earning a giggle, and head for the door. Before I slip out, my eyes meet hers. "I'll be back."

"Wait," she says, grabbing the small bag with the burger and fries. "Don't forget your food."

A grin sweeps across my lips as I unlock the door and pull it open. "That's yours, Mal. Eat up, and I'll see you soon."

Then I walk through the door, making sure it's secured tightly behind me before I leave.

Mallory

I stare down at the bag of food, my stomach reminding me I haven't eaten much today.

"Nuggies!" Lizzie says with a mouth full of food, sauce dribbling down her chin.

"Don't talk with your mouth full, remember?" I remind her, taking the empty seat across from her.

My daughter nods in understanding and dips the nugget back in the sauce. I reach for the small bag, the scent of French fries almost making me deliriously hungry. I ate a few crackers for breakfast and then a granola bar for lunch, but nothing of real substance. I'm not trying to starve myself. I'm not on a diet, though I think I could afford to lose a few more pounds, but my priority will always be my daughter.

I pull out the fries and the burger, irritated by Walker. At his insistence at getting us food and his white knight tendencies that showed brightly today. And then I get annoyed at my irritation, because I know he was just trying to be nice. I mean, he's fixing my battery, for God's sake! He didn't have to do that. He could have called me an Uber and went about his day, but he didn't. He also was super sweet to my daughter, which is a side of him I wasn't expecting.

"Mommy eat too," Lizzie says between fries.

I give her a smile and stick a few of my own fries into my mouth. They're not very hot now, but still taste like heaven, all salty and rich. I find myself eating them, two at a time, until they're gone before I even touch the sloppy double burger. It looks nothing like the ones I serve at Burgers and Brew. These are flat, with condiments seeping from the sides, while ours are huge, with quarter or third pound patties and fresh produce. They even handmake the fries.

When our food is gone, I get Lizzie cleaned up and put a movie on in the living room. She chose Dora today and is happily watching it and playing with toys while I clean up the kitchen. Walker returns to my mind, front and center, and I know I'm going to have to talk to him about today. While I appreciate his help, I don't want him to feel like taking care of us is his responsibility. I've been working my ass off to make a better life for Lizzie and me, and I will continue to do it.

Without a man dictating and running the show.

When the clock hits seven, I help Lizzie into the bathtub and get her washed up. I start to worry about my car too. He's been gone for more than two hours, which tells me there was something else wrong with it. And it's probably going to be expensive.

Trying not to cry, I get Lizzie dressed in princess pajamas and brush her blonde hair. The curls straighten as I brush them, but it won't last long. They'll pull up as they dry, soft little ringlets like an angelic halo.

Just as I finish, there's a knock on the door. "I'll be right back, sweetie," I tell her, getting up from the floor. A quick glance through the peep hole confirms it's Walker. "Hey," I say, after unlocking and opening the door.

"Hey, sorry it took so long," he starts to say, stepping into my small apartment, which feels like it's getting smaller and smaller by the second. He's a large man, tall and muscular, and takes up a lot of real estate wherever he goes.

"Walk!" Lizzie yells, jumping up and running for the man standing in the living room.

"Lizzie Lou, how are you?" he asks, picking her up one-handed and resting her on his hip.

"I watch Dora and Backpack," she tells him, placing her tiny hands on his cheeks and giggling as the stubble tickles her palms. This is actually the second time she's done that today.

"Sounds interesting," he says, carrying her to the small table. He glances up at me. "Do you mind if I eat? Jasper made me and Jameson burgers before we took off."

"Oh, not at all," I insist, realizing it's the least I could do, letting him sit at my kitchen table to eat his dinner.

He sits down in the only seat that doesn't have a booster strapped to it and positions my daughter on his thigh. She helps him pull the Styrofoam lid off the burger and dumps the fries out on it. Lizzie reaches for one and takes a bite. "Lizzie, that's not nice. That's Walker's dinner."

Her big green eyes look up at me and then at Walker. "You can have as many fries as you want, Lou," he insists, holding out a second one for her other hand.

"What do you say?" I ask.

"Tank you," she replies sweetly before shoveling the fried potatoes into her mouth.

"You're going to need another bath," I mumble, smiling and shaking my head.

"Sorry," Walker says, those ocean blue eyes locking on mine.

I wave a hand and lean against the wall. "Don't worry about it. You get used to having to constantly wash something sticky off them," I tease.

"Oh, I wouldn't doubt it," he says. I watch as he opens the top bun and checks out what's on his burger. He catches my eye and adds, "I have to make sure he doesn't put any weird shi—stuff on it. Sometimes, Jasp gets inventive and we find unusual toppings on our food. But this one's okay."

"Ride a Cowboy," I state, noticing the fried onion rings drizzled in sweet barbecue sauce. I've heard it called a western burger before, but nothing like the name on our menu. In fact, all of the burgers' names are slightly inappropriate or funny.

"My favorite," he confirms before taking a massive bite, one-handed.

I almost offer to take Lizzie, but I realize he's not having difficulty. In fact, they seem to both be enjoying their time together. Walker is eating and sharing his fries, and Lizzie is nibbling on them and talking about all the things inside Backpack. He listens intently, asking a few questions along the way, like what exactly is Backpack.

After my daughter gets her fill, Walker glances up at me. "Want some? You can have what's left."

I shake my head, my stomach still full from the large fries and double cheeseburger from earlier. "No thank you."

He finishes off the rest of them and places his trash back in the bag. "Me do it!" Lizzie hollers, climbing down off Walker's leg and taking the bag to the trash.

"Thanks, Lou," he says, holding up his hand for a high five. Lizzie gladly obliges, slapping his hand. As soon as he shakes it, as if her smack hurt him, she starts giggling. "Man, you're a strong girl," he says dramatically.

She reaches for his hand and pulls on him. When he gets up off the chair, she drags him into the living room. "Com'on, Walk. We watch Dora."

"Lizzie, I'm sure Walker has plans tonight," I start, but stop when I realize neither of them are really listening to me. All I can do is watch as Walker sits down on my couch and my daughter curls up on his lap. They watch the child's cartoon together, both smiling from time to time. Every time Lizzie giggles, Walker smiles, as if he's hearing the greatest sound on earth.

I happen to agree with him.

When the episode ends, I try to help give him an out. "Lizzie, I'm sure Walker has things to do. He wasn't planning on having to help us on his only night off."

He just seems to get even more comfortable. "I had no plans, Mal. Besides, I can't think of anything better to do than watching *Dora the Explorer* with this little lady," he says, playfully tugging on a curl and making Lizzie giggle.

They end up watching another episode, but I can tell she's getting sleepy. Her eyelids are heavy as she snuggles into his chest more. My eyes are drawn to them, mostly because it's been a while since someone paid her attention like this, besides me. Devon was a good father, until he wasn't anymore. Early on, he made sure he was home to help with the pre-bed routine and to tuck her into bed. But things started to change almost a year ago. The man I knew and loved slowly disappeared. Literally. He'd leave and wouldn't return until the wee hours of the morning, and when questioned about it, he told me not to worry about it.

I did.

Worry about it, that is.

Turns out, I had good reason, even if I didn't know it at the time.

"I think she's out," Walker says, pulling me from my thoughts.

When I glance down, I see Lizzie sleeping against his chest, her jaw dangling open as she snoozes. "I can take her to bed."

He adjusts his arms and slowly stands up. "I got her, Mal. I'll follow you."

I hesitate but end up walking to the hallway and into my daughter's room. All I can do is stand back, my heart pounding in my chest like a drum as he carefully lowers her into her toddler bed. Lizzie opens her eyes, just long enough to see Walker and smile. "Night, night, Walk."

Walker grins and kisses her forehead. "Night, night, Lou."

When he stands up, I make sure her purple princess blanket is pulled up to her chest and her favorite teddy bear is in her arms. "Love you, sweetie."

"Night, night, Mommy," she says through a sigh before closing her eyes and falling asleep.

Walker leaves the room first, while I make sure her window is locked, shutting off the light, and pulling the door until it's almost closed. When I turn around, he's standing in the doorway across the hall, taking in the empty room. "Is this your room?" he asks, his eyes drawn together in confusion. "Where's your bed?"

I place my hand on his arm. A jolt of electricity zips through my blood, causing me to pull back. His eyes widen and he looks down to where I touched him, as if he felt it too. "Come back to the living room so we don't wake Lizzie," I tell him, though I know that's unlikely. If my child can sleep through an argument and the make-up sex next door, I'm sure she'll sleep through Walker and I having a conversation. As soon as I sit down on the couch, I ask, "Do you want something to drink?"

Walker takes the seat beside me and turns to face me. "No, thank you. Where's your bed, Mal?" His voice is soft, his eyes confused.

Taking a deep breath, I reply, "You're sitting on it."

He glances down at the old floral cushion between us. "You sleep on the couch." It's not a question, but a statement.

"I do. For now, anyway. When we moved here, I just had my car and whatever I could fit inside it. I made sure Lizzie had everything she needed."

"So you left your bed," he deduces, sitting back. "Where are you from?"

"Gibson, Indiana. The circumstances in which we left weren't the best, and maybe someday I'll share them with you. But for right now, just know this was our fresh start. As long as she's happy and healthy, I'll endure as many nights as needed on this old couch," I tell him.

Before he can reply, the door slams on the other side of the wall and the muffled sounds of voices filter through the walls. Walker turns and stares at the wall, as if he can actually see my neighbors. "Thin walls?"

I snort a laugh. "At least they're not fighting. Or having sex," I mumble, casting my eyes downward.

"Really?"

"Oh yeah. *Loud*."

"Interesting. Maybe I should stick around? I could give them pointers through the wall," he adds, his blue eyes shining with amusement.

I can't help but laugh. "I'm not sure they'd hear you over the bed slamming against the wall or the constant moaning."

Why am I telling him this?

Clearing my throat, I add, "Anyway, I wanted to thank you for everything you've done tonight. Let me know how much the repairs were, and I'll pay you back. Gas money too."

"That's not necessary, Mal," he replies, moving closer to me on the couch. My heart starts to strum a little quicker in my chest as he reaches for my hand. His palm is so much larger than mine, his long fingers extending well past my own fingertips. "I want to help."

Swallowing over the tightness in my throat, I close my eyes and try not to fall under the spell of his hand against mine. "I appreciate that, Walker, really, but I need to do this on my own."

When I open my eyes, he's watching me intently. "Do what?"

"This. Life. I need to prove to myself I can support Lizzie and me on my own."

He continues to stare at me as our fingers link. "What did he do to you?" he whispers, my eyes drawn to those full lips.

"He hurt me, but not physically." Walker seems to visually relax with relief. "He put my daughter in jeopardy, and I didn't even realize it," I find myself confessing, the tears burning my eyes.

"I'm sorry he did that. When you're ready to talk about it, I'll listen. But you should know, you're not getting rid of me that easily, Mal. I'm drawn to you in a way I've never felt before, and as much as I've tried to fight it, I just can't anymore," he says, sliding his hand up my neck and holding me tenderly.

"What does that mean?"

He shrugs. "Damned if I know, but what I do know is I can't stop thinking about you and want to be near you all the time." His thumb strokes over my spine and sends goosebumps flying across my burning skin.

"I need to pay you back," I insist, the words coming out in a little gasp of air.

"Okay," he agrees. "The battery was forty bucks."

"Forty? That's all?"

Walker shrugs. "It was on sale."

I don't believe him but have no real experience with batteries and the costs associated. "I'll get it for you." I jump up off the couch like it were on fire and grab my purse. There's a slight tremble in my fingers as I pull today's tips from my wallet. I wasn't able to store them in my hidden jar yet, which is convenient.

When I turn and hold out my hand, he stands up and approaches. He doesn't make any moves to take the money, so I extend it out even farther, until my hand is practically against his chest. "Are you safe here?" he asks, his eyes never wavering from mine.

"Yes," I reply instantly. "It's old and rundown, and the neighbors are loud, but I've never felt unsafe here. I wouldn't have Lizzie here if I did."

He absorbs my words and nods. "Okay," he replies, turning and heading for the door.

I follow, still holding the money. "Wait, don't forget this."

He seems reluctant to take the cash, but eventually does, shoving it into the front pocket of his jeans. "You'll call me if you ever need anything?"

"Yes." Though I don't have his number. The only one programmed into my prepaid phone is Isaac's.

"Do you have my number?" he asks, as if reading my thoughts. I shake my head. "Grab your phone. I'll put it in there."

I do as instructed and retrieve my phone. There are only a few numbers saved in the contacts. When I left Gibson, I left my old phone behind, right along with my old life. He adds his number and shoots a text message. The phone in his back pocket dings. "Now I have yours too."

He hands me back the device. "Thank you."

Walker steps closer, his body heat warming my skin without even touching me. He lifts his hand again and wraps it around the back of my neck, his fingers dancing against my skin. "Call anytime, Mal."

"Okay," I reply.

Then, he moves. His mouth lingers beside my own, and I suck in a gasp of air and wait, anticipating. He doesn't kiss me though. Well, at least not full-on lip action. Instead, his lips glide softly across the corner of my mouth in the most sensual way possible. "Lock up behind me," he whispers against my skin.

But then he's gone, pulling open the door and walking through it. "Wait," I reply, trying to catch my bearings. "You don't have a car."

Walker smiles and shoves his hands in his pockets. "My Jeep is downstairs. Jameson and Isaac helped me jockey vehicles so mine was here."

"Oh."

He grins again. "Lock up."

"I will," I tell him.

"Now, Mal. I'm not leaving until you're inside."

I let out an exasperated sigh. "Fine. Thank you for all your help tonight. The food and the battery."

"You're welcome, beautiful. See you tomorrow."

I toss him a little wave and close the door, locking both the knob and the sliding the chain into place. Only then do I feel like I can finally breathe. Not because he's suffocating, but because he takes my breath away. He's gorgeous and attentive and the way he looks at me makes me feel like I'm the only one in the world he sees. Not to mention the reaction of my body when he touches me.

Oh, Walker Meyer is trouble with a capital T.

And I'm certain I'm not strong enough to resist him.

Walker

It took everything I had to walk out that door last night.

First, there was the fact she's living in a dump. Don't get me wrong, it was clean and tidy, but you could tell it was old and worn down, just like the building itself. Then, there's the whole sleeping on the couch thing. I wanted to grab her shit, throw her over my shoulder, and get them out of there. To my house.

To my bed.

But I can understand her desire to prove to herself she can do it. I'm the product of a young, single mom. I totally get it, probably better than most. My mom did everything in her power to raise me, working her ass off at two jobs to make sure I had clothes, food, and a roof over my head. It wasn't easy, and when I close my eyes, I can still hear her crying late at night when she thought I was sleeping. But we got through it and made it work. My grandparents and Aunt Edna were a big part of the solution.

I pull in, a shiver of excitement sweeping through me as I spy her Escape parked in the lot. Granted, I'll only be seeing her a few minutes before she leaves, but I'll take them. I'll take whatever I can get at this point, which is completely unlike me. It just proves she's wormed her way under my skin. Her *and* Lizzie.

I slip down the hallway and head for the dining room. Mallory is over at a table, talking to a group of women. Her smile lights up her face, and I find myself smiling too. "Look at you, all in love," Gigi coos, as she moves beside me at the servers' station.

"You're crazy," I grumble, shoving my hands into my pockets, my eyes automatically seeking her out.

Gigi makes a tsking sound. "We'll see," she singsongs, ripping off a receipt and heading to her final table of the afternoon.

"Hey," Mallory says, stepping up beside me and tapping on the touchscreen.

"Have a good shift?" I ask, leaning against the wall to watch her work.

"Yeah, not too bad," she replies. I want to run my fingers through the soft curls in her ponytail.

"Did you get to take a break today?" I ask, casually, though it's anything but. The truth is I called Jasper last night on my way home and chewed his ass. He didn't realize the servers weren't all taking advantage of the burger and fries for their break deal. He told me he'd make sure she ate, and if there wasn't much time, he'd send her home with food before she left. Of course, he teased the hell out of me for even being concerned in the first place. He knows me well. I've never been one to fret over the staff or making sure they ate a decent meal while at work, but Mallory's different. As much as I've tried to deny it or fight it, I've come to accept the fact that she is. Period. I still don't know what that means really, but there's no running from these crazy feelings she conjures up, namely the need to protect and take care of her.

She glances at me out of the corner of her eye. "I did," she states, her eyes narrowing a little. "I take it you had something to do with their insistence I sit and eat."

I just shrug my shoulders. "All servers get a free burger or sandwich." That's all I say.

"Mmhmm," she says, fighting a smile, as she steps around me and heads back to her table.

When she collects the check and the customers leave, she starts to clean up the table. Gigi is in the kitchen and Marla off on the other side of the restaurant with her own customer. "Why don't you and Lizzie come in tonight?"

She looks up, her eyes widening. "You want me to bring my three-year-old to a bar?"

"Well, not the bar, per se. You can sit in the restaurant or even one of the pub tables in the back over there," I tell her, pointing to the grouping of tables on my side of the business. "We allow kids with adults over there up until a certain time."

She seems to be considering the offer. "I don't know."

"Come on, Mal. I can make Lizzie a kiddie cocktail."

"I don't let her have soda, Walker."

"Fine. I'll mix up the best chocolate milk she's ever had," I insist. I don't know why I'm pushing so damn hard for this. The only thing I can think of is I want to see them, and with our work schedules not jiving well, I'm limited on when I can do it.

She sighs and cocks her head to the side. "She won't eat one of those big burgers."

"Of course not, but you know she likes the fries. She ate half of mine last night. Besides, there's a kiddie menu. She can have a grilled cheese."

Mallory finishes collecting the dirty dishes and slips the tip from the table into her apron. "We'll see."

"We'll see?" I parrot.

"Yes, Walker, we'll see. I need to hit the laundromat, and depending on how many are there, sometimes it takes a little longer."

"Afterward. Come by. Please."

Those emerald eyes gaze up at me, and I can tell I've got her. "Fine."

I'm already grinning. "Great. Come sit over at a pub table so I can take care of you," I tell her, turning and heading to the large doorway leading to my bar, with a little extra spring in my step.

Fifteen minutes later, I watch as Mallory heads for the back door, ready to head home for the day. Before she disappears, she turns and finds me watching her. I throw her a wave, which she returns, and then she's gone.

I spend the next two hours serving drinks and retrieving burger orders. When I glance in the dining room, I see it almost filled to capacity. Several of the pub tables and barstools over here are filled with the after-work crowd, some eating food and others just looking for a few drinks and to unwind.

It's just after six when I catch movement in the hallway and see Mallory and Lizzie. My feet carry me toward them a moment later, those waiting for drinks second fiddle to greeting them. "Hey," I say when I approach.

"Walk!" Lizzie hollers, letting go of her mom's hand and jumping into my arms.

"How's my favorite little girl? Are you hungry?" She nods, glancing around at the bar. "I have the perfect table for you," I add, leading them toward a pub table toward the back of the room, yet in the perfect line of sight for me to watch them. "How's this?"

Lizzie points to the booster seat already strapped to the chair.

"Pretty confident we were coming, huh?" Mallory teases, noticing the seat prepared for her daughter.

I shrug. "I had hoped," I reply, placing Lizzie in the booster and strapping her in. "And look at this," I add, pulling the coloring book and crayons off one of the other chairs.

Her green eyes light up with delight as she squeals, reaching for the colors.

"Thank you," Mallory says, taking the seat right next to her child.

"I'll go get drinks. What would you like?"

"Water is fine," she replies, glancing down at Lizzie. "And chocolate milk for her."

"Yay!" Lizzie exclaims, already scribbling across the picture of a dragon. "Chocy milk!"

"Coming right up," I tell them, heading back behind the bar. I quickly make the two drink orders for the dining room and slide a refill for one of the bar patrons across the hardwood. Then I grab a glass and fill it with ice water and make the best chocolate milk I can in a lidded cup from the restaurant.

I'm just making my way back to their table when I hear, "Drinking heavy tonight, I see?"

I scowl at Jameson and walk right by him. "One chocolate milk for my Lou."

She looks up with those big green eyes and smiles at me, so much joy lighting up her sweet little face. I'm pretty sure she just stole my heart. "Tank you, Walk. I wove chocy milk."

"You're welcome. Now, what are you gonna eat for dinner? Grilled cheese and fries?"

"Yes, pwease!" she replies enthusiastically, as she goes back to her coloring.

"And you?" I ask, as Mallory scans the menu card. "You don't have that memorized yet?" I tease, tapping her in the arm with my pen.

"I do," she insists, sliding the menu back into the rack in the center of the table. "I just wanted to try something different than the basic burger."

"Want my recommendation?" I ask, leaning against the table and shifting so I'm a little closer. Out of the corner of my eye, I see one of the servers heading for my bar, so I know my time is limited. When Mallory nods, I tell her, "Strip and Go Naked."

Her eyes widen. "W-what?"

I lean in, my face damn close to her own. I know if I were to move just so, my lips would align with hers. Holding her gaze, I restate, "Strip and Go Naked. It's one of my top three favorite burgers, assuming you don't mind avocado."

"I don't mind," she whispers, her warm breath tickling my lips.

"Hmmm," I murmur, devouring those lips with my eyes. Fuck, I want to kiss her so damn bad right now. "I wouldn't mind that either."

"Walker," the server hollers from the bar, grabbing my attention.

Sighing, I stand up straight and take a step back. "I'll be back with your food," I say, noticing how her gaze is zeroed in on my own lips still.

There's an extra hitch in my step as I head back to my bar to complete their order. I hold up a finger to the server to let her know I'll be there in a second and stop at the computer to key in Mallory and Lizzie's dinners. When they're set, I finally head over and make the drink order.

For fifteen minutes, I fill drinks, and take another burger order from Eddie, a regular weeknight patron, all while keeping one eye on the pub table in back. I catch Mallory watching me several times. I know this because I'm watching her. She hasn't experienced this side of the business yet, though it's one of the slower nights.

Jasper comes around the corner with two plates and heads over to Mallory's table. She smiles when she sees him and greets him cordially, even introducing her daughter to him. It raises my hackles that he's over there and I'm not, so the first free second I have, I move in their direction.

"Hey, everything all right?" I ask, grabbing a bottle of ketchup from the cooler on my way by.

"Great," Mallory says, glancing at the burger I recommended.

"Yucky crust," Lizzie grumbles, taking in her gourmet grilled cheese. The thing is made with four kinds of cheese on lightly toasted Texas toast, so it's a little thicker than normal.

Without being instructed, I grab a knife out of the silverware roll and start slicing off the crust. When I have it cleared away, I pick up a fry and hold it out to her. She happily takes it and shoves it in her mouth. "Ketchup?" I ask, pointing down to her plate. When Lizzie nods, I squirt a big blob of red sauce onto her plate and slide it over to her.

When my eyes meet Mallory's, she's just watching me, a look of surprise on her pretty face. It's as if my interaction with her daughter is astonishing.

"Mind if I join you?" my friend asks, pulling out one of the remaining pub chairs.

"Not at all," Mallory replies, offering him a smile before she eats a fry.

"I thought I'd watch you enjoy the last burger of my shift," Jasper says.

"You were supposed to be off two hours ago," I remind my workaholic friend.

He just shrugs. "I stayed to help the night cook make patties. I saw this order come in, so I thought I'd whip it up real quick and head out."

"Then why are you still here?" I ask, only teasing a little.

Jasper just grins a knowing smile. "Company is much better here than at home, friend."

I roll my eyes, unfortunately having to return to the bar, but I keep my eyes on them. Jasper talks to both and makes silly faces at Lizzie while she's eating. Their laughter floats through the air like a song, familiar and soothing, and I find myself smiling as I pour a draft beer. Even after the server takes it away to the dining room, I'm still grinning.

"When are ya gonna tell her?"

Glancing up, I find Jameson sitting at the end of the bar, his gaze cast toward Mallory's table.

"Tell her what?" I ask, busying myself with wiping down the bar top.

"That you like her and want to fuck her."

His words give me pause, and I'm standing directly in front of where he sits moments later. "What the fuck, Jame? I don't want to fuck her," I argue. "I mean, yeah, I do, but that's not it," I stammer, trying to find the right words. When I look up, he's just smiling, and realization sets in. He set me up. "Fuck you," I mumble.

Jameson shrugs. "You gonna let your stupid 'I don't date women from work' bullshit stop you? All it would take is one guy like numbnuts over there," he starts, pointing over his shoulder at Jasper, "to swoop in and steal your girl. He wouldn't mean to, because that's not how we roll, but if you don't stake your claim now, someone else will. That's all I'm saying."

I sigh and glance over to where Jasper and Mallory visit, jealousy burning in my gut. "I told her last night I was interested."

"Interested in what?"

Again, I exhale loudly. "Hell if I know, man. The truth is I can't stop thinking about her. And her daughter? Fuck, I'm already gone where that little girl's concerned."

Jameson takes a sip of his water. "A kid adds a whole new level of complication."

"No kidding," I tell him, pouring a quick drink and grabbing two bottles of brew for some guys at the bar. When I return, I continue. "But have you seen her? She smiles up at me with those big green eyes and her pigtails, and I want to slay dragons, man. I legit would do anything and everything I could to keep her safe. Is that crazy? I've known her for like…two days."

Jameson shrugs. "Hell if I know, but I agree. Cute kid. Just make sure you're not with the mom because of her daughter, okay? The last thing you want is a dead-end relationship because you like the kid."

I get what he's saying, but I don't think that's a problem. I was drawn to Mallory before I even knew about Lizzie. If anything, it makes my protective streak that much more intense when it comes to her, because now there's two. The fact there's a kid involved doesn't even seem to faze me, which I find odd. Not that I'm against dating single mothers or anything, but it can add a whole new level of complication I'm not looking for.

I nod at my friend and head over to Mallory's table. When she sees me approaching, her eyes light up, and that right there is why I can't stay away. The light in her eyes that seems to shine a little brighter when I'm near. The look of excitement and anticipation, which I'm sure is reflected in my own eyes.

The way she tells me she's interested without so much as fluttering her eyelashes or nibbling on her bottom lip. It's not about seduction or desire but about honesty and hope. That's what I read from her gaze when those green eyes lock with mine.

Courage and bravery.

Yeah, I'm already a goner.

Mallory

It's Saturday afternoon when my phone rings. Finding the number for Burgers and Brew on the screen, I answer quickly. "Hello?"

"Hey, Mallory, it's Isaac. We have a problem."

"What's up?" I ask, stepping into the kitchen and away from little ears.

"Jakki quit thirty minutes before her shift is supposed to start. Any chance you want the hours?"

"Oh, uh, I wish I could, but I don't have a sitter available." And that's the truth. Mrs. Fritz is playing Euchre at the YMCA tonight, and there's no way I could ask her to cancel. She's been talking about it all week.

"What if I could help?" he asks, sparking a little bubble of hope. I've heard the stories of tips on Friday and Saturday nights, and if I could work a shift, I could secure my rent and utilities for next month. Of course, I'd have to have a sitter to make that happen.

"Help how?"

"What if I watched Lizzie for you?"

That makes me pause. "You?"

Isaac chuckles into the phone. "Yeah, me. I'm actually one of four kids, Mallory. Remember, I was raised by a single mom. I have six nieces and nephews, and I watch them regularly for my siblings. I wouldn't mind helping you out."

I swallow hard over the emotions. No one has volunteered to help me out as much as Isaac and Walker. Sure, I had some friends in Gibson who would take Lizzie for a few hours, but the moment the shit hit the proverbial fan, they all seemed to turn their backs to avoid the spray, leaving me to take the brunt on my own. "Umm, are you sure?" I whisper, grateful for the offer, yet not really allowing myself to believe it.

"Of course I am. I wouldn't have volunteered if I wasn't."

"Okay, uh, can I call you back in a minute? I want to talk to Lizzie."

"Not a problem. The other servers are pitching in and covering the tables right now, but I will need to call someone else if it's not going to work out," he says before signing off.

I go to the living room and find Lizzie playing on the floor. "Hey, sweetie, can I talk to you a minute?" She nods and comes over, taking a seat on my lap. "Do you remember my friend Isaac from work? The man who had the coloring book and crayons in his office for you?" Again, she nods. "Well, he asked me if I could come in and work for a while tonight, and Mrs. Fritz isn't home. My boss Isaac volunteered to come play with you."

"Will he color?"

I smile down at her. "I'm sure he would."

"And pway dress up?" A bark of laughter slips from my lips. "That I'm not sure about, but you could ask him."

She seems to think for a few seconds before answering, "Otay."

"Okay? That means Isaac would have to get you dinner and help you get ready for bed. Mommy won't be home when you go to sleep, but I'll be here when you wake up in the morning."

I can tell the wheels are spinning. "But Isaac will be here wiff me?" I love the way she says his name. I comes out I-sick.

"He will be with you the whole time until I get home tonight."

"Otay, he can come pway." And just like that, she's up and running away from me.

"Where are you going?" I ask.

She slows but doesn't stop. Instead she hollers, "I have to get my pwincess stuff weady!"

Laughing, I grab my phone and call the last number in my call log. "Burgers and Brew, this is Isaac."

"Hey, Isaac, it's Mallory. If you haven't found anyone to fill the shift, I'd love to have it. That is, if the offer still stands to hang out with Lizzie tonight."

"Of course it still stands. I have my bag already packed with some office stuff and can be out the door in a few minutes. I'll be there shortly."

"Okay. Thank you. See you soon," I tell him, hanging up the phone, a mix of emotions swirling in my chest. I'm anxious to go to work, and hopefully, make good tips. Not that I don't make decent ones during the week, but I've heard the talk about the weekends. Marla said one girl made almost a hundred and fifty bucks one night. Do you know what I could do with that much money? Well, it would definitely go toward next month's rent, but it would also put me a lot closer to securing a bed.

I head to my bedroom and grab a polo shirt from the stack, as well as my last pair of clean black slacks. I'll either have to hit the laundromat again tomorrow, which I'm not looking forward to, or I'll have to wash them in the sink and hang them to dry.

When I'm dressed, I head across the hall to Lizzie's room. Her space looks like a princess castle threw up in it. There are a few dress-up outfits and some tiaras on her floor, as well as dolls and pink building blocks. "Wow, that's a lot of stuff," I say, observing her.

She doesn't stop setting out her toys. "We have lots of pwaying to do, Mommy."

Smiling, I head to the bathroom and swipe some mascara across my eyelashes. I find a black rubber band and pull my hair into a low ponytail. Just as I'm finishing up brushing my teeth, a knock sounds at the door.

"I get it!" Lizzie hollers, taking off for the front door.

I head that way too, grateful she can't reach the chain yet. "You're not supposed to open the door, remember?" I ask, peeking through the hole to confirm our guest.

"Hi, Lizzie," Isaac says, as soon as I open the door.

"Isaac! Where's Walk?" Lizzie asks, glancing around his leg.

Isaac gives me a questioning look that has my cheek flushing. "Walker isn't with Isaac, sweetie. He's working too."

"Oh," Lizzie says, a look of total sadness crossing her face. "It's otay. He pway pwincess wiff us nest time."

Isaac laughs. "Oh, I'm sure Walker would *love* to play princess with us. Definitely, next time we'll ask him to come too. I saw the picture you hung in his office. Maybe we should make him another one," Isaac suggests, pulling out another brand-new coloring book and a big box of crayons from his bag. He sets it down on the kitchen table. "I brought stuff for after she goes to sleep. You don't have to worry about me working before then."

I give him a smile. "You're a lifesaver, Isaac."

He just grins back. "I remember what it was like for my mom, so anything I can do to help. I know tips are pretty good on the weekends," he says, leaning against the wall.

"Thank you," I reply, a bubble of emotion catching in my throat. I try to clear it away, glancing over at Lizzie, who's eagerly waiting to steal away the man in the room. "Her bedtime is eight. Don't worry about a bath, even though she'll probably tell you she needs one. She took one this morning, so she's fine. She thinks she needs to play in the bubbles every night before bed, regardless of her day's activities."

Lizzie giggles. "Bubbles are fun."

"There's a pair of pajamas on her bed, but if you don't feel comfortable changing her, she can sleep in the clothes she's wearing."

"I don't mind that, as long as you're both comfortable with me doing it. My nieces are four and two, so I'm used to the drama that comes with changing someone for bedtime."

Smiling, I step forward and throw my arms around his shoulders. I know it's completely unprofessional of me, but that doesn't stop me from doing it. "Thank you, Isaac."

He returns the hug, but keeps his hands carefully positioned on my upper back. "You're welcome, Mallory. Now go so you can start earning those tips," he says, practically pushing me out the door.

"Bye, Lizzie. Be good for Isaac, okay? I'll be home after you go to bed, remember?"

She nods. "Otay. Wove you," she says, giving me a tight hug and a kiss.

"Love you too." I stand up and look at my boss. "Call me if you need anything."

"We'll be fine, Mal. Promise."

I take a deep breath and step out the door, listening for the sound of the locks engaging. When I hear them, I head for the stairs and make my way down all three flights. It's crazy I'm not more nervous about this. It wasn't that long ago I trusted a man with my child, and I almost lost her as a result, but I don't feel apprehensive now. I truly believe I can trust Isaac and Walker and the rest of the guys of Burgers and Brew with my daughter.

But I thought I could trust her with her own father once before too, and that bit me in the ass.

Pushing those thoughts out of my mind, I drive to work, surprised when I pull into the parking lot a few minutes later and find it completely packed. It's barely five, and I can tell the place is busy. I jump out and use my key to slip in the back door. I toss my purse in my locker, tie on my apron, and drop my phone inside, praying I'll have some free time tonight to call and check on them.

As I barrel through the door, I slam into a warm wall, much like I did not that long ago. His now familiar scent wraps around me, bathing me in comfort and hormones. Damn, this man smells sexy as hell.

"We have to stop meeting like this. Where's the fire?" Walker asks, holding me against his chest.

"No fire, but I'm filling in for a server tonight. I don't want the others to have to cover for me any longer than necessary," I tell him, knowing I need to get going, yet completely unable to make my feet carry me in that direction.

"Well, you better get in there. It's already a packed house," he says, letting go of my arms and taking a step back.

"Yeah," I reply, smoothing down my hair and taking a deep breath.

"Hey, Mal?" When I glance up, he continues. "Don't worry about Lizzie, okay? If there's anyone I'd trust with my child, it'd be him. He's a stand-up guy. Plus, he loves kids. He'll probably have a dozen of them someday," Walker says, giving me a half-smile.

I exhale. "Thank you." He nods in reply and turns to head in the opposite direction. I catch a good view of his attire. The well-fitting dark jeans. The black sleeveless shirt that shows off his ink and the definition of his arms. That ass. Holy shitballs, that's one mighty fine ass.

"Hey, Mal?" Walker asks.

When I glance up, I can already tell he busted me checking him out. "Get your fine ass in the dining room and make that money."

I give him a wide smile and take off like a bullet.

When I reach the servers' station, I find the table assignments with Jakki's name on them. I'm lucky because they're almost the exact same tables I cover during my shifts. "Hey, I'm Duke. We've covered drinks for all your tables and took orders for tables seventeen and nineteen. The rest have menus and are all yours."

I give him a grateful smile. "Thank you so much. I appreciate the help," I say, taking the order tablet he started for my tables.

"No prob. We help each other around here. Sucks that Jakki just up and quit, but whatevs. You'll earn her tips tonight, sweetheart." He gives me a flirty smile, not seeming to care that I'm several years older than he is. I peg him for early twenties, much younger than the twenty-nine written on my driver's license.

"I better get to it," I tell him, stepping around the corner and hitting my tables. I stop by each one and introduce myself, taking food orders for those who still need to order and refilling drinks for the others.

The time flies by, and before I know it, an hour has passed. I'm able to slip into the hallway and fire off a quick text to Isaac.

Me: *Everything good there?*

He replies right away with an image, which takes only a few seconds to load up.

Isaac: *Does this tiara make me look fat?*

When the picture fills the screen, I can't help but laugh. It's taken selfie-style, with Isaac and Lizzie sitting on the floor, both wearing princess tiaras and matching grins. Isaac looks to be wearing a sash, while Lizzie holds a wand.

Me: *Wow, good thing she doesn't have any princess makeup yet.*

Isaac: *I'd make that look good too.*

Just as I giggle, I feel a presence behind me. I startle when two hands wrap around my hips and hold me steady. "Everything okay?" Walker whispers, his voice a gravelly, deep whisper.

"Fine," I reply in somewhat of a squeak. "I was just checking on Lizzie and got this," I say, holding my phone out so he can see the photo of his friend.

"I'm a little jealous right now," he says, beaming at the image on the screen. He looks at it for a few more seconds before stepping back and glancing down at me.

"Jealous? Why?" I ask, slipping the phone into my apron.

"I'd be smiling like that too if I had a cute little princess sitting on my leg," he says, swiping a wisp of hair from my cheek and placing it behind my ear.

"You enjoy playing princess and dress-up?" I ask, teasing.

He shrugs. "For the right woman," he says with a wink.

I swallow over the lump in my throat. "I need to get back in there. We're super busy, and I only wanted to take a quick second to check on Lizzie."

"I saw you head off and thought I'd just check on you."

I can't help but grin. "Stalking me, are you, Meyer?"

Again, he shrugs and leans against the wall. "Protective, Sargant. Very protective."

A shiver sweeps down my spine. Something tells me that's a very accurate description. "Anyway," I say, pointing over my shoulder to where I came from.

"Go." He doesn't move until I do, and I can feel his eyes on me.

I spend the next three hours hopping from table to table, running to the bar for drinks, and basically working harder than a normal lunch rush. Wow, there's something to be said about an evening shift at Burgers and Brew.

Each time I text Isaac, he replies right away, assuring me they're fine. At eight, he made sure she was in bed, having read two princess stories before lights out, and now, he says he's working at the kitchen table on some stuff for the business.

At nine, the dining room starts to clear out, but some of them just move over to the bar. Duke pulls the rope across the doorway, separating the two large rooms. It ensures no one comes over from the bar side while we close down the restaurant. I go through my normal routine of stocking silverware and napkins and making sure the tables are cleared off. Duke puts the chairs on the tables, while the other server, Shannon, runs the noiseless vacuum.

My eyes are drawn to the bar, as the noise level carries over. Everyone is clearly having a good time, laughing and talking. I can't see one seat left open, at the bar or the pub tables around the perimeter.

Suddenly, the entire room goes quiet. So quiet, it catches my attention and I wonder if something's happened. The silence is replaced with the sound of a guitar, the music soft and seductive. My feet carry me toward the doorway, my eyes searching for the source. There, sitting on the small stage, is Jameson, strumming a guitar. I find myself completely pulled in, drawn to the melody like a moth to a flame. I lean against the doorway and just watch as he plays. It's soothing, cathartic almost, and he hasn't even opened his mouth yet.

I can feel eyes on me. When I look to my left, I find Walker behind the bar, his gaze the only one not cast toward the stage. No, his is on me. At first, I wonder if I'm in trouble. I'm supposed to be working, right? But here I am, caught up in Jameson's smooth spell. Yet, I realize the intensity in his eyes has nothing to do with work and everything to do with desire. I can feel it burning, practically see the smolder of want from across the room. Honestly, it makes me a little uneasy. I've never had a man look at me the way Walker does, with such raw yearning and lust.

"He's pretty good, huh?" Duke asks, coming up beside me.

"He is," I reply, my gaze returning back to Jameson.

"He plays Friday and Saturday nights from nine to eleven. This place is always packed."

Jameson starts singing, and my mouth falls open. This big, somewhat scary-looking man, with shaggy hair and tattoos covering his arms can sing like a bird. Soft, beautiful, and on-key. I could stand here and listen to him for hours.

"Let's get finished up and then we'll head over and listen," Duke says, placing his hand on my back and guiding me back into the room.

"Oh, uh, I can't stay," I tell him, heading over to finish the job I started earlier.

"No? Not even for a little bit?" he asks, closing down the iPad register and pulling the drawer. He takes it into the kitchen, presumably to Jasper, but I couldn't be sure. When he returns, he stops and says, "One drink, Mallory. It's your first evening shift and you did a damn good job. Let's go celebrate with a drink." He's very insistent.

I'm about to tell him no, to maintain I head home to my daughter, but before I can answer, Walker is there. "You coming over?" he asks Duke and Shannon, who both nod. "You?" he asks, those blue eyes focused solely on me.

"Uhh, I probably shouldn't."

He steps up to where I stand. "Isaac has her. He says he's working and wants you to stay."

"You talked to him?"

He shrugs. "He texted to check on everything here. I told him we were fine and that you were listening to Jameson play. He insisted you stay."

"I don't know," I stammer, trying to wrap my head around this. I haven't been out since I got pregnant. If I went anywhere, it was work or dinner with Devon, baby in tow.

"Come on, Mal. I've got you," he says, holding out his hand.

Without giving it a second thought, I place my hand in his and let him lead me down the hallway. I can feel Duke and Shannon behind me, but don't catch what they're saying. All I can focus on is the feel of his hand wrapped around mine, his fingers grazing against my palm. It's the most electrifying, yet comforting feeling at the same time.

I want more.

Walker

I can't stop wanting to touch her. Her hand in mine feels so fucking good, it's messing with my brain, because all I want to do is pull her flush against my body and kiss her sweet mouth. Maybe it's the song Jameson's playing about finding someone and falling for them, or maybe it's just having her in my domain. Either way, I'm getting hard as hell and completely turned on just holding her hand.

I guide them to the reserved seats at the end of the bar. This is where my partners usually sit later in the evening or after they finish with their job for the night. "What can I get you?" I ask the three as a whole, yet my eyes only for her.

"Pale ale draft for me," Duke says.

"Malibu and pineapple juice," Shannon adds.

"Oh, uh, just Coke or Sprite," Mallory replies, glancing around.

"Nothing in that Coke or Sprite?"

She shakes her head. "I'm not a big drinker, and I'll have to head home to Lizzie soon."

I let go of her hand, missing the contact instantly, and tap on the bar top. "Coming right up."

Mallory and Shannon take the two stools, while Duke practically hangs on Mallory's arm. He's way too close for my liking, but I force myself not to rush over there and make that fact known. Instead, I focus on their drinks. A tall, leggy brunette tries to grab my attention, but I hold up a finger. I quickly deliver their drinks, sliding Mallory's Coke in front of her, earning me a smile. "Thank you," she says, turning back to watch Jameson play.

"Holler if you need me." Those words are for her, but also for Duke. I can see his interest written all over his young, acne-covered face, but I can also tell it's not on hers. Years behind the bar has made me a pretty good people-reader, and though she smiles at him politely, I notice the way she gently pulls away from him. She's not interested in Duke, and that's the only reason I don't stake my claim right here and now.

I head back over to the brunette, who practically throws her tits in my face. "Sex on the Beach," she requests, her voice low and meant to be seductive. I ignore her unspoken offer and mix up her drink. When I reach for her card, her fingers stroke mine, and it takes everything I have not to roll my eyes. I've seen women like this a thousand times before, and I know what'll happen next. When she signs her name, she adds her cell phone number to the slip. "Just in case you're lonely later," she adds with a wink before strutting away.

Sighing, I slip the ticket into the drawer and move down the bar. Kallie is working the far end of the bar, while I have the side closest to Mallory. As if completely on their own, my eyes keep seeking her out, watching her as she just sits there, enjoying the music. It's not silent anymore, but everyone respects those around them enough that they keep their voices down so everyone can hear Jameson.

He's singing about a breakup when I notice Mallory typing on her phone. I finish pouring a draft beer and collecting the money before I head down to where she sits. "Still good?" I ask, grabbing her glass and topping off her Coke.

"Fine. Lizzie's still sleeping. Isaac is insisting I stay," she says, worrying her bottom lip with her teeth. I can tell she's nervous to be away from her daughter, and to be honest, I wouldn't blame her if she left and went home.

"Do what makes you comfortable, Mal, but know he wouldn't offer to keep her if he didn't want to."

Those green eyes meet mine. "He said that on the phone earlier."

"And you should believe it. He's a pretty blunt and straightforward guy. If he was ready to head out, he'd tell you."

She nods and sets her phone back down on the bar. "Okay. I've just never left her at night like this before."

I give her a small smile. "I know, but try to enjoy yourself. You've earned it tonight."

She grins from ear to ear. "We did have a great night."

"The best," Duke adds, interrupting our conversation. He throws his arm around Mallory's shoulder and gives it a little squeeze.

A growl erupts from my gut, completely out of nowhere. While Mallory's eyes widen, Duke's register understanding. "Ahh, so it's like that."

I just meet his eyes, silently confirming it's exactly what he thinks. Well, maybe not exactly. I'm sure he thinks I'm screwing her, which I'm not—not yet, at least—but I'm not about to confirm nor deny anything.

Duke laughs and turns to Shannon. "You still need a ride home?"

"Yep," she replies, glancing at her watch. "Wow, it's already after ten thirty."

"Yeah. I'm supposed to meet up with some friends," he says, pushing his empty glass across the bar. "Thanks for the drink, Walker."

I nod once, clearing off their empties and setting them in the sudsy clean water. "You okay to drive?"

"Yeah, of course. I just had one and it's been gone a while. I feel fine."

"Okay. If not, let me know. Jasper should be done in the kitchen and he can run ya both home."

"Naw, I'm good. Thanks though." Duke turns to Mallory. "Great working with you tonight. You did great." He squeezes her knee lightly and takes off toward the back hallway.

"I'm glad you were able to fill in tonight. Maybe we'll work together again soon," Shannon says to Mallory before following behind Duke.

When Mal turns back to me, she gives me a shy grin. "They seem nice."

I nod, wiping down the area around her. "They are. We have good kids here," I tell her.

"Duke is...friendly," she adds, trying her damnedest to fight a grin.

"He's a smart kid," I tell her, resting my elbows on the counter and leaning toward her. "He knows a gorgeous woman when he sees one."

"Kid, huh?"

"I think he's twenty-three."

She mimics my position and bends toward me. "Maybe I like younger guys," she whispers, just over the noise around us.

"Do you, Mal? Like younger guys?"

It takes her a second before she slowly shakes her head. "Nope. Six years is a little too young for me."

"Hmm, so that makes you twenty-nine. What about older guys? Do you like older ones?"

She shrugs, her blonde ponytail falling over her shoulder. "Depends on how much older," she replies, teasing.

"Three years older."

"That's not so bad. As long as he has a nice smile. I'm a sucker for that," she says, grinning.

My own smile is slow and definitely reaches my eyes. "Good smile. Got it. What about a nice ass too? I've heard a lot of pros about my ass, Mal."

She barks out a laugh, and before she can reply, I catch movement out of the corner of my eye.

"You better get your dumb ass over to where they're backed up two deep, or your *nice* ass is gonna be out of a job soon," Jasper says, leaning against the end of the bar and basically sticking his nose right between us.

"I'd like to see you try my job for just a day," I smart off to Jasper.

"I would dance circles around you, my friend. Everyone knows my hip action is much better than yours." He winks at Mallory, who seems a little confused. "Ahh, this is your first night shift. Well, sit back and relax, Mal. You're in for a treat." He gives me a wide grin and shoos me away.

Reluctantly, I back away and start filling drink orders. Jasper takes the seat Shannon vacated and gets comfy beside my girl. *My girl.* No, I haven't made it official, but after seeing guys try to flirt with her all night, I know there's no fighting it any longer. She's mine, whether she knows it yet or not.

When the timer goes off behind the bar, I stop by one last time at the end of the bar. "It's almost time," Jasper says, smiling so widely he resembles the Joker.

"Time for what?" Mallory asks, glancing between the two of us.

"Oh, just watch, love. You're in for a real treat tonight," my friend adds, relaxing on his stool beside her.

I turn my attention to the woman at the end of the bar. "Don't hold this against me, okay?"

"Oh, now I'm nervous," she replies with an uneasy chuckle.

As Jameson finishes his song, a round of applause echoes throughout the room. It's immediately followed by silence as I make my way to the jukebox for our weekend ritual. I slip a quarter into the machine, as everyone waits. I already know which song I'm looking for and find it easily in the playlist. I press the correlating buttons and wait for the opening notes to play. As soon as they do, the room erupts into cheers.

"Kickstart My Heart" plays, fast and full of energy. It's not lost on me that it's exactly how I feel when I see her. My heart starts to pound heavy in my chest and sometimes it's even hard to breathe when she's near.

Bar patrons start to sing as I make my way back to my bar. This time, I stop in front of it, at the place where our servers order their drinks. Placing my hands on the hardwood, I hoist myself up to cheers and accolades around me. First thing I do when I'm on the bar is glance down to Mallory, who's watching with wide, laughing eyes, her mouth hanging open.

With one quick wink for only her, I start to shake my hips in rhythm with the song, which is fast. I completely ignore the hands on my calves as I dip and grind. Kallie throws me a ball cap, which I place on my head backward. I start to move, my hips, but also my feet. They carry me toward the end of the bar.

Toward Mallory.

When we hit the final refrain, I reach down and steal Jasper's drink. He knows it's coming and just shakes his head like he does every weekend. I throw back the shot of tequila, drop the glass in his hand, and throw my arms to the side. When I belt out the lyrics I know by heart, my eyes connect with hers. She seems shocked, but excited by the scene playing out directly in front of her.

As the song nears the end, glasses are raised in the air as everyone sings along. I extend my hand down to her, but she quickly shakes her head. The happiness I saw in her eyes rapidly replaced by fear, like the thought of getting up here terrifies her. Instead of insisting she come up and dance with me, I just wink and finish my dance.

When the song officially ends and the next one in the jukebox begins, I hop down off the bar to more cheers and head their way. Jasper's grinning, sipping the fresh drink he grabbed himself behind the bar.

"So, you're a stripper," she says, her eyes sparkling with delight.

I bark out a laugh. "No way. My clothes always stay on. *Here*." That last word is a little lower and a whole lot dirtier.

"Walker, let's go," Kallie hollers, as bodies line up around the bar. This is when we get the busiest. Jameson is done playing, and the Mötley Crüe dance reminds them closing time is near.

"I'll be back," I tell her, tapping the bar top, and jumping in to start pouring drinks.

The last hour flies by, and before I know it, the clock reads midnight. Last call was ten minutes ago, and now it's Jameson's job to start pushing the patrons toward the front door. The brunette from earlier makes eye contact, a well-manicured eyebrow arching in invitation. I wave her away, having no intention of going anywhere with her, and set out to clean up.

"What can I do?" Mallory asks, glancing around.

"Not a damn thing, Mal. You've already worked your shift tonight," I tell her, closing out the registers.

"I want to help," she says, watching as Jameson starts picking up pub stools and placing them on the tabletops. Before I can say anything, she goes off to the opposite side of the room and helps, though it's a little harder for her shorter frame.

"I'll grab some cases. What do you need?" Jasper asks, glancing at the coolers behind me.

I point to four beers that are very low, and he takes off to the walk-in cooler to start pulling product. Just as I pull the drawers and set them on the counter, Mallory appears beside me. "Can I wash those?" she asks, pointing to the trays of dirty glasses ready to be washed.

"If you insist, though I'd be fine with you sitting down and relaxing."

"I've been sitting for the last couple of hours, Walker. I need something to do or I'll fall asleep."

I snort. "Not used to staying up so late?"

"Not in the last year or two."

I watch as she refills the sink with hot, soapy water and uses the stationary glass scrubber to start cleaning the glasses. "Just set them on that mat, and they'll get put away tomorrow when we open," I tell her.

With Mallory's help, we're able to close down the bar within thirty minutes. Everything is cleaned and restocked and ready for Sunday. "Thanks, Kal," I say, waving, as the young woman clocks out on the iPad.

"See you next week," she hollers, heading out the back door with Jameson on her heels.

"Ready?" I ask Mallory, who giggles when she yawns.

"Ready."

Jasper confirms all the doors are secured and sets the alarm as we all head for our vehicles. "Later, guys," Jasper says, approaching his fancy sports car. "Mallory, great to see you again this evening."

"You too, Jasper," she says, tossing him a little wave as she reaches her Escape.

"I'll follow you home," I state, unlocking my Jeep.

"That's not necessary," she insists, pushing hair behind her ear.

"It is necessary, Mal," I tell her, helping her with that erratic strand of hair blowing in the wind.

"Later," Jameson calls, jumping on his Harley.

"Won't he get cold?" Mallory asks, watching him take off in nothing but a sleeveless T-shirt and jeans.

"He's used to it." My fingers graze over her forehead, the slightest touch causing my cock to jump in my pants. "After you," I add, waiting while she climbs into her vehicle. Only when it's running do I jump into my CJ and back out.

I follow her through the familiar streets as she heads for home, the sounds of Stevie Nicks floating through the air. When she pulls into the lot, I do the same, parking beside her car. I hop out and meet her at the back of her Escape. Shoving my hands into my pockets, I tell her, "I'll escort you up."

"You don't have to," she says, but must realize it's a losing battle. No way am I letting her go up by herself this late at night. I don't think anything would happen, but I'm not taking the chance. Not here. "I texted Isaac to tell him I'm home so he can remove the chain," she adds, as we open the front door of the building and head for the stairs.

"I wish this place had security. Even just a lock on the doors that tenants have keys to," I observe, making a mental note to find out who owns this dump.

Mallory doesn't reply, just walks up the two flights of stairs to the third floor and uses her key in the door. When she pushes it open and enters her apartment, I move inside, closing it tightly behind me.

"How'd it go?" she asks Isaac, who has his bag of work shit gathered up.

"She was perfect. We made pigs in a blanket with hotdogs and crescent rolls," he boasts.

"I'm glad she wasn't too much trouble."

"Are you kidding? She's fucking awesome. Anytime you need a sitter, Mallory, just call."

Mal smiles and it looks like tears fill her eyes. I don't think she has much of a support system since she's moved, but that's okay. We've got her. Me and my friends.

The Brew Crüe.

"Thank you," she whispers. "Oh," she adds, pulling a wad of cash from her purse. "Let me pay you."

"Hell no," Isaac says, looking insulted. "You're not paying me, Mallory."

"I don't mind," she says, but he cuts her off.

"Not happening. I don't charge my family, and that's what you are now, Mal. Family."

"Thank you," she whispers, heading over and giving him a hug. "For everything."

"No problem." Isaac heads for the door but stops before he gets there. "So, your neighbors. Wow. I wasn't sure if I was supposed to be appalled or turned on."

"Oh my God," she grumbles, holding her hands up to cover her mouth. "They did *that* tonight?"

"Oh yeah, I think twice. Your girl slept through everything though."

Mallory exhales. "She usually does, thank goodness. I'm not sure if the walls are just that thin or if they're just that loud."

"I'm pretty sure it's both," Isaac says, pulling open the door. "That lady is definitely a screamer, and I'm positive no amount of insulation would keep her contained." Isaac throws me a wave and heads out the door, pulling it tightly closed behind him.

"At first, I thought they only did it against the wall right where my couch is, but then I realized I could hear it just about anywhere. I bet the neighbors downstairs get an earful too."

I smile and reach behind her to lock the door. She doesn't say anything as I slide the chain across and step back. When I reach for her hand, she willingly places hers inside mine. "Come on, Mal. Let's go check on our girl."

Mallory

Our girl.

Those two words keep replaying in my head as I walk to Lizzie's bedroom to peek in on her. Walker is close behind. I can feel the heat from his body in the too-small hallway and the press of his hand to my back as I slowly push the door. My daughter is sleeping soundly in her toddler bed, curled up with her favorite blanket and a teddy bear. When I know we've both seen with our own eyes that she's safe and snoozing, I pull the door back, leaving it cracked just a bit.

Back in the living room, I turn to him nervously. Suddenly, the room feels way too small. I can hear his even breathing and smell a mix of his soap and sweat. Needing something to do with my hands, that doesn't involve me grabbing that sleeveless shirt and ripping it from his body, I head for the kitchen. "Would you like a glass of water?"

Walker follows me, of course, and leans against the wall, watching. "Sure." When I pull two glasses from the cabinet and a gallon jug from the fridge, he adds, "If you're tired and ready for bed,

I can head out. I'm usually pretty amped up after work and tend to stay up later than I should."

Pouring the liquid, I shake my head. "No, I'm fine. I'm not really tired yet."

He moves beside me, taking the jug from the counter and recapping it, before replacing it back in the fridge. I grab the first glass and chug half the contents, my throat suddenly extremely dry and parched. Even in the low lighting of the room, he's stunningly beautiful.

Walker grabs the second glass and reaches for my hand. "Come on. Let's go sit in the living room."

I'm not sure what to do. Do I sit in the middle so we're close, or do I take an end and let him choose where he sits? Gahhhh, why is this so weird? It's not the first time I've been around a man—well, maybe not one this hot—but I'm acting like a teenager about to experience her first kiss.

I end up halfway between two cushions. Getting comfortable, I kick off my shoes, turn to face the other end, and crisscross my legs. He takes the other end cushion, throws his arm over the back and turns slightly to face me. We're not too close, but casually close enough that we could touch if we wanted to.

"So," I start, leaning my shoulder against the couch. "Tell me what I witnessed tonight."

He laughs, low and gravelly. I wiggle in my seat. "*That* was a five-year tradition that began on opening night after too many shots of tequila."

Smiling, I relax against the couch, not even caring how uncomfortable it really is. "Tell me about it."

"It took us six months to get Burgers and Brew operational. We opened on a Friday night and were so amped up on excitement,

I ended up doing a few shots with some of our patrons. At eleven, I went to the jukebox and played 'Dr. Feelgood,' in honor of our favorite band. I ended up dancing on the bar and singing along," he says, shaking his head at the memory.

"The next night, at eleven, they started chanting for me to do it again. So I walked over the jukebox and picked another Crüe song to dance to. Suddenly, every Friday and Saturday night, we were playing a Mötley Crüe tune and celebrating."

"What were you celebrating? Well, besides the obvious," I ask, leaning my head against the cushion and listening.

"The success of the business, first, but to our friendship too. We met in college, though Jameson and I kinda grew up together. One night, we met Numbers in the bathroom. Wait, that sounds bad. We were in there...engaging in recreational pot, when he came in to piss. Turns out, the bathrooms were a horrible place to smoke, and we set off the sprinkles and fire alarm. We ran from the place, me, Jameson, and Jasper, with Isaac in tow. He was so pissed off at us because we ruined his fancy dry-clean only, button-down shirt. We haven't been able to get rid of him since," he says with a chuckle.

"So that's why we call ourselves the Brew Crüe. We were smokin' in the boys' room when we became friends."

Grinning, I reply, "That's funny." But my heart is still beating in my chest, my mind going back to his confession of smoking pot. Pot never bothered me before, but that was before. Before Devon. Before the arrest. Before I almost lost my daughter.

"That was the last time any of us smoked pot," he says, taking a sip of his water. "I never really saw the appeal anyway, but when you're in college, you do stupid shit."

I feel myself visibly relax, because as much as I like Walker, that's sort of a hard limit for me now. Too many bad memories revolving around them to want to get caught up again.

Needing a change of topic, I ask, "So you grew up here?"

Walker kicks off his boots and gets comfy on the couch, his hand resting on my arm. "I did. Jameson and I both. As I said, we met Jasper and Numbers in college. Jasper had a dream to run his own restaurant, and one night over a few beers, we made a plan for a place with both good food and a casual place to have a few drinks. Isaac was working at a financial place and hating it, so he sat down and started putting numbers together. The rest was history."

"And Jameson?"

"He was working as a mechanic at a shop, playing guitar at a local pub on the weekends. He was easy to convince to join the business venture. Believe it or not, he's the one who came up with most of our startup capital."

"Really?"

"Yep. Working since he was sixteen and didn't go to college. Just came and hung out with us all the time. He worked his ass off and saved. Jameson looks rough, but don't let that fool you. He's actually very smart, especially in math. He just chooses not to utilize those skills."

"He's crazy talented. I never imagined him to play and sing so beautifully," I tell him, yawning.

Walker leans back into the corner of the couch and motions for me to join him. I nestle myself against his body and he wraps his arm around my shoulder. The warmth and comfort is instantaneous as I relax against him.

"Are you saying I can't sing?" he asks teasingly, adjusting his legs so they're extended on the couch.

"Well, to be honest," I start, resting my cheek against his chest, "I was too distracted by your hip thrusts to pay any attention to your singing voice." My face burns with embarrassment at my admission. Thank God I'm not looking directly at him anymore.

Not only do I hear the rumble of his laugh, but I feel it against my skin. "Well, hopefully you found them adequate. I'm pretty proud of those moves, you know."

I can't stop from giggling. "Oh, I'm sure."

We're silent for a few long seconds, both relaxing and trying to ignore the springs trying to kill us through the old cushions. "So you didn't know anyone here when you moved?"

I shake my head and exhale. "Nope. I found the listing for this apartment on Craigslist. I knew my budget was going to be small with the move, and what I had been able to save before we left Gibson wasn't much."

I swallow hard and continue. "When I moved in, I met Mrs. Fritz. She found me in the stairwell, trying to move Lizzie's toddler bed up to the third floor, with my daughter wrapped around my ankle. I was on the verge of tears, ready to quit and go home, when she sat down on the old steps and started talking about Cinderella and Belle.

"After a few minutes, she volunteered to come up to my apartment to keep Lizzie busy so I could move everything up. That moment was the first act of kindness I'd experienced in God knows how long."

Walker's quiet, the only sound is his heart thundering in his chest against my cheek. "When you're ready, I hope you'll tell me about the circumstances that brought you here, Mal. It doesn't have to be today, or even tomorrow. When you're ready, I'm here for you."

I don't know why, but a tear slips from my eye and lands on his black shirt. Actually, wait. I do know why. Because of him and the kindness he is continually extending to me and Lizzie. "Thank you," I reply, choking on my emotions. "Tell me about your family," I add, closing my eyes and relaxing even more.

"My mom had me when she was young, and I've never known my father."

"I'm sorry to hear that," I tell him, yawning.

I feel him shrug. "It's okay. My mom made it work. She had my grandparents and tons of siblings that helped, but she still worked her ass off and did it on her own as much as possible."

"You have a big family?"

"Too big sometimes," he teases. "My mom was adopted by my grandparents at a young age and is one of seven they took into their home and raised. My grandparents have since moved to Florida and most of my family is scattered around the country, but those still in the area all get together at my aunt's house on Sundays."

I smile, my eyelids too heavy to open. "That's nice."

Walker sighs. "It is. And so is this," he says, holding me tightly. "Is it okay if I stay just a little longer?" I can hear the drowsiness in his voice now.

"Yeah, this is okay," I reply, feeling myself start to succumb to the exhaustion.

The last thought to filter through my mind is how easily it could be to get caught up in the sense of security and warmth he provides, and I'm not just talking about being held by Walker Meyer. There's something else there. Something that draws me in and won't let go. I'm not sure what it is or what it even means, but I do know one thing. Being in his arms is the best place I've ever been.

A girl could get used to this.

"Walk!"

I'm startled awake, pulled from the hot cocoon of sleep I've been resting in. My pillow moves and sighs, muscular arms wrapping around me and shifting our bodies until I can feel his erection pressed firmly against my back. "Morning, Lou," Walker croons, his rich, deep voice raspy with sleep.

When I open my eyes, I see Lizzie staring at me, her green ones full of delight. I go stiff, my body as rigid as what's pressed against my lower back. "Good morning, Lizzie," I stammer, trying to pull out of his embrace, but his arms tighten around me and hold me in place.

"Mommy," Lizzie giggles, "you sweeping with Walk."

My face turns red as I pull against his arm. This time, he lets me go. "Uhh, yeah, we fell asleep last night," I tell her, sitting on the edge of the couch, taking stock of my appearance. I'm sure I look rough, what little makeup I was wearing smeared around my eyes like a raccoon. I'm still wearing my uniform from last night, and when I glance behind me, I realize Walker is too.

As soon as I'm out of the way, Lizzie jumps on the couch and climbs on Walker. He adjusts himself, concealing the erection I felt pressed against me just a few moments ago. He pulls her onto his chest and returns the hug she gives him.

"I have an idea," he says, grabbing her complete attention. "How about breakfast?"

My daughter nods eagerly.

"Mommy can go take a shower, and you and I will fix her something yummy. Want to help me cook her some breakfast?"

Lizzie claps and jumps up and down on his chest. He doesn't seem fazed in the slightest. "Pancakes!"

Walker laughs. "Mommy likes pancakes or Lizzie likes pancakes?"

Lizzie just nods, making me giggle. Truth is, pancakes are her favorite, which in turn makes them my favorite too. Watching the sheer elation in her eyes as she devours a syrupy, fluffy pancake is the best feeling.

"Let's go make Mommy some breakfast, Lou," Walker says, turning and sliding off the couch. Before he gets up completely, he turns and faces me. "Good morning, Mal." His warm lips brush against my forehead as he adds, "Go shower before breakfast."

Then he's up and moving, his big arms holding my greatest treasure in the world, as they disappear into the kitchen. I stare at where they stood moments ago, trying to wrap my head around the fact I've let a man into not only my life, but my daughter's. I swore I'd never do it again, never risk seeing the hurt and pain in her eyes. Yet here I am, standing back while Walker tears down every wall I carefully constructed over the last year.

The crazy part is, I'm not afraid. Sure, I'm a little worried about letting Lizzie form a bond to the man who could as easily walk out of my life as he walked in, but I'm not afraid of the feelings he evokes. In just a short amount of time, I've learned to trust a man again, enough with my daughter. And not just him, but his friends too.

Listening to the sound of cabinets opening and closing, of Lizzie talking about her favorite princess movie, hearing the happiness in Walker's laughter has my eyes burning with unshed tears. I don't let them fall though. I've cried enough over the last year, and now isn't the time for it.

Now, I need to get in the shower, because my daughter and the man who is making himself comfortable in our life asked me to.

As I make my way to the bathroom, stopping in my empty bedroom to grab some clothes, there's a smile on my lips. A real, honest smile. One that gives me hope and fills my heart with something I haven't felt in so damn long.

Faith.

Walker

As I watch her eat her second pancake, a crazy idea fills my head. At first, I tried to dismiss it, but the thought just wouldn't go away. In fact, the more I contemplated it, the calmer I felt.

"Go with me to lunch at my aunt's house."

There. Said it.

Her eyes are wide as they meet mine from across the table. "What?" she asks, her mouth full of fluffy pancakes.

"We get together every Sunday at my great-aunt's house. There's only a few of us, but she cooks up a storm of some of the best food you'll ever eat," I tell her, taking a sip of my coffee. I found an old pot in the back of her cabinet, and after a little cleaning, was able to brew a pot with the old ground beans left in the fridge. It's not the best, but it'll do in a pinch.

She glances at Lizzie, who's shoveling another bite of breakfast in her mouth, syrup dripping down her chin. "Is that a good idea?"

I shrug. "Why not? You gotta eat, right?"

She seems to be contemplating, while she plays around with the food on her plate with the fork. "Can I ask you a question?" Her words are soft and full of vulnerability.

"Of course."

"Why do you want us to go? Honestly."

I meet her gaze and speak from the heart. "Because my family would love you and Lizzie. Because you don't have a lot of people in your corner, and you would from the moment they meet you. Because I've never taken a woman to meet my family, and for the first time in my life, I *want* to have someone there with me. You're the one I want there. Well, besides maybe Scarlett Johansson, but she's always so busy."

A slow smile spreads across those beautiful lips. The ones I've dreamed about kissing more often than not anymore. Yet, I can't seem to just do it. I don't know why, but I know kissing Mallory will be a turning point for me. There'll be no going back. There will simply be a before Mallory and an after, like those major life-changing events you read about in the history books. She's my life-changing event.

I can feel it.

"Okay," she whispers, sucking in a deep breath and letting it out. "I'd love to meet them."

"Good. Now finish up your breakfast. I'm gonna run home and shower and get ready. I'll be back. We'll probably be outside, so don't put her in something she can't get dirty in," I add, dropping off my cup in the sink and grabbing the dish soap.

"I can get that," she says, as the bottom of her chair legs scrape across the linoleum.

I finish washing the cup, rinsing it in clean water, and place it in the drying rack on the counter. Just as I turn, she wraps her arms around my waist and presses her cheek to my chest. "Now you don't have to," I tell her, kissing the crown of her head and holding her against me. The scent of her fruity shampoo fills my senses and makes my cock jump in my pants.

"Thank you," she whispers, her warm breath seeping through my T-shirt.

"You're welcome, Mal."

With Herculean strength, I pull back and drop my arms. Even though I'd much rather hold her for the next few minutes, or a thousand years, I know we'll never make it to Edna's house if I don't leave now.

She follows me to the door. "What time should we be ready?"

I glance at my watch and notice it's just after nine. "Is ten okay? I usually help my aunt with some of her yardwork, and I have a few things to finish up at my place."

"Ten's good," she replies, twisting her hands together nervously.

Stepping forward, I slip my hand into her hair. Her breath hitches, and fuck, do I want to kiss her. But I know I'll never be able to stop once I start, so instead of taking her lips with mine, I kiss the corner of her mouth. "Lock up behind me," I whisper before pulling back. "Bye, Lou," I add a little louder.

"Bye, bye, Walk!" Lizzie hollers from the table, her plate almost empty.

Then I force myself to leave, even though an invisible force is drawing me back, pulling me to where she is.

Once I hear the lock engage and the chain slide into place, I set out for the stairs. I could tell she wanted me to kiss her. It was written in her eyes and echoed in the way her breathing hitched.

I will.

I want that kiss more than my own next breath, but I know one won't be enough. She's a hit I crave. That's why I have to wait. At least for a little longer.

Tonight.

Tonight, I will finally taste Mallory.

When I knock on her door, I hear the sound of Lizzie on the other side. "He's here!" she yells, twisting and turning to knob.

"Lizzie, you're not supposed to open the door, remember?" I hear Mal say, as she slides the chain and releases the lock. "Hey."

"Hi." I barely get the words out before Lizzie jumps in my arms. "Did I hear you trying to open the door?"

She gives me a shy nod.

"You have to make sure your mom opens it, okay, Lou? You're too short to see who's here, and you always have to look before you unlock the door. Got it?"

She lowers her eyes but keeps them locked on me. "Otay. I will."

"Good girl," I reply, kissing the top of her head. "You ready to go?"

She wiggles in my arms until I set her down. "I'm bwinging my bag, Walk," she informs me, going over to retrieve the backpack-style bag on the couch. Mallory goes over and helps her put the Dora bag on her back, and the moment it's in position, she turns and proclaims, "Weady!"

I pick her up again and turn to face her mom. "How about you? Ready to go?"

She nods, twisting her fingers together again. "I think so."

I step up to her and place a hand on her hip. "They're gonna love you guys."

Mallory takes a deep breath and exhales. "I feel bad for not bringing anything."

I bark out a laugh. "Oh, don't feel bad. Wait until you see the spread Aunt Edna puts on every Sunday. It doesn't matter if there're four people there or forty. Plus, she usually sends me and my cousin, Jamal, home with leftovers. It helps get me through the first half of the week," I state, as Mallory grabs her purse and we head for the door.

Lizzie chats the entire way down, but my eyes are focused on her mom. She's wearing a fitted T-shirt and shorts that make her legs look a million miles long. All I can picture is how fabulous they'd look wrapped around my waist. Preferably while we were both naked.

Mallory is quiet as I drive to Aunt Edna's. I can tell the wheels are spinning and decide to let her try to work through it herself. She'll talk when she's ready.

It only takes a few minutes, actually, before she turns in the passenger seat of my CJ and asks, "So, Jamal? That name sounds..." she starts, but suddenly stops.

"Black? It is," I tell her, keeping an eye on the road as I fill her on my family. "I mentioned my mom was adopted as a young girl. Well, my grandparents, Hershel and Alma Washington, are black. They adopted seven kids of all races and walks of life. My mom and Aunt Cynthia are white. My uncle, Donald, will probably be there today. He's part Vietnamese. His dad was white and in the military. He was born over there and immediately placed in an orphanage. Not too long after that, he was brought over to the United States and placed for adoption here. Donald was the youngest child they took in. My uncle, Padro, was the oldest, at fourteen when he came to live with Grandma and Grandpa."

"That's amazing," she says, the smile evident in her voice.

"Jamal is my uncle Andre's boy. He's one of the only ones who stayed around here."

"Are you close?"

"Yeah, pretty close, though he's a little younger than me. He worked at Burgers and Brew when it first opened to help us get it off the ground. He worked in the kitchen, washing dishes for the first year. Now he's a carpenter, and actually refinished the bar top and all the pub tables a year ago."

"Really? They're beautiful!" she proclaims.

"They are. He did a great job. He's working for a small furniture outlet in Savoy, making custom pieces at ungodly expensive prices."

Mallory laughs. "Well, if the other furniture he makes is anything like the bar, I'm sure it's worth it."

"It is. I actually have one of his first dining room tables at my place. I'll show you someday."

"I'd love to see it."

I glance over and see her smiling, that relaxed look finally back on her gorgeous face. I'm glad, because I know how nervous she is about today.

Pulling into the driveway, I see all the usual vehicles. My cousin's truck is backed up to the front of the house, what looks like a mattress in the back. He watches me pull in, casually leaning against his truck bed, as he waits for me.

"What's that?" I ask, hopping out of the driver's seat.

"Aunt Edna bought a new bed," he hollers, his eyes catching the fact I have a passenger.

I reach through the opening of the Jeep and help Lizzie unbuckle her harness. Once she's on my hip, her bag tucked under my elbow, I ask, "Didn't she get a new bed a few months ago?"

"It was too soft! I have to practically roll out of bed every morning. The other day, I got stuck and couldn't get out. Almost had to call the fire department," Aunt Edna yells as she walks outside through the open doorway.

"You weren't stuck. You were just hoping they'd send the good-lookin' firemen like on those YouTube videos," I yell back, smiling.

"Darn right, I was. Oh, for heaven's sake," Aunt Edna says, clearly noticing Mallory and Lizzie. I feel Mal's delicate hand grip the side of my T-shirt as my crazy aunt makes a beeline for us. "Where are my manners? Here I am talking about hot, shirtless firemen, and we have guests."

"I never said anything about shirtless," I state, the corner of my lip turning upward.

"Oh heavens, child. Those hot men are always shirtless. I'm Aunt Edna," she says, reaching out and pulling Mallory into a big hug.

"This is Mallory and her daughter, Lizzie. She works with me."

Edna pulls out of the hug. "Oh my, child, you are a beautiful little girl. Look at the hair," she says, pulling on one of Lizzie's curls and making her giggle. "Do you like chocolate chip cookies?" Lizzie smiles big and nods her head. "You come inside with me, and I'll get you one."

"I thought we don't eat cookies before the meal," I sass my aunt.

"*You* don't eat them, but this baby can eat whatever she wants at Aunt Edna's house. Would you like to come with me?" she asks, not reaching for the girl yet. Lizzie looks from me to her mom. "How about your mama comes too? I think Jamal is gonna put Walker to work for a few minutes."

"Otay," Lizzie says, shimmying until I set her down on the ground. Then, she reaches up her tiny hand toward my aunt and is led away to have a cookie.

"You okay?" I whisper before Mallory takes off.

"Yeah, I think so."

"Good," I reply, kissing her forehead. "I'll be inside in a few minutes. Oh, and don't let Aunt Edna fill her up on cookies before lunch."

Mallory just smiles and turns toward the house, following behind my aunt and her daughter. "Hello," she says to Jamal as she walks by.

"Hey, I'm Jamal. Nice to meet you."

"The work you did at the bar is beautiful," she says, making my cousin preen like a peacock.

"Thank you."

Mallory turns and gives me a little wave before disappearing inside.

Jamal whistles. "Damn, boy, where'd you find her?" I don't miss the way his eyes glance down at her bare, shapely legs.

"Eyes up, jackass," I mumble.

He busts up laughing. "Who knew you were so easy to rile up?" He tugs on the mattress. "So you gonna help me carry this in or watch me do all the work like normal?"

I roll my eyes and grab the end of the mattress. "How old was her old bed?"

"Four months," Jamal confirms, lifting the other end and heading for the front door.

"What's she gonna do with the old one?" I ask, jimmying the new mattress through the front door.

"She wanted to sell it, I guess. The secondhand store won't take mattresses that are used. Body fluids and all that gross shit. I told her I'd post it on the buy and sell page on social media."

Suddenly, I'm hit with an idea. "How much does she want for it?"

"She told me fifty bucks, just to get rid of it. It's worth way more than that, but you know how she is," he replies, as we maneuver the mattress into Edna's room and lean it against the wall.

She already has the bedding stripped off, so we grab the old mattress and head back out the front door. As we set it against the truck, another idea hits me. "Hey, Jamal? Would you be able to drop this off somewhere after lunch? Not that far from here," I ask.

He shrugs. "I guess. Anything would be better than storing the damn thing until she finds someone to buy it."

We take the box spring and do the same as before. When we set it down on the old frame and place the mattress on top. "Come on, let's go load up the old stuff and get in the kitchen before Uncle Donald eats all the appetizers."

Jamal chuckles and leads me back outside for what should be the last time. Once the older mattress and box spring are loaded and strapped down, we finally make our way to where our family is gathered.

First thing I do is seek out Mallory. She's sitting at the small table in the kitchen, talking to my mom. I bend down and place a kiss on Mom's head. "Good morning," I tell her.

Mom gives me a wide smile. "Hey, you. I was just visiting with your friend, Mallory. You didn't tell me you were bringing someone," she says, her tone slightly accusatory.

"It was a last-minute decision," I reply, reaching over Mom's shoulder for a carrot stick. I dunk it in the dill dip and pop it into my mouth, winking at Mallory. She gives me a smile and goes back to talking to my mom.

I glance behind me and find Lizzie sitting on the counter, her face covered in gooey chocolate from her cookie. "Walk!" she proclaims, holding out her hand that has a small bite of cookie in it.

"This is for me?" I ask, bending down and taking the treat from her hand, causing her to giggle. My face sobers as I slowly chew. "Why is it soggy?" I ask without swallowing.

"I wicked it!" she says, causing my stomach to drop to my boots.

Everyone in the room laughs. "Never take food offered to you by a toddler," Mom states, her voice full of amusement. "You never know where it's been."

"That's disgusting," I mumble, turning to the three-year-old on the counter. "You licked my cookie?"

Her eyes sparkle as she nods. "Mine."

I grab her sides and give her a little tickle. "I thought we were pals. Pals don't lick each other's cookies, Lou," I tell her, sighing dramatically, before stepping up to her and kissing her forehead.

Turning to my great aunt, who's smiling like the cat who ate the canary at the stove, I say, "You're selling your bed?"

"Mmhmm," she replies, stirring the pot of gravy. "Jamal is gonna post it on that interweb thing."

"Facebook," Jamal hollers from the living room, where he's watching some car show with Uncle Donald.

"That. He's gonna post it for me."

"Well, I might know someone who wants to buy it," I tell her, casually. "How much?"

"Fifty dollars. Do you think that's too much?" she asks, looking up from the gravy.

"Not at all. If anything, it's probably too cheap."

Aunt Edna just waves off my comment and goes back to finishing lunch.

To be honest, I almost just offered to pay for it right then and there, but I knew that's not what Mallory would want. Not after her big speech about doing things on her own. Even though this decision seems minute to me, it's not mine to make.

So, I'll talk to her after lunch and see what she thinks about purchasing it. If she does, and fuck, I hope she does, I'll have Jamal drop it off after we eat.

I'll be able to sleep better at night, knowing she's in an actual bed and not on that shitty couch anymore.

Edna shuts off the heat and removes the pot from the burner. "All right, Walker, go finish setting the table. Time to eat!"

Mallory

"Want to go for a quick walk?" Walker asks, as he approaches the chair I'm sitting in.

"Oh," I reply, glancing over to where Lizzie plays with Jamal. They're kicking an old Smurfs ball around the yard, making up rules to their game as they go.

"Just a short one. We'll be back in just a bit," he adds, throwing me those sexy blue eyes that seem to make me weak in the knees and my heart all fluttery.

"Go ahead, kids. I'll keep an eye on Lizzie," Marie, Walker's mom, says, smiling at where my daughter plays in the yard.

"We'll only be a few minutes," he says to his mom, before reaching for my hand.

I place mine in his, catching the way Marie openly grins at where we're joined. As he leads me around the house, I ask, "Should I tell her I'm stepping away for a few minutes? I don't want her to look for me and get scared."

Walker stops, considering my words. He turns back to Lizzie and hollers, "Hey, Lou?" She stops and turns to face him. "Your mom and I will be right back, okay? You can keep playing and beating Jamal. Sound good?"

"Otay!" she yells back, kicking the ball as hard as she can. He pretends to stumble for it, allowing the ball to slip between his legs.

"She's fine. Come on," he says, guiding me toward the front of the house.

It's a small subdivision on the edge of Stewart Grove with smaller family homes. Edna's house is probably the smallest on the street, but it seems just right for her. It has two bedrooms and two bathrooms, plus a large dining room, which Edna said over lunch was the reason she bought the place. She loves to cook, and since she has such a large extended family, she wanted a place that was comfortable for a crowd.

I also learned over lunch that Walker tends to the property each week. He mows, trims the bushes and trees, and takes care of snow removal in the winter. Jamal helps too, but it's Walker who's the closest and who does most of the work. He doesn't seem to mind, though. I can tell by the way he smiles at her, he loves her.

She's a sweet woman, who instantly took a liking to Lizzie— and me too. But it was Lizzie who stole everyone's attention today. Between Edna and Marie, my daughter ate more sweets than she has all year. That's why I'm glad she's outside burning off some of that energy. Naps aren't really her thing anymore, but I'm sure once she lies down to rest, she'll be out like a light.

"So, I wanted to run something by you," Walker says, leading me toward the sidewalk.

"Okay."

"Aunt Edna is selling her old bed," he starts, as we head away from Edna's home. "I was thinking, since you needed one, maybe you'd be interested."

"Oh. How much is she selling it for?" I ask, mentally running through the amount of cash I have in my purse and in the can at home.

"Fifty bucks."

I stop walking. "That's all?"

He turns those all-seeing eyes on me. "That's all. She asked Jamal to post it online when he gets home. She donates a lot to the local Goodwill store, but they can't take used mattresses. She's only used it a few months, and when I loaded it into the truck, I could tell it was in great shape."

I start to get a little excited about the prospect of sleeping on an actual mattress again. It's been weeks since I had a bed. Hell, just over a month since I found my way to Stewart Grove. Even if it's not the most comfortable bed, it has to be better than the couch, right? "Can I see it?" I find myself asking.

Walker immediately turns us back to the house, leading me straight to Jamal's truck. "It's a queen."

When I reach the truck bed, I take in what looks like the biggest bed in the world. It's not, of course, but after sleeping on a two-foot wide lumpy couch, it looks like a big slice of heaven. I press down on it, even though I can't really get enough leverage to really push. "It feels really soft," I tell him, my mouth practically drooling.

"That's her problem. She needed something a little firmer."

I glance his way once more. "Fifty bucks?"

He nods once. "You can pay it whenever you're ready," he starts, but I cut him off.

"I have it now. I actually have it with me."

"There's no frame, so we'll have to stop by the furniture store and grab one," he says.

"And sheets," I add absently. All I can do is stare at the bed. *My* new bed. Who cares if it's used? Not me.

"There's the supercenter right down the road from Jenkins Furniture. We can hit it up after we get the frame."

I take a deep breath, realizing I'm about to make my first big purchase since moving. It's thrilling and a little scary, but only because I worry about spending the money I may need for something else. But I know I'm okay financially. I've already paid next month's rent and have set aside utilities. I can purchase the bed and new sheets and frame and barely touch the savings I have stashed away. Last night's tips were a big help, and it looks like I'll be able to get a bed because of them.

I find Walker's gaze and offer him a small grin. "I'll take it."

Now, that grin turns into a full-watt, panty-melting smile. "Perfect. I'll let Edna know."

"How will we get it to my apartment?" I ask, thinking about all those stairs to go up to reach my apartment.

"Jamal can follow us over there. He can help me carry it up, and then when we're done, we'll run and get the stuff we need."

"You don't have to do all that running. I can find a frame and bedding."

Walker shrugs and shoves his hands in his pockets. "I don't mind helping. In fact, I rather like it." I can feel my cheeks heating up at his words. "Actually, it's more than that. I like you."

"I like you too," I find myself confessing, almost immediately. Nothing like laying all your cards down on the table before the bets are thrown. I should be holding my hand close to my chest, yet here I am, showing my hand and hoping he isn't bluffing.

He steps closer and grabs my hip gently. His right hand threads into my hair, as his left one slides around to rest on my lower back. I hold my breath, waiting and anticipating what's next. Will this be the time he finally kisses me? I've never wanted a kiss as badly as I want his.

I'm sadly disappointed though when he places his lips at the top of my forehead. Again. "We better head back," he says, his voice a little dry and hoarse.

"Yeah," I reply, trying to hide my dissatisfaction.

Walker takes my hand once more and leads me around to the backyard. Just as we come around the corner, I see Lizzie kick the ball wide, throw her arms in the air, and declare, "I'm the beater!"

Jamal just stands there. "What? How? You didn't kick the ball between my legs."

She just smiles, batting those sweet little eyelashes, and says, "I'm the beater!"

Walker chuckles, as I shake my head. "She plays by her own rules," I mumble.

Spying Marie and Edna at the table under the tree, we head that way. The moment I take an empty seat, Walker says, "I'm going to go play with Lou. You okay here?"

I nod, feeling the eyes of both ladies on me. Walker releases my hand and heads over to where Jamal sits on the grass, looking exhausted, as Lizzie kicks the ball around him. Walker jumps right in, trying to steal the ball away from her, but is "too swow" as my daughter makes a diving grab for the ball.

"I always knew he'd be good with kids," Marie says, watching her son play with my child, a small smile on her face.

"He's been wonderful," I confirm, glancing to Edna, who's watching me. I try to dip my chin, but I'm certain she catches my blush.

"So, you two work together?" Edna asks, getting comfortable in her chair with a glass of sweet tea.

"We do. I'm a server at the restaurant."

"It's such a nice place there, isn't it?" Marie asks, so much love and pride in her smile.

"It is, and the guys are all super great," I add.

Edna scoffs. "They are, but that Jasper thinks his pecan pie is better than mine, but I assure you, it's not."

I can't help but smile. I've never had any of the desserts Jasper whips up, but I hear great things about them.

"So, tell us a little about you? Where are ya from?" Edna asks.

"Edna," Marie chastises.

"What? I would like to get to know the woman who stole my nephew's heart," she argues with her niece.

My eyes must show my shock. "Oh, stop being dramatic. We don't know their situation," Marie says.

"Child, that boy of yours hasn't so much as brought another human being here, except that Jameson. The fact he has not one, but two guests, says somethin'."

"Maybe, but that's not any of our business," Marie argues, giving me an apologetic grin.

"Oh, it is our business, and you know it," Edna states, making both Marie and me laugh. "So go on. You were about to tell us all about you."

"Uh, well, I'm from Indiana and only recently moved here."

"Family?" she asks, getting into her inquisition.

"Unfortunately, not much. My parents divorced when I was little, and my dad left town. I haven't seen him since I graduated high school," I confess, hating the feeling of longing and sadness that seeps into my soul when I talk about him. It's not that I didn't try to reach out to him, on numerous occasions, but he just moved on with his life, leaving me behind. He got remarried and had more kids, which he's completely devoted to. It hurts, honestly, and I've just learned if I stay away, I can avoid the painful reminder I've never been a priority in his life.

"And your mama?"

"She passed away a few years back. She was hit by a drunk driver on her way home from work."

Marie's eyes fill with sadness. "I'm so sorry. That must have been very rough on you."

I smile, but it's one of grief. "It was. I actually found out I was pregnant with Lizzie about a week after she died."

"It was like she was sent to you from heaven," Edna adds, reaching over and patting my hand. "A gift from God, and your mama."

I didn't even realize a tear slipped from my eye, not until it hit my hand.

"Your baby girl is the sweetest. She's the spitting image of you," Edna observes, as we all glance over to where Walker and Lizzie are playing. He has her up in the air, spinning her around like she's flying.

"She is."

It only takes a few heartbeats before Edna asks the question I knew was coming next. "And her father?"

I sit back and try not to fidget. "He's currently not in her life." *Not anymore.*

"I'm sorry to hear that too. I raised Walker as a single mother. It definitely wasn't easy, but I had my parents and family," Marie says.

"I had some friends who helped, and at the time, my ex was there. We made it work, at least for a while."

"Did you tell Edna about the bed?" Walker asks, stepping up beside me with Lizzie on his shoulders.

"Oh, no, not yet."

"Mallory wants to buy your bed," Walker tells his aunt.

"You can have it," Edna says with a big smile on her face.

"No, ma'am, I'm more than happy to purchase it from you," I insist.

Something passes in those dark, soulful eyes when they meet mine. It's as if she sees and understands my determination, and if the way she smiles at me is any indication, I'd say she respects it as well. "Well, I was going to ask fifty dollars."

"I would happily pay more," I whisper, grateful for the deal, yet acknowledging the fact she's undercutting the value.

"And I would happily give it to you."

An hour later, we're pulling out of the driveway, Jamal's truck following behind us. Inside is my brand-new bed. Well, new to me.

Lizzie is chatty, but only for a few minutes. As we pull into the parking lot of my apartment building, her talking falls to silence. I glance back and smile the moment I see her sleeping. "Figures. She used to do that all the time when she was a baby. Fall asleep right before we arrived to wherever we were going."

Walker pulls into a parking spot and glances back, his own smile crossing his lips. "I can carry her up," he says, shutting off the ignition and unbuckling his seat belt. He points to the front door, motioning for Jamal to back up to the steps. Then he heads to my daughter, carefully unbuckles her harness, and slowly lifts her awkwardly from the car seat. Lizzie remains like a limp noodle as he cradles her against his chest and heads for the building.

I dig out my keys, stealing glances of Walker and Lizzie. She's always been an easygoing, carefree child, who warms up eventually once the shyness wears off, but I don't recall seeing much of that shyness where Walker was concerned. She took to him right away, probably much easier than he did. I could definitely see the apprehensiveness in his eyes that first time he met her in Isaac's office, but it only lasted a short while. Now, they're fast friends, which makes my heart do little somersaults in my chest.

I unlock my apartment and watch as Walker carries Lizzie into her room. He places her on top of the tiny mattress and kisses her forehead, before covering her up with the princess blanket. "Why don't you stay up here while we carry the bed up?"

Nodding, I reply, "Okay." As he heads for the door, my eyes seem to drop to his ass, all on their own. I mean, it's such a nice one, probably the best I've ever seen in a pair of Levis, so why not enjoy the view while I have it, right?

Several minutes later, I'm standing at the front door while Jamal and Walker carry up the mattress. "Are you even helping lift it?" Walker asks, clearly teasing his cousin.

"Fuck you. You made me go up backward on purpose. Quit trying to knock me down," Jamal argues as he hits the landing for our floor.

"Thank you so much," I insist, as they maneuver through the doorway.

"It's no problem, Mal. If only Walker was a little stronger and actually helping me," Jamal says with a big dopey grin as the walks by me.

I can't help but return his smile. Walker throws me a wink as he goes by, without so much as breaking a sweat or showing any sign of exertion.

They head back down to retrieve the box spring, and while I wait for their return, I grab two glasses and fill them with water from the fridge. Once they place the second piece with the mattress, leaning against the wall in the bedroom, I offer them both the cold liquid. "Thank you both so much. I couldn't have done that without you."

Walker takes a drink, his eyes locking with mine. "I would hope you wouldn't have tried that by yourself."

I shrug, but he's right. No way would I have attempted to carry a queen-sized mattress and box spring up two flights of stairs by myself. Even I, a woman who has made questionable life choices, wouldn't have ever thought that was a good idea. I couldn't even carry a toddler bed up without almost having an emotional breakdown.

"All right," Jamal says, finishing his glass of water and setting it on the table. "I'ma head out. You need anything else, just call," he says to his cousin, but gives me a look, letting me know he's talking to me too.

"Thank you, Jamal."

"You're welcome, Mal. You ever get tired of this shmuck, give me a call." Jamal barely has the words out before he's punched— playfully—in the side. Well, at least I think it's playfully.

"Get out of here," Walker demands with no heat behind his words. He gives his cousin a smile and walks him to the door.

Once he leaves and the front door is locked again, the apartment feels a bit smaller. I don't know what it is about this man. He makes my heart skip a beat and my breathing hitch whenever he's near. He makes me nervous, but not in a bad way. I feel anxious because, for the first time in forever, I feel safe. I can relax.

But then he looks at me with those heavenly blue eyes, and not only can I see the desire—but I can feel it too—as if it were a living, breathing entity. It's there, very much present whenever he's near. In the slight ways he touches me, setting my skin on fire. In the way he watches me from across the room, as if he can't stop his eyes from seeking me out. In the way he held me close all night long on the uncomfortable couch. I think Walker wants me, and the truth is blatantly obvious, something I can no longer ignore.

I want him too.

Walker

When Lizzie wakes from a thirty-minute power nap, we prepare to head out again. It's midafternoon, and while the stores will be busy with Sunday shoppers, I'm determined to get the things Mal needs so she can sleep on a comfortable bed tonight.

Just the thought of her tangled up in sheets has me adjusting my crotch, trying to relieve a little discomfort from the erection I've been sporting half the day. From the moment I woke with her in my arms to the time I turned around and saw her standing in the doorway between her kitchen and living room, I've been fighting getting hard.

I want her.

Bad.

"Why don't we take your car?" I ask, as we head down the stairs, Lizzie in my arms. "The frame should come in a box, but you have a little more trunk space than I do."

Mallory stops on the stairs and glances over her shoulder. "Is that a butt joke?" she asks, her pale face turning beet red the moment the words leave her lips.

I can't help it. My eyes drop down to take in the luscious view of her ass in a pair of denim shorts. "I have absolutely no complaints about your trunk space, Mal. In fact, you have the perfect amount of *trunk*."

When I meet her eyes again, I'm sure she can feel the fire burning in mine. It's been there since the first time I saw her, smoldering and breathing, waiting on that one little spark to ignite the blaze. The more I'm around her, the harder it is to contain.

She giggles before continuing down the stairs. We move Lizzie's car seat from my Jeep back to the Escape. "You know, it would be easier if we grabbed another car seat. This way, we don't have to keep moving it back and forth all the time," I say in observation, as she secures the seat in her vehicle.

When she stands up, her eyes are wide, as if she's shocked by my statement.

"What?" I ask, setting Lizzie down in the seat and watching as she buckles herself into the harness. "You think you're getting rid of me that easily?"

The moment the girl is secured, I pull back and shut the door. Mallory is close but doesn't back away to add space. I take that as a sign she's okay with me touching her. My hand reaches up and threads into her blonde hair, while my other grabs her hip. I feel her hands grip the back of my T-shirt as she gazes up at me with those incredible green eyes. Eyes I realize I'd do just about anything for. For a man who has kept women at arm's length for most of his adult life, this is still a startling revelation, but one I'm not afraid of.

"I'm not going anywhere," I whisper, bending down and kissing her on the forehead.

Again.

Fuck, do I want to kiss her lips. I want to kiss her *everywhere*. I'm hard as steel at the thought.

I drag myself away from her and reach for the keys. She doesn't even bat an eye, just hands them over and makes her way to the passenger seat. I adjust my crotch before slipping into the seat, nailing my knee on the steering wheel.

"Sorry, the lever is under the seat," she instructs, closing her door and fastening her belt.

Once the seat is moved all the way back and I can comfortably drive, I start the small SUV, adjust the rearview mirror since it's pointed down, and pull out of the lot. The entire ride, Lizzie talks, about what, I'm not even sure. That nap apparently was just what she needed to recharge her battery, because she's been nonstop since.

Our first stop is the small family-owned furniture store in the heart of town. I park along the street, surprised to grab a spot along the main artery of Stewart Grove. I glance down to the next block, to where Burgers and Brew sits. The lot looks full, as well as the road, which puts a smile on my face.

"Looks busy down there," Mallory observes, standing on the sidewalk beside me.

Before she has a chance to open the back door, I'm there, helping her daughter unbuckle. "I was just noticing that," I reply, lifting Lizzie and setting her down beside me. "Sundays are usually busy, especially after church," I add, smiling as one tiny hand slips into mine.

We walk silently to the furniture store, where a bubbly man who quite possibly had too many Monster energy drinks greets us at the front entrance. "How may I help you today?"

"We're looking for a queen-sized bedframe," I tell him.

"Wonderful. Do you need the mattress to go on the frame?" he asks, his eyes sparkling at the commission prospect.

"Not today, just the frame."

"Oh," he replies, his face falling faster than a lead balloon. "I'll run and verify we have one in stock."

I glance over at Mallory, who raises an eyebrow in question. Surely she caught his swift change of attitude when he realized he was making a fifty dollar sale, as opposed to the one he thought he might be getting.

"Walk! Wook!" Lizzie hollers, pulling me toward their living room furniture displays, where there are a few small kid recliners for sale. The one she drags me toward is a pink one with small white crowns all over it.

"Well, look at that. They have Lizzie-sized chairs," I reply.

She lets go of my hand and takes a seat, fitting perfectly in the small pink chair. When she glances up at me, her green eyes dance with happiness and her grin is contagious. I almost reach into my wallet and grab my credit card, ready to buy the two-hundred dollar recliner for my little buddy, but then I glance back at Mallory. There's a smile on her lips, but it's the apprehension in her eyes that makes me pause. This woman is working her ass off to provide for her daughter and doesn't want a white knight. She's told me that much. A pink recliner isn't something you just randomly buy on a Sunday afternoon. It's an expensive item, one that would make a great gift, but I know if I were to pull out some cash and make this purchase, she'd shut down on me. I feel it in my bones.

So instead of taking the chair with me today, I make a mental note to keep it in mind for Christmas. It's only three months away.

"You're in luck. We have one in stock. I can have it brought up for you," the salesman says, joining us at the tiny recliners. "Those are a great deal," he adds, seeing the little girl sitting in one.

"Just the frame today, thank you," Mallory says, grabbing her wallet from her purse and following him to the front counter.

I stand with Lizzie, who's damn comfy in the kiddy recliner, but keep an eye on Mal. She uses cash to make the purchase and smiles when she rejoins us. "They're bringing it up."

"Let's get ready to go, Lou," I tell Lizzie, reaching out my hand.

She reluctantly stands and takes my hand. Before we walk away, she says, "Bye, bye, chair."

Mal smiles and shakes her head, leading the way to the front door. A man from the back warehouse meets us with the box containing Mallory's new bedframe. He offers to carry it out for us, but I'm already passing Lizzie's hand off to her mom and reaching for the box. "I got it. Thank you," I tell him before we head out the door.

Five minutes later, we're buckled in the Escape, bedframe in the back, and driving toward the Walmart superstore. "Walk, did you wike the chair?"

I glance in the rearview mirror and find those piercing green eyes locked on mine. Jesus, I wish I would have bought the damn chair. Yes, it would have probably pissed off Mallory, but I can't take the look she's giving me. It's hopeful and curious, yet with a tinge of sadness there. I know you can't buy a child everything they want, but dammit, I want to buy her the fucking chair. I want to buy her everything she wants. I don't care how much it costs.

I want to do anything and everything to make her happy.

Both of them.

171

Surprisingly, that only brings a smile to my face instead of scaring the hell out of me.

"I did like the chair, Lou," I finally reply, my throat thick with emotion.

Lizzie just smiles at me. "It was pwitty."

That all she says. She doesn't beg for it. She doesn't cry or throw a temper tantrum because it wasn't purchased for her. She just grins, blonde whisps of hair blowing from the open window. I vow right then and there to go back and purchase that chair tomorrow. Even if this thing with Mal doesn't progress, or even if it ends before it even begins, Lizzie will have that princess recliner.

Finding a parking spot at Walmart isn't nearly as easy as it was at the furniture store, so we have to hike through half the lot to reach the doors. Mallory grabs a cart from the bay and meets me at the sliding doors. The moment we step inside, it's chaos. Sighing, I remember exactly why I hate shopping on Sunday afternoons.

"Yeah, it's a little busy," Mallory mumbles, as we make our way to the bedding section. "Lizzie, do you want to ride in the cart?"

Her daughter shakes her head. "I want to walk with Walk."

Mallory smiles before meeting my eye. "What can I say? I've got a way with the ladies."

She snorts a laugh. "Oh, don't I know it," she replies, shaking her head.

There are a few other shoppers in the bedding aisle, but we're able to browse the selection of sheets without much interruption. Mallory seems to be contemplating and considering all her options. She mentions thread count versus cost, before moving on to those beds in a bag. She finds a white, gray, and pink set in the size she needs, and I fucking love the way her eyes sparkle with happiness.

"This one look okay?"

I realize right there, even if it was the ugliest bedding in the world, I'd still tell her yes. Why? Because something as simple as new bedding makes her giddy with excitement, and I want to see that smile on her face every day for as long as possible. "It's perfect," I reply, returning her grin. Stepping up close as she mulls over the bedding, I whisper, "Your blonde hair and fair skin against that pink color will haunt my dreams tonight."

Her face blushes its own three shades of pink as she nibbles on her bottom lip. I've seen the action a thousand times before. You don't work behind a bar and not become accustomed to that particular movement on females. Ever since that Christian Grey book came out, women have been using their lip and teeth as a form of seduction, and while I'll admit it can be alluring, I've since learned it's not about the act.

It's the woman.

I saw fifteen women nibbling their lip Saturday night alone and felt nothing.

But Mallory? One little bite, and suddenly I'm half-mast in the bedding aisle at Walmart, visions of her clamping down on that very lip while I slide inside her body.

"Do you, uh, is it okay if I grab a few other things while we're here?" she asks, clearly flustered by my comment.

"Get what you need," I state. One less trip she has to make.

We move through the store, grabbing toilet paper and a few cleaning supplies. Mallory also adds cereal, a gallon of milk, and some canned goods to the cart. When we reach the meat section, she heads over to the hotdog and lunchmeat section, Lizzie and I lagging behind.

"Well, if it isn't Walker Meyer."

That voice.

Way too familiar.

I glance over my shoulder and find Bethani, the crazy patron who wouldn't leave me alone two years ago. She's smiling widely, her makeup flawless, her lips a deep shade of purple. I'll admit, she's pretty, but I'm having a hard time recalling why I was attracted to her. She's not really my type, if I have one. There's only one reason I can think of, and it was because I was horny, and she was easy and willing. Plain and simple.

"Hi," I reply, turning back around and trying to move away from the situation.

"Look, Amie, it's Walker," Bethani coos. Suddenly, the other woman is directly in front of me.

"Hey, Walker. How's Jameson?"

I roll my eyes, unable to stop myself. "Why don't you ask him?" I ask, trying to step around her.

I feel Lizzie tug my hand, so I reach down and pick her up. The faster I leave, the better off we'll all be.

"Oh, I plan to see him later tonight," she replies, playing with a strand of her long hair.

Again, I step to the right, but this time, I bump into Bethani. "I didn't know you had a wife and kid," she says, smiling at Lizzie.

"I don't," I mumble.

"I mean, I wouldn't care if you did." Both women giggle and block my exit.

"Have a nice day," I reply, retreating backward.

"Wait, can I stop by later?" Bethani asks, my mouth dropping open in disgust.

"No. I thought I made my position pretty damn clear two years ago," I tell her.

She laughs. "Oh, that little piece of paper didn't mean anything. Plus, you let it expire."

I sigh, regretting ever letting the Order of Protection I had to take out on her end, but she left town. At least for a while. "Not happening, Bethani. Stay away from me and my bar. You're not welcome near either." With that, I turn and walk away.

The moment I step beside Mallory, she asks, "Friends of yours?" There's a smile on her face, but it doesn't reach her eyes. They're tight with anxiety, as if she knows she may not want to hear the answer to the question.

"Absolutely not. I'll explain later," I tell her, setting Lizzie in the cart, and gently pushing it toward the checkout.

We use a self-checkout station because the lines at the other lanes are too long. I hate lines. Mallory pays for her purchases and is smiling as we make our way to her Escape. Once we're loaded up, I jump behind the wheel and get the hell out of the busy supercenter.

Something hits me as I'm heading back to her house. "I have an idea," I say, catching her attention. "You'll probably want to wash your bedding before we get everything put together. How about we stop at my place and use my washer and dryer? This way, you don't have to worry about babysitting the machines in the basement."

Mallory seems to consider the offer. "We could go to the laundromat downtown. It's pretty clean and usually isn't too busy."

I shrug. "We could, but you don't have laundry soap with you. I have some at my place. Plus, Lou can play in the backyard while we wait on it to wash and dry."

She's silent for almost a full minute before she finally speaks. "Okay, I guess that would be all right. Thank you."

Feeling like this is a small victory, I pass the apartment complex and head for my place. I don't know why, but the thought of having Mal and Lizzie there calms me. I like the idea of having them at my house. It's nothing special, but maybe that's not what makes a house a home anyway. Maybe it's not the walls or the number of bedrooms or the amount of living space.

Perhaps it's the people you invite inside.

Mallory

By the time we wash and dry two loads of laundry and head back to my apartment, it's well after five. Lizzie is dirty and tired from playing outside on the swing set Walker has, left by the previous owner of the house, and I'm anxious to get my new bed put together. The prospect of not sleeping on that lumpy old couch has me all sorts of excited.

It takes two trips to get everything up to my apartment, but once we do, a renewed sense of happiness sweeps through me. It's partly because of the bed, but it's more than that. Today was...nice—wonderful, actually—and I can't argue the reason. Walker. He's sweet and caring, even though he tries to act a little gruff and can be blunt, and not just with me, but with Lizzie. He's the kind of man any woman would want, especially if you have a child.

I've felt this attraction to him pretty much since the moment I laid eyes on him in a darkened hallway, and that hasn't waned in the slightest. In fact, it's only growing stronger and stronger the more time I spend with him and get to know him. Is it too soon to welcome him into my home—and maybe my bed? Probably. Am I creating more heartache and hurt with allowing my daughter to get so close to him? Possibly. Will that stop me from wanting to get to know him more and see where this *thing* between us goes? Nope.

Because in just a short amount of time, I've become addicted to Walker Meyer.

"I have an idea," he says, coming up behind me, as I put away the few groceries I picked up.

"What's that?" I ask, trying to play it cool, even though my body is on fire. His hands rest on my hips, his chest pressed gently to my back, and his strong jaw angles right over my shoulder.

"How about I order pizza tonight, so we don't have to cook while putting together your bed?" His warm breath fans across my cheek.

"You don't have to do that," I state, wanting to turn around. Wanting to throw my arms over his shoulders and press my chest to his. Wanting to climb on the counter and wrap my legs around him. Wanting all of that, but not giving in to the desire. Instead, I hold completely still.

"I want to. Lou's eyes are already getting droopy. I think she'll be out early tonight," he whispers, his lips lingering so close to my ear. There's a hint of something...dirty in his innocent statement, and my word, do I want to explore the dirty.

"I'm sure you have other things you needed to do today, Walker. You hadn't planned on spending the entire day with us."

"No, maybe not, but this was way better than anything I might have done today. Besides, I can mow and shop and do chores on Tuesday when I'm off," he says, resting his chin on my shoulder. "I like spending the time with you."

I exhale, not realizing I was holding my breath. "I like spending time with you too."

He kisses my shoulder, my skin's sad there's material between us, and says, "Okay. I'm gonna order a pizza. What do you like on it?"

"Anything. Get what you like."

"No, that's not what I asked. What do *you* like on it?"

I can't help but grin. How long has it been since someone asked me what I wanted on pizza? Years, I think. Devon hated mushrooms, didn't want them on a pizza, even just half. He swore the juices tainted the whole thing, so I got in a habit of getting what he liked. The last pizza I ordered for just me and Lizzie was cheese, because it was cheaper, but also because it was just easier than to pick off what Lizzie won't eat.

"I like sausage and mushrooms," I tell him, my voice soft and hesitant.

"Yeah? Me too. That's my favorite," he says, the smile evident in his voice. "What about Lou?"

"She doesn't like mushrooms, but I can pick those off."

"I'll get part of it without the mushrooms then," he states, stepping back and severing our connection.

I glance over my shoulder. "You don't have to do that. I'm sure it's easier to get the whole pizza one way."

He just gives me a cocky, crooked grin. "I got this, Mal. Don't worry about a thing."

After we ate the pizza—with one quarter of it without mushrooms—Walker starts to set up the bedframe. "Where do you want the head?" he asks, glancing around the mostly empty room.

I just started to fill the bathtub for Lizzie, and poked my head inside the room. "Umm, maybe there?" I reply, pointing to the far wall without the window.

"Doesn't that butt up against your neighbors?" he asks, arching an eyebrow and giving me a slow, sexy smile.

"Oh. Yeah. That might be a bad idea."

"How about this one? It's an inside wall, so you might not feel like you're a third wheel in their all-night sex-athons."

I can't help but giggle. "Definitely. If it's that loud in the living room, can you imagine what it's going to be like in here?" I ask, suddenly wondering if moving into my bedroom is the best idea.

"We'll invest in earplugs," he quips, sliding two pieces of the frame together and locking them in place.

We'll.

"Mommy, I weady!" Lizzie hollers before streaking from her bedroom completely naked, her giggles trailing behind her.

"We have company, Lizzie. You can't run around naked," I state, taking off after her, and unable to hide my smile.

She giggles loudly in reply and waits for my help to jump in the tub. She uses cups to douse herself in water, helping me rinse the suds away as I go. Lizzie yawns once, so I decide to pull the plug and not let her have the usual extra time to play in the water. She doesn't seem to mind, though. I help her out, dry her off, and wrap a towel around her little body. The moment I do, she takes off out of the bathroom, giggling once again.

"Walk! I cwean!" she announces as she hits the threshold to my bedroom.

"I see that. Go get some jammies on, and you can help me make your mommy's bed," he says. I notice he has the frame together and the box spring and mattress positioned on top.

"Otay," she replies, running across the hall to her bedroom.

I help her dry off and dress in a pair of Dora pajamas that have seen better days. They were a garage sale find earlier this summer, but she loves them. As fast as she's growing, I'm not sure how much longer she'll be able to wear them.

"Weady," she announces, as she runs into my bedroom, me trailing behind with her hairbrush.

I quickly set her on the bed and run the wide-toothed comb through her locks. Her hair tangles easily with the curls, but as long as I use conditioner, it's not too bad. It doesn't take long to comb out her hair, and she's ready to help.

"Okay, you take this corner," Walker instructs, handing it to her across the bed. "Hold it tight." When he pulls to tuck in his end, he pulls it out of her hand and makes her laugh. "I said hold it tight, silly," he adds, laughing right along with her.

I end up on one side of the bed, while the other two pull and secure the fitted sheet. We work as a team to make the bed, and the moment the cases are on the pillows, Walker picks Lizzie up and carefully tosses her onto the mattress before jumping on himself and lying beside her. "What do you think? Did we do a good job?" he asks, resting his head on my pillow.

"Yep!" she replies, yawning.

I glance at my watch, realizing it's after seven. Bedtime is usually eight, but I can definitely see an earlier bedtime for my girl tonight. "How about we go start a movie and relax?" I ask, catching her attention.

"Cat and Hat," she bellows, as she bounces off the bed and heads for the television in the living room.

Walker crawls off the bed too, and there's definitely something sexy about the way he moves. It catches and holds my attention, riveting me in place as he heads my way. "I don't think I've seen *The Cat in the Hat*."

"Who doesn't like Mike Myers?" I ask, my voice a little breathless.

"Mmm," he replies, pulling me into his chest and running his nose along my hair. I can hear him inhale, as a shiver sweeps down my spine.

"I'm sure you have better things to do," I whisper.

He pulls back and meets my eyes. "Do you want me to leave?"

I realize quickly the answer. Even though I'm sure he has other things he can be doing, I decide to answer him honestly and shake my head.

Walker's grin starts off slow and lights up his entire face. "Good. I want to stay."

I get the DVD player set up with the movie, smiling when I turn to see Lizzie sitting on Walker's lap. He's watching me intently, those blue eyes like a caress over my skin. I press play on the remote and move to where they sit. I don't have time to contemplate where I'm going to land, because Walker lifts his arm, inviting me to sit beside him.

We're fifteen minutes in when he nudges me with his arm. I glance over, only to find Lizzie sound asleep, curled up on his lap with her head resting on his chest. "Do you want me to take her?" I whisper, even though, deep down, I already know the answer.

Walker carefully moves to stand, slipping his arm from around my shoulder and cradling my daughter. He moves so easily, so effortlessly, as if he's been taking care of a child for years. As he did the other night, he carries Lizzie to bed, kissing her forehead as he tucks blankets around her body. "Night, night, Walk."

"Good night, Lou."

"Wove you," she whispers, turning on her side and snuggling into her pillow.

Walker clears his throat before murmuring, "Love you too, Lou." He runs a hand over her forehead before he stands and moves toward the doorway.

I crouch down and grab her teddy bear, placing it right beside her. With a quick kiss on her forehead and a whispered "I love you," I turn on the night-light and slip out of her room.

In the hallway, I find Walker, casually leaning against the doorframe of my bedroom. His hands are in his pockets, and he gives off the appearance of calm and collected. But that's not what I see in his eyes. They're dark and stormy, thundering with desire and want, yet he doesn't move from his position.

Feeling a boldness I've never felt, I step forward, placing my hands on his chest. I feel his heart thundering beneath my palm and can see his jaw tighten. Still, he doesn't move.

I think about all those times I thought he would kiss me but didn't. How badly I want him to now. But something is holding him back, and frankly, I'm tired of waiting. I *need* to kiss him. It's like he's the oxygen my lungs demand.

Gazing up into his blue eyes, I find the strength to ask the one question I can't stop thinking about. "Walker, can I kiss you?"

His lip ticks, but he still doesn't move. "You can do anything you want."

Leaning forward and up on my tiptoes, I swipe my lips across his, reveling in the warmth and softness. "Why haven't you kissed me yet?" I whisper, my eyes closed.

He exhales, his breath fanning across my face. I feel him pull his hands from his pockets and slide them up my back. He grips my shirt and pulls me even closer. "I've wanted to. So fucking bad, but I wanted to take things slow, and I knew I wouldn't be able to stop once I started."

I open my eyes to meet his, mine pleading and burning with a desire I've never felt in my life. "Then don't stop."

That's all it takes. His lips slam into mine, hungry and full of want, as he devours my mouth so expertly, all I can do is hold on. My hands thread into his hair as he lifts me to meet his height. As my legs wrap around his hips, I can feel how hard he already is, and I grind against him, seeking that glorious friction.

"Fuck," he hisses, rocking into me.

"Yes. That."

His looks up, his eyes searching mine, as if seeking confirmation. He swallows hard, his voice raspy when he finally speaks. "I wanted to take things slow."

"I know, but sometimes fast is good." I move, sliding along his hard length. "Real good."

As if someone flipped the switch, he moves, carrying me into my bedroom. We fall onto the mattress together, his mouth claiming mine once again. This kiss is full of urgency and passion and makes me a little dizzy with lust.

Walker lifts my shirt and slides a hand along my stomach, branding me with his touch. I've never felt this...hot before. I push his shirt up, exposing hard abs and tanned skin. My fingers graze over his flesh, and I can feel goosebumps rise.

"Let's take off this shirt, shall we?" he whispers, running his lips down my neck and nipping at my chin.

"Yes, please." I tug upward on the back of his shirt.

He chuckles. "I meant yours, but I'm an equal opportunity clothes remover." He sits up and grabs the material behind his head and pulls it up and over his head in one swift motion.

My eyes feast everywhere. His broad chest, the ripple of abs, the hard muscles. He's a vision in a shirt, but without? I practically swallow my tongue.

"Now you," he instructs, helping me sit up and removing my T-shirt.

Usually this is the part where I'd ask to turn off the lights. I'm not hard or ripped anywhere. If anything, I'm carrying a little flab in the middle and my boobs are nowhere near as perky as they once were. But the way his eyes devour me, it's more liberating than anything else. What used to be embarrassment when I got naked is now replaced and fueled by something else.

Desire.

"You're so fucking beautiful," he whispers hoarsely, his large hand sliding up my side and slipping beneath the cup of my bra. My nipples pebble as he runs the pad of his thumb over the top of one hard peak. Walker adjusts the material, exposing my breast. The moment he does, his mouth descends, licking and sucking until I can barely breathe.

I grip his upper back, holding on while he teases one nipple before moving on to do the same to the second. My heart is trying to pound out of my chest, my panties too wet to be useful. I can't seem to catch my breath, as he softly bites down on my nipple, making me cry out.

"Mal, I'm going to jump up and shut the door, okay? Then I'm going to finish undressing you and taste every inch of your body."

Before I can even wrap my head around his words, his warmth is gone as he gets off the bed. He peeks in across the hall, making sure Lizzie is still sleeping, before he returns, shutting the door tightly behind him. The look in his eyes has me squirming where I lie, anxious, yet slightly nervous. My expertise in this area isn't very broad, and I don't want my lack of experience to show now.

Walker returns to the bed, slipping a hand behind my back and unclasping my bra. He tosses it onto the floor, as his mouth descends once more. I rock my hips, seeking more of that delicious friction. He runs a hand down my hip and slides it between my legs. A gasp slips from my lips, his fingers rubbing across my clit.

"Let's get rid of these shorts," he suggests.

Lifting my hips, Walker slides both my shorts and panties off, giving them the same treatment as he did my bra. My legs spread to accommodate his body as he positions himself where I need him most. His focus is down, and when he licks his lips, I know what's coming next.

"You're wearing more clothes than me," I remind him, but it falls on deaf ears. He has a plan, and I know exactly what it entails.

The first swipe of his tongue across my clit causes me to buck. Walker places his hands on my thighs and spreads my legs even more before he lowers his mouths and devours. That's the only way to describe it. His lips suck on my clit and his tongue delves deep inside my pussy. All I can do is hold on and enjoy the ride.

I moan in pleasure as my body starts to coil tighter. He slips a single finger into my body as he sucks hard on my clit. The orgasm rushes in fast, sweeping through my body in the most spectacular fashion. Walker uses his tongue to coax out every drop of my release possible, and the moment I fall limp and sated onto my bed, he sits up, watching me. A slow grin spreading across his lips as he reaches down to release his belt.

"I'm not done with you."

Walker

My God, that was the most spectacular sight I've ever seen. Watching her come under my tongue and on my fingers will forever be etched in my brain. I'm already addicted, determined to do it again and again.

And then once more.

Right now, the only thing I can think about is watching—no, feeling—her come on my cock. She lies limp on the bed, a vision of beauty. Her hair is mussed, her breathing slightly labored, and her fair skin just as gorgeous against the pink and gray bedding as I suspected.

I pull my belt from my jeans, my eyes locked on her content face. A sense of pride sweeps through my body, and I can't help but smile. I did that. I'm the reason she looks completely sated and happy right now.

Only I'm not done with her.

As I pop the button on my pants and slide down the zipper, her eyes slowly open and watch my every move. Even when I slip off the bed to rid myself of shoes, socks, and jeans, those emerald eyes are locked on me. There's also no missing the way they flare with excitement as I lower my boxer briefs down my thighs.

I grab my jeans and pull my wallet from the back pocket, retrieving the two condoms I slipped in there earlier today. I was hoping to get to use them someday in the near future but wasn't expecting it to be tonight. Not that I'm complaining. I've thought of nothing but taking Mallory to bed since the moment I laid eyes on her. However, she's the first woman who felt different than just a romp in the sheets. The first one who made me want to get to know her before I took her to bed. The first one who made me look past the superficial and want to explore the person deep down.

I rejoin Mallory on top of her bed, moving between her open legs and lying over top of her. She wraps her legs around my hips, aligning her pussy with my cock. I realize my mistake right away. I should have suited up before even climbing back into this bed. Before I felt how amazing her wetness feels against my bare skin, and almost said fuck it and went in without protection.

But I'd never risk her.

Ever.

So I reach for one of the foil packets I dropped on the edge of the bed, rip it open, and roll the protection into place. Once I'm repositioned between her thighs, I thread my fingers into her hair and hover my lips over hers. "Are you sure?" I whisper, holding back, even though my cock is nudging anxiously at her entrance.

"I'm sure," she murmurs, the softest, sweetest words I've ever heard. "Please, Walker."

I slowly push forward, sliding into her tight, wet body. Mallory gasps, tightening around my cock and making my eyes cross. "Relax, sweetheart," I say softly before taking her lips with my own.

I feel her body relaxing under me as she deepens the kiss. It allows me to pull out and thrust back inside, filling her completely. While she tenses around me, she digs her heels into my ass and tilts her hips upward, allowing me to go even deeper. Our joint moans fill the room, her nails digging into my shoulder blades as I rock my hips, burying myself to the hilt.

Mallory squeezes around me, and the pleasure almost makes me lose it, but I'm not about to blow in ten seconds like a high schooler. No, I'm drawing this out as long as possible. Holding myself up on my elbows, I move my hips, fighting the urge to just let go. With each thrust, every gyration of my body, I feel her tightening around me, her body climbing closer and closer to a release.

Nails dig into my flesh as her sweet pussy starts to squeeze. She gasps, her eyes falling closed, her mouth dropping open. I run my lips over her jaw and down her neck before pistoning inside her body hard. It pushes her over the edge, her body milking and pulsating around my cock in the most amazing way possible.

I try to hold myself back, but can't. I'm too far gone. With her pussy vise-gripping me, I let myself lose control, rocking and thrusting, chasing my own release. It doesn't take long before my spine starts to tingle. Ignoring the burn in my thighs, I let go, coming hard with a grunt and her name on my lips.

Exhaustion sweeps in, the remnants of an epic orgasm pulling me toward sleep, but I refuse to just pass out. I roll us to our sides, tucking Mallory against my body. We're both sweaty, but neither of us seems to mind. She snuggles into my chest, her warm breath tickling my neck. I hate snuggling, but for some reason, this is the most comfortable thing in the world. Even with her long hair sticking to my arm, I've never been more content.

It's the first time I realize how well I actually slept last night. On that lumpy, shitty couch, with her curled up beside me, I slept like a fucking baby. No music. No noise. Just six hours of blissful sleep, and I realize I want that again.

Even though her breathing is starting to even out, I need to get up. I have to remove the rubber, but also shut off the television and light in the living room. Carefully, I extract myself from under her body and slip from the bed. Grabbing my boxer briefs, I head for the bathroom and clean myself up, disposing of the protection. I take a clean cloth from the pile, warming it with water, and slip on my underwear. The last thing I want is for Lou to come out and find me naked.

Slipping quietly out of the bathroom, I shut down the TV and flip off the lights before making sure the front door is secure. I knew it was, but you can never be too careful. Only when that's done, and I've checked on Lizzie once more, do I make my way back to the master bedroom. It's still a long way off from being perfect, but at least she has an actual bed, and by the way she's curled up in the middle, passed out, I'd say she's happy about it.

I carefully slip under the sheet, moving her so she's beneath the bedding. She murmurs as I run the warm cloth over her thighs, my cock suddenly taking notice of how wet she still is. But I ignore the way my dick starts to get hard again, anxious for round two, and pull her against my chest.

"Walker," she whispers, her lips grazing across my pec as she nestles in close.

"Do you want me to head out?" I ask, running my hand over her bare back.

"Stay."

Relief fills my entire body. One word, and all feels right with the world.

Stay.

So I do. I hold her tightly in my arms and drift off to sleep.

"Hey," I say, slipping onto the only available chair at our table for four.

Jasper glances up and meets me eye. "You got laid."

"What?"

He snorts. "I knew it!"

"All I said was hey," I argue, taking a drink of my Coke.

"It wasn't what you said, but how you said it."

I can feel all eyes on me, but I don't twitch. Instead, I sit back in my chair and give nothing away.

"At least someone is getting laid," Jameson mutters.

"What are you talking about? I ran into Amie yesterday and she said she was coming here last night," I tell him.

He snorts and shakes his head. "Oh, she did. I snuck out the back when she was getting another drink at the bar." His eyes meet mine. "She was with Bethani."

My friends know what happened with her and about the restraining order I was forced to file. "Ran into her yesterday too."

"What happened?" Isaac asks, setting aside his stack of papers and pulling off his reading glasses, giving me his full attention.

I shrug. "Nothing, really. She wanted to come over, as if nothing happened two years ago, and I told her that wasn't fucking happening. I told her she wasn't allowed here. I had Lizzie and Mal with me, but that didn't seem to deter her in the least. In fact, I think she looked at them as a challenge."

Jasper grins. "So you *did* get lucky."

"Shut up," I reply, giving him a pointed look. Just then, Mallory walks in from the restaurant and heads for the bar. Jillian is there and starts making whatever drink order she has. Mal glances over her shoulder and sees me, offering a small smile.

"You have it bad." Jasper laughs and takes a drink.

I don't reply. Not because he's wrong, because he's not. I do have it bad. Waking up with her in my arms this morning was the best fucking thing ever. So was the shower we took together immediately after. Taking her against the cool fiberglass wall, water cascading down her naked body, and my name on her lips as she came on my dick will be something I won't forget anytime soon.

Adjusting myself casually, I glance back over my shoulder and watch her retreat back into the restaurant, ignoring the snickering and teasing from my closest friends. Someday, they'll understand. They'll get what it feels like to be so wrapped up with one woman you can't think straight. A month ago, I would have scoffed and fought it, but now?

Now I embrace it and want more.

"All right, let's leave Walker alone and get to our meeting. I looked over the material Jameson presented last Monday," Isaac says, slipping back into manager mode. He glances across the table and meets our friend's eyes. "I like it."

"You do?" Jameson asks, seemingly surprised.

"Yeah. In fact, if we do this right, this could be an incredibly profitable venture for us. I talked with a man in Illinois who owns a restaurant and brewery and got some tips and ideas. He's more than willing to help in any way he can. In fact, he sent over his vendor list for the brewery, along with a few contacts."

We spend the next hour going over everything. P&L sheets, startup expense projections, and a contract for the building next door. It's been empty for a while, and when Isaac contacted the bank about leasing it, the owner decided he'd be willing to sell. The initial expense is going to be big, mostly due to the cost of leasing or purchasing the equipment needed to start manufacturing our own beer, but I can tell by the look on everyone's faces, this is a venture we're all excited about taking.

"I want to run it." Jameson clears his throat and sits up straight in his chair.

"Will you have time for that?" Jasper asks, finishing his burger and setting his plate on the table behind him.

"I don't feel like I pull my weight around here. Not like you guys," Jameson says, finally vocalizing one of the issues I know he's battled since we started the business.

"What? That's bullshit. You work harder than anyone," Jasper argues, but stops when Jameson holds up his hand.

"I'm here, but I don't feel like I contribute as much as you guys do. Isaac practically runs the entire back end of the business, working seven days a week. Jasper, you take care of the restaurant, also working seven days a week, and Walker has this side. I know I help keep order on the weekends and play some music, but I really think I can do this. No, I *want* to do this. I *need* to do it."

Isaac sits back and takes in our friend. "Well, if you want to oversee the setup and day-to-day of the brewery, I don't have a problem with it." I can physically see Jameson relax at those words. "And for the record, I don't work seven days a week. I was off Saturday night," he counters, clearing his throat and shuffling his papers.

"That's right. Babysitting duty," Jasper teases with a laugh.

"And I'd do it again in a heartbeat," Isaac quickly replies, cutting a glance my way, an unspoken message written in his eyes.

"And I'd like to add no one here feels like you don't contribute or pull your weight. You do just as much as the rest of us, but your duties are pulled in all sorts of directions. I may focus on the bar, but you're a big part of that. Not only do you help me, but you help Jasper and Isaac. Cut yourself some slack, Jame. You do more than you realize."

"Agreed. I have a meeting scheduled for four," Isaac adds, glancing across to Jameson. "It's with the realtor. Wanna go with me to check out the property?"

"Hell yeah," he replies, a wide grin over his scruffy face.

"Good." Isaac moves on to talk about a few more issues before wrapping up today's meeting.

Jameson and Jasper head off to the kitchen, and when Isaac gets ready to take off to his office, I reach out and grab his forearm. "Hey, got a quick second?"

"Sure."

"It's about the babysitting duty," I say.

He instantly smiles. "Not a problem. It was fun. She's a great kid," he replies.

"She is," I agree, shoving my hands into my pockets and rocking back on my heels. "I was kinda hoping you wouldn't mind doing it again."

Isaac arches and eyebrow in question.

"Tomorrow night."

Isaac blows out a breath. "Tomorrow? Yeah, I guess I could help out. What's up?"

Nerves flutter in my stomach, which is something that's never happened before. "I want to take her out on a real date, and tomorrow's my night off."

"Okay, sounds good. Just shoot me a text on what time."

"Thanks, man. I owe ya."

Isaac glances over my shoulder and smiles. "I'll let you pick me as best man for the wedding."

I turn around and find Mallory there, waiting on a table, yet stealing glances my way. "I'm not so sure about that," I tell him, but even I know I'm full of shit.

"If you say so," he teases, slapping me on the shoulder and retreating to his office.

Before I can make a break for my own office, Jameson joins me in the middle of the bar. "You wanna head over with us at four? Jasper's in."

My eyes seek her out once more, all on their own. She's laughing at something the group of women says, her blonde hair pulled back in a ponytail with a few escaped locks hanging around her ears. "Count me in, as long as Jillian can stay a little longer."

Jameson chuckles, pulling my attention. "I never thought I'd see the day."

"What day?" I ask, preparing myself for what I know is coming.

"The day the almighty Walker Meyer falls in love."

I open my mouth to argue, but I can't. It's futile. "I've only known her a couple of weeks, man," I argue, even though there's no punch behind my words.

Jameson shrugs. "When you know, you know."

I glance back at Mal, who's turning and heading toward the server stand. She spies us standing there and gives me a little wave and smile.

Am I in love with her?

Possibly.

I know I like spending time with her and making her laugh. I enjoy kissing her lips, now that I know what that feels like. I want to see her smile and hold her hand and wake up next to her. I want to snuggle with both of them before bed and make sure they get enough to eat at dinner. All that doesn't mean love, but it sure makes a damn convincing argument.

"I like her, Jame. A lot."

He grabs my shoulder and squeezes. "I'm glad, man. You deserve to find a little happy."

"You too."

"Ehh, that shit's not for me. I'll just be the cool uncle who lets the girl have too many cookies."

I snort a laugh. "You'll be a great uncle. Your sister, BJ, ever gonna settle down?"

Now it's Jameson's turn to laugh. "Hell no. You know her, always having one foot out the door."

"She sounds like her brother."

"Pretty much," he replies, giving me a crooked grin before walking toward the back door, cigarettes in his hand.

Finally making my way to my office, I think about his words. No, I can't say I'm in love with Mallory, but I'll agree I'm intrigued and enjoying my time with her, and if that leads to something more, then so be it.

I'm not afraid of taking the next step, whatever that is.

I'm afraid of the fall.

Mallory

I'm just finishing up my shift when a group of three women come in. It's nearing shift change, and I already know I'll be starting their table, but someone after me will finish it. We're supposed to split the tip when that happens, as long as we've both worked as close to half of the service as possible, but I know that doesn't always happen. Not when Manda is working my section.

"Good afternoon," I tell the trio as I deliver glasses of water to their tables. "Can I get you something else to drink?"

"Definitely. Something fruity and fun. We're celebrating a birthday," the redheaded woman says, a warm, pleasant smile on her face.

"We'll all have to call for rides home," the shorter of the two brunettes adds, taking a menu from the center of the table.

"That's fine. Rusty gets off work at five and can come get me," the third and final woman says.

"Do you have any recommendations?" the redhead asks. "Tish has been here a few times, but this is my first visit. I'm new to town and have heard nothing but rave reviews everywhere I go."

"I'm fairly new too, but everything I've had has been amazing," I say.

"I think I'll have a pina colada," the shorter brunette, Tish, says.

"Throw in extra rum for her birthday," the taller woman throws out there.

"I'll have the same."

"Me too."

"I'll give you a minute to look over the menus and grab your drinks," I tell them, taking a step back. "Oh, and I really like the Panty Melter Burger."

"Ohhhh, that sounds like heaven," the redhead moans, glancing down at her menu and searching for the suggested burger.

"I'll be back," I reply with a smile, leaving them to look at the menu.

After I have the three drinks, I return to my table. I try not to eavesdrop on their conversation, but it's hard when I'm standing right there and they continue as if I weren't.

"I was so proud of Jackson today. He worked hard during class and even raised his hand when we were talking about things that start with the letter A."

"That's good. In the four years I've been teaching, I've never seen a kid shyer than that one," Tish replies. "Even just passing your class in the hallway, I can tell he's going to be a struggle to pull out of his shell."

"We've only been in class three weeks, and he's made great strides," the redhead says, glancing up and noticing my rapt attention. "Oh, I'm sorry. We're a bunch of preschool teachers and most of the time, we don't leave work at the school."

The other two laugh in agreement.

"You teach preschool?" I find myself asking, setting down the drinks.

"We do. Little Learners. It's my first year. Tish is on her fourth year as the four and five-year-olds teacher, and Stephanie is the director."

I look over at the taller woman, Stephanie, who's wearing a pleasant smile. She's older than the other two, probably in her thirties, with big brown eyes. "Our preschool is through the Lutheran Church on Madison Street. Have you heard of it?"

I shake my head. "Sorry, no, but I'm new here. My daughter and I moved about a month ago."

"Daughter?" Tish asks.

"Lizzie. She's three," I tell the trio.

"Three? She'd be perfect for my class," the redhead says. "Sorry, I'm Addi, or Miss Hanson, and I teach the three-year-old class. Is she in preschool?"

Guilt sweeps through my body as I slowly shake my head no. It's not something on my radar yet, which makes me feel even worse. My life turned completely upside down in the last year, and sadly, my daughter is suffering. I didn't realize they offered preschool at such a young age. I thought maybe four or five, but three?

"You should bring her by," Addi adds, pulling me out of my funk.

"Really?"

"Absolutely. We have an opening in the three-year-old room, actually. One of the littles had to move last week, when his dad started a new job. We have an opening in the Tuesday and Thursday mornings class," Stephanie says.

My heart starts to pound with excitement. "Really? What time is class?" I ask, mentally trying to work it out.

"Nine to eleven thirty," Addi replies.

My heart falls. "Oh, I'm not sure that would work with my hours." I'm sure I could probably pay Mrs. Fritz a little more to help with transportation, but I imagine the cost of preschool—a private church-based one at that—isn't going to be cheap. I'm not sure I can swing any extra money to the older lady right now.

"I can tell you're thinking about it, but maybe have a few reservations. Come by tomorrow morning before work and we'll discuss it," Stephanie instructs politely.

"Okay," I find myself saying, even though my mind is racing a thousand miles per hour. Even if it's too expensive and doesn't work out, it wouldn't hurt to meet with them, right? Maybe this isn't the right school for my daughter, but that doesn't mean I can't start researching options for her.

"Great. Now, let's talk about that Panty Melter Burger," Stephanie says with a grin.

A knock echoes through the apartment. Running a sweaty, nervous hand down my thighs, I remove the chain and release the lock on the front door. There in my doorway is the most handsome man I've ever met. His hair is styled a little and he's freshly shaved. Walker's wearing a navy polo shirt and dark jeans, a pair of nice boots on his feet, and a smile that makes my legs quiver.

"Hey, beautiful," he says, stepping inside and reaching for me. "You look gorgeous."

I glance down at my dark skinny jeans and red cold-shoulder top. It dips low in the front, revealing a slice of cleavage, but not in a slutty way. Or at least it doesn't feel that way. I've only worn the shirt once, and that was more than a year ago. I had to dig into the bottom of the box containing my old clothes in order to find something I felt was date worthy. "Thanks, you look good too."

He tightens his hold on my hip and brings his lips to mine. The kiss is slow and tender, but still packs a punch to my lady parts. In fact, I can feel wetness pooling between my thighs as I grip his shoulders and hold on tight. Walker slips his tongue inside my mouth, the taste of his toothpaste assaulting my senses.

"I didn't realize I was getting a show tonight too." The words hold a hint of laughter, the voice familiar. I pull away from Walker and find Isaac standing in the doorway behind him, smiling.

"Horrible timing, as usual," Walker grumbles, stepping aside and allowing his friend to enter the apartment.

"I can go, if you'd prefer," Isaac teases his friend as he sets a bag down on the couch.

"Walk!" Lizzie hollers, running down the short hallway and bursting into the room in a flurry of pink ruffles and silver sparkles. She launches herself at him, but he catches her easily and brings her to his chest.

Walker kisses her forehead and positions her on his hip. "Hey, Lou. Did you have a good day today?"

"Yep! I pwayed with the dollies."

"That sounds fun. And guess what? Isaac is here to play with you tonight."

"Yay!" she bellows, throwing her hands in the air. "We pway pwincesses again."

"Yes, Isaac loves being a pretty princess," Walker says, unable to hide a big grin.

"Fuck you," Isaac grumbles quietly as to not be heard by little ears.

Walker glances over my daughter's head and meets my eyes. "You ready to go? We have reservations at seven."

I glance at my watch and see we have fifteen minutes. "I'm ready," I tell him, heading over to grab my purse. I hear the little pitter-patter of feet on the old flooring moments before Lizzie's arms wrap around my legs. Picking her up, I ask, "Are you going to be a good girl for Isaac?"

She nods. "Walk says I can paint his nails. Can I, Mommy? Pwease?"

I look up to find Isaac glaring at a laughing Walker. "Well, that's probably up to Isaac, but boys usually don't like to have their nails painted, sweetie."

Lizzie turns to Walker. "But you'd wet me paint yours, wight?"

"Anytime, Lou," he replies with conviction.

She just grins up at him, as if he hung the moon and the stars. "Otay. I be dood for Sic," she confirms, heading over to collect whatever toys are on the floor. "Weady?" she asks, turning to look at the man closest to the door.

"As I'll ever be, pumpkin. Let's do your worst," Isaac states, following behind Lizzie, who disappeared into her bedroom.

"Come back out and lock the chain after we leave," Walker hollers after his friend, who just holds up a hand and waves.

"Ready to go?"

"Yes," I answer, slipping my purse over my shoulder and following him to the door. Walker opens it, allowing me to exit first, before making sure the door is secure behind him. He takes my hand as we descend the stairs to the ground floor, where his CJ is waiting in the lot.

As soon as we're settled inside and I secure my seat belt, I ask, "So, reservations where?"

"The little Italian place near Freeman Pond. Have you ever been there?" he asks, starting up the Jeep and shifting into reverse.

"No, but I've heard about it." I don't tell him that everything I've heard revolves around the expense.

"I think you'll like it. From what I can recall, they have a decent menu selection," he says, turning onto the main road and heading into the heart of town.

"You haven't been there in a while?"

Walker shakes his head. "No. We went for my mom's birthday a few years back, but I haven't been since."

"No hot dates?" I find myself asking with a laugh, then wishing I would have kept my mouth shut. That's not exactly first official date etiquette.

He glances my way. "No hot dates. I don't date," he says, turning his eyes back to the road.

"Me either," I whisper, looking at the landscape as we drive by.

Walker reaches for my hand and links our fingers. We drive in silence, and he only releases my hand when he has to downshift for a stoplight. "This may be the first time I've ever wished for an automatic Jeep," he mumbles, taking us from first to second gear easily and smoothly.

"Why?"

He glances my way and gives me a cocky smirk. Then, he grabs my hand and brings it to his lips, kissing my knuckles. "Because I can't do this when I'm shifting."

My heart skips a beat and my breathing hitches. There's a hint of desire in the pools of those blue eyes, but before I can dive in, he turns his attention back to the road. The restaurant is positioned along a large pond with fishing piers and gorgeous landscaping. There are paved paths with families and couples taking leisurely strolls, as well as a few pavilions for picnics.

"Wow, this place is great," I murmur, watching a small group of women power-walk around the far side.

"It is," he replies, unfastening his seat belt. "Admittedly, I haven't been here lately, but it's always pretty busy. It's a great place for families to gather. The park is always packed," he says, pointing over to a grouping of trees and the playground equipment scattered within.

Walker jumps out of the Jeep and meets me at the passenger door. He slips his hand around mine and steers me toward the restaurant. "Maybe we can bring Lizzie here this weekend. It's supposed to be fairly decent weather."

"That sounds nice," I find myself agreeing with a smile on my lips.

He stops when we reach the door, returning the grin. "Good." Then he brushes his lips across mine and opens the door. "Come on."

The moment I step inside, I'm hit with all the comfort scents of Italian food. Marinara sauce, garlic, and fresh baked bread. My stomach growls anxiously as we approach the hostess stand. "Good evening, and welcome to Avanti's."

"We have a reservation for seven, under Walker."

She checks her computer screen and gives us a polite smile. "I have you down for two on the back deck. Is that still okay?"

Walker glances at me, as if asking permission to be seated outside. It's such a gorgeous evening, the sun starting to set over the trees, and I find myself nodding eagerly.

"Follow me," she instructs with a smile, leading us through the restaurant and out to the back deck.

It's slightly cooler back here under the shaded canopy, but the view is amazing. It feels like we're right on top of the water, even though there's space between. "This is perfect," I say, as Walker pulls out a chair for me. We're seated along the railing with a view of the setting sun.

"Here are your menus, and your server will be out shortly to take your drink order," the hostess says, before disappearing back inside.

As I glance over the menu and try not to gasp at the prices, I can't help but recall what he said in the Jeep. "So why don't you date? I mean, you're hot. Half the women here were checking you out as we walked past."

Walker glances up, his eyes sparkling with humor. "I'm hot?"

Rolling my eyes, I look back down at the overpriced linguini options. "You know you are. Stop being coy."

He snorts out a laugh. "That's something I've never been called." He reaches over and sets my menu down in front of me, before taking my hand in his. "I've dated, just not a lot, especially in the last few years. Growing a business is hard work and left me little time for anything else. And to comment on your other statement, I don't care what half the women in here think. I only care about you."

I feel the blush sliding up my neck and burning my cheeks. Apparently, even under the dimness of the setting sun and the hanging lights, Walker can see it too. He reaches up and caresses my cheek. "I love it when you blush."

"I hate it." My reply is automatic.

Our server arrives with two glasses of water and takes our drink order. He's young and seems to struggle to keep himself organized, even with a simple task like writing down drinks. I can't help but wonder how new he is at this job, and instantly feel empathy for him. It's not easy, especially when you start to feel overwhelmed.

"I'll be right back to take your orders," he replies, scurrying off to grab our drinks.

"You know, you blush *other* times too." Even though he's looking down at his menu, I can see his smile. There's also no doubt in my mind as to what he's referring to.

My cheeks burn even hotter.

When my eyes lock with his, he just grins wider, which makes me squirm in my seat. My panties are soaked in a matter of seconds and I'm pretty sure my nipples are poking through my top—and it has nothing to do with the temperature outside.

Setting his menu aside, he leans in and whispers, "I have to admit, Mal. I'm looking forward to seeing that blush spread across your entire body later. While you ride my cock."

Just like that, I melt right off my chair.

Walker

"How was your day?" I ask as we walk hand in hand around the dark pathway. Fortunately, the moon is full and shining brightly in the night sky, reflecting off the pond beside us.

"Good. Something happened though."

I tense beside her. "What?"

"Oh, nothing bad. I met some teachers from a local preschool. They invited me to come by tomorrow to discuss enrolling Lizzie."

"Wow, that's great. I think Lizzie would kick ass in preschool," I say honestly.

Mallory chuckles. "Yeah, I bet she would, but I'm not sure," she replies, shrugging uncomfortably.

"What aren't you sure about?" I ask, stopping in the middle of the path and turning to face her.

"I'm not sure if it's the right place for her," she replies, glancing down at the earth at our feet. "The opening is for Tuesday and Thursday mornings from nine to eleven thirty. I'd have to see if Mrs. Fritz would be able to pick her up, and I'm not sure she'd be all that thrilled to do it. It's right in the middle of her soap operas. She'd hate to leave."

"I'll do it." The words are out of my mouth before I can stop them, but as soon as they're out there, I realize it doesn't matter. I'd really do it for her.

"You? You work too," she argues, but it falls on deaf ears.

"First off, I'm off on Tuesdays, so that doesn't matter, but also I don't go in until four on Thursdays. I can easily pick her up from school." I place a hand at the back of her neck, my thumb sliding over her spine. She shivers at the contact and leans a little farther into my chest.

"I couldn't ask you to do that," she adds, closing her eyes as my hand gently kneads the neck muscles.

"You didn't ask. I volunteered."

She opens her eyes and gazes up at me. "That's a lot to ask of you."

I lean forward, brushing my lips across hers. "I'd be honored to do it, Mal. For you, and for Lizzie. She's an awesome kid, and like her mother, she makes me smile."

"Yeah?" she asks, smiling against my lips.

"Hell yeah. In fact, I'd be okay if she hung out with me those afternoons. Tuesdays you can swing by after work and grab her from my place, and on Thursdays, I can bring her to the restaurant. You could save yourself a few bucks by not paying Mrs. Fritz."

"I'd want to pay you," she insists, just like I knew she would.

"The only payment I'd take is like this," I say, right before plastering my lips to hers and deepening the kiss. The moment she's breathless and pliant under my touch, I add, "I collect in kisses, Mal. *Your* kisses."

We spend the next several minutes making out like teenagers. We're far enough away from the restaurant that anyone lingering on the deck shouldn't be able to see us, but if there happens to be anyone out on the path, they'd surely discover us. Not that I'm worried. There's something so urgent about kissing this woman. It's as if I *need* to do it, right this moment.

"Walker?" she gasps, pulling her lips from mine.

"Yeah?" I whisper, sucking in a greedy breath of oxygen.

"Will you stay with me again tonight?"

I pull back, meeting her gaze. Her green eyes are full of lust and determination, the combination making my already hardening cock twitch with excitement. I swear I can see down to her soul so vividly and clearly, it's as if I can read her desire, her purpose, and even her trust in those emerald orbs. That last one causes me to pause, but not because I don't want it or deserve it. Because she's giving it to me, willingly.

When I don't answer right away, she quickly speaks. "You don't have to."

"I want to," I insist. "I want to more than anything, Mal."

In fact, I wanted to last night but made myself leave. I was there Saturday and Sunday night, and the last thing I wanted was to suffocate her. So I went back to my place, alone, and fucking hated it. Even with the music playing, it was too quiet, too lonely. I needed to smell her shampoo and feel her skin against mine, not the cold sheets in my own bed. I felt more isolated than I ever have, which fucking sucked.

She smiles up at me and my cock tries to Hulk out of my jeans, but I refuse to maul her right here in the middle of the damn park. Taking her hand back in mine, I lead her the way we came, retracing our steps to the parking lot. Once we get to my Jeep, I press her against the door and kiss her again. I can't stop. My lips crave hers.

"Let's get back to your place," I growl, opening the door and practically picking her up and setting her inside the vehicle.

Mallory giggles and reaches for the belt. It actually takes her two tries to secure it into place, but the moment she does, I slam the door and run around to the driver's seat. I'm not sure how many traffic laws I break on our way back to her apartment, but there were definitely a few. All minor infractions, but still.

When we reach her place, I practically pick her up over my shoulder and run up the stairs. "Walker, put me down," she says, a mixture of laughter and shock.

"In a minute, beautiful," I state, only setting her down on her own two feet when we reach her front door. Before she can pull out her keys, the door opens, and my friend is standing there with an amused grin on his face. "You waiting up for me, sweetheart?" I ask Isaac.

"Heard a ruckus on the stairwell. Should have known it was you and your caveman tendencies," Isaac argues, stepping aside to let us in.

"How was Lizzie?" Mallory asks, setting her purse down on the couch.

"Great," he informs us, glancing around nervously. I pick up on it right away and look around myself. That's when I see it.

A doll.

I look at my friend in question. Isaac sighs, knowing I'm not going to let it go, and pulls out his cell phone. He types in his passcode before handing it over. "She asked me to braid her hair, which of course I couldn't do, so I've been watching YouTube videos on how to braid. Did you know there are dozens of variations of hair braiding?"

I can't help but smile as I glance down at the instructional video on his phone. "And the doll?"

Isaac sighs. "Practice. I think I finally have it down," he confirms, showing us the doll with long blonde hair, much like Lizzie's. It's a little crooked, but the doll has a well-executed French braid down its back.

"Wow, that's impressive," Mallory chimes in, smiling down at the doll in his hand. "You may be on braid duty from here on out."

Isaac grins. "I'm just a call away," he says, turning and grabbing his work bag from the kitchen table. "Now, I imagine I'm holding up whatever end-of-date activities you want to engage in, so I'm out. She fell sleep just after eight and hasn't made a peep since. Good night, and don't forget a condom."

With that, Isaac slips out the front door, the echo of his shoes descending the stairs following in his wake. I make sure the lock is engaged and the chain secure before turning back to face Mallory. The look in her eyes is all I need to know.

I stalk toward her, as if she were my prey. Her green eyes widen and dilate as her breath hitches in her throat. She takes a step back, then another, until she's backed against the living room wall. I slowly advance, my eyes devouring her from head to toe. Her breathing is slightly panted and her nipples strain against her shirt. She's a vision, and fuck, if the fact she's *mine* doesn't make me hard as steel.

Instead of pressing my body against hers the way I long to, I keep a few inches of separation. She gazes up at me, her eyes glassy with lust, as she says, "Well, now that we're alone..."

I place my hands on the wall beside her shoulders and lean in, inhaling her sweet scent. "Now that we're alone," I parrot, allowing only my nose to touch her as I slide it up her neck.

The slightest gasp spills from her lips as she tilts her head, granting me access. I lower my lips and slide them over her soft, creamy flesh, following the trail from my nose just a moment ago. "You taste like heaven," I whisper.

"You touching me is even better," she murmurs, pressing her chest forward and gliding her tits across my own chest.

"Is it?" I ask, moving one hand from the wall to grip her hip.

She rocks into me, brushing against my cock and making me groan. "I think you agree."

"I do agree, sweetheart. Touching you is one of my favorite things ever."

She gazes up at me and grips my shirt at my sides. "Then touch me. Please, Walker."

My mouth slams into hers with an urgency of a possessed man. Mallory opens her mouth, granting my tongue entrance, as she rips my shirt up and claws at my flesh. "I'm going to need you naked, Mal. When I get you naked, I'm going to taste and touch every square inch of your body," I practically growl with insistence. Then she's in my arms, her legs around my waist, as I sprint to her bedroom.

The moment I cross the threshold, I press her into the wall, loving the sweet friction she creates against my cock. "I wish we were already naked. I'd fuck you against this wall."

"Yes, that. Do that," she pants, clawing at my shirt and trying to push it up and over my head.

I nip at her neck with my teeth. "But I told you I was going to touch and taste you."

"Later. You can do all that later, Walker. Right now, I need you."

I realize right then and there, I'm a weak man. I'm not strong enough to fight what I feel for her, and I'm not just talking sexually. I mean all of it. All that bullshit I tried to hide from, tried to keep at arm's length. Here I am, ready to completely submit to a tiny blonde with the most amazing green eyes I've ever seen. Not to mention her daughter, who has completely stolen my heart.

Setting Mallory down on the floor, I strip her as quickly as possible, while she grips and tugs at my clothes. It takes me a bit to unlace and kick off my boots, but Mal keeps herself occupied by touching her pussy. My eyes are riveted to those delicate little fingers as she slides through her lips, coating her fingers in wetness. "Fuck, I could watch you do that all night long," I mumble, blindly reaching for my jeans and digging out my wallet. When my fingers wrap around a condom, I rip it open and sheath my cock in record time.

Then, I reach for my woman and pull her into my arms. "Later, I'm watching you fuck your fingers, Mallory."

She juts her chin up at me and declares, "Only if I get to watch you stoke your cock, Walker."

Groaning, I lift her up and thrust, hitting pay dirt in one swift motion. Together, we moan in pleasure as I fill her completely, her pussy gripping my cock with resolution. "Shit, sorry. I could have done that with a little more finesse," I whisper, kissing her lips softly and sliding my palm along her forehead to brush back her hair.

"Does it feel like I wasn't ready for you?" she asks, using her muscles to give my dick a little squeeze.

"Shit, baby, do that again, this'll be over quickly."

The temptress does exactly that once more, causing my body to thrust all on its own. "Did I give you any indication I wanted you to take this slow?"

I can't help but gaze down at her with wide eyes. Never has she been this bold and brazen. This sexy and confident. Clearing my throat, I give her short little thrusts that are more like teases. "So you want this fast and hard, beautiful?" I ask, rocking my hips and hitting deep inside her.

The nails digging into my shoulders and the whimper on her lips are her answer.

"Hang on tight."

Then I move.

My hips piston repeatedly, as I press her back into the wall. My arms and thighs start to burn a little from holding her up, but the adrenaline pumping through my veins takes over and any muscle discomfort quickly fades. All I can think about is how tight her pussy grips my cock. Her hands grasp the back of my neck and her legs clamp around my hips, as she tilts her pelvis upward, taking me so fucking deep, it makes my eyes cross and my cock thicken.

That familiar tingle starts at the base of my spine, and I know the end is near, but I'll be damned if I'm going to get off before Mallory does. "Slip your finger between us and touch yourself," I demand, not breaking my stride.

Mal worms her hand down between our bodies and grazes her fingers across her clit. Her gasps fill the room, followed quickly by a moan so loud, I clamp a hand over her mouth. A moment later, a loud thumping pounds on the wall opposite where I stand. We both still, listening intently.

"Was that someone pounding on the wall?" she whispers.

I thrust, her lower back thumping against the wall and another moan emanating from her sweet lips. It's followed quickly by a second pounding on the wall. "I think your neighbors aren't a fan of our noise."

"I'm a pretty big fan of what you're doing to me," she confesses, wiggling against my body and moving on my cock.

"Yeah? Of this?" Thrust.

"God, yes," she groans, gripping my dick.

"Let's give the neighbors a taste of their own medicine," I vow, readjusting my grip and starting to move. Faster. Harder.

I can feel Mallory's fingers between us as she plays with her clit. Her body starts to jerk as her orgasm rips from her body. I almost silence her with a kiss, but my own release rears its head, sending me barreling down the mountain of bliss. My hips spasm, my legs shake, and my breathing is choppy as I lean into the wall, pressing firmly against the woman in my arms.

"How was that?" I ask, kissing her shoulder.

She glances up, a sated glaze in her eyes, and says, "Let's ask the neighbors."

"Walk, I frowded up."

I crack my eyes open and stare straight into sleepy green ones. A smile slowly spreading across my face at first, and then my tired brain seems to register what Lizzie just said. I jump up, grateful to be wearing my boxer briefs, and glance down at the sad ones in front of me. She's wearing a nightgown with chunks of brown mush on the front.

"Shit."

"What's wrong?" Mallory mumbles, reaching for me.

"Uh, Lizzie's here, and I think she got sick."

That gets a reaction from Mal. She quickly tosses back the blankets and runs around to where her daughter stands. Like the super woman she is, she carefully picks her up and scurries off to the bathroom across the hall. I jump up, my foot landing in a small pile of something gross and wet. Sighing, I reach for a towel tossed in the hamper and wipe the bottom of my foot. Then I set out to cleaning up any trail of vomit left behind on the old, worn carpet.

Quietly, I head to the bathroom and peek inside. Mallory is there, kneeling over the tub and helping Lizzie take a bath. She runs cool water over her head, murmuring soothing and soft sentiments as her daughter whimpers.

"What can I do?" I ask softly from the doorway.

"Will you grab the thermometer and Tylenol? They're in the kitchen cabinet by the sink. When I get her out of here, I'll take her temperature."

I nod, glancing at Lizzie once more, before taking off for the kitchen. I open every cabinet in a rush, looking for the device in question. It's behind the last door I open, the one closest to the sink, my hand slightly shaking as I grab the bottle of medicine and thermometer and set them on the counter.

I pace the small room, hating the feeling of helplessness that overcomes me. I want to stomp into that room, pick Lizzie up, and hold her until she feels well again. Actually, better yet. I'd take the sickness away in a heartbeat, if I could.

Ten long, agonizing minutes later, Mallory comes into the kitchen, a tired Lizzie wrapped in a pink hooded towel on her hip. "Walk," Lizzie mumbles, reaching for me. "My tummy hurts."

She's in my arms moments later. I inhale the scent of her fruity shampoo as she tucks her head into the crook of my neck. Rocking her slowly back and forth, I watch as Mallory gets the thermometer ready and sets the device on her daughter's forehead. "One oh one point two." I'm about to ask if that's bad, when she opens the Tylenol and pours some into a little plastic cup.

"Lou, let's take some medicine and then we'll go snuggle, okay?" I ask, moving her back so I can see her face.

"Otay, Walk," she mumbles, as she turns toward her mom for the medicine.

She swallows the purple stuff before nestling back against my chest, her body sagging against me.

"Let's hope she keeps that down," Mallory whispers, running a hand down Lizzie's back.

"What do you need from me?" I ask, rocking back and forth gently.

Mallory yawns. "Nothing, Walker, really. If you'd rather go home, I'd understand. She must have a little stomach bug or something, and I'd hate for you to get it."

"I'm already exposed, so I might as well stay and help," I tell her, kissing Lizzie's forehead as she drifts off to sleep in my arms.

"Well, there's nothing we can do but go to sleep and hope she's done throwing up," she says. "I need to pick up her bedding and rinse it in the shower."

"I can do that," I insist, even though the thought of cleaning puke doesn't exactly rate high on my fun-o-meter.

"No, it's okay. I'll do it," she replies, heading down the hall toward Lizzie's bedroom. I head across the hall to the master bedroom and carefully lie the sleeping girl in the middle of the bed. I find my shirt from last night and put it back on to cover my chest. Then, I slip under the covers, careful to only pull the sheet up on Lizzie.

"Okay, I think it's fine until the morning when I can run to the laundromat," Mallory says, slipping quietly into the room and crawling into bed.

"I'll take it home with me and wash them," I insist, glancing at Mal over Lizzie's head. We're both on our sides facing each other, Lizzie snuggled in between us.

"You don't have to do that."

"I want to, Mal. If Lou is sick, you shouldn't be going out to do laundry. I'll run and wash it and grab some chicken noodle soup on my way back. I can get all that done before you have to leave for work. You can either go in and I'll stay here with Lou, or you can call in sick. I'm sure Isaac and Jasper can find someone to take your shift."

She smiles softly at me and closes her eyes. "You're too good to be true, Walker Meyer."

I reach over and run my hand over her cheek. "I could say the same about you."

Mallory

"Walker is going to pick you up after school," I tell Lizzie, as I walk her into school.

"I know, Mommy," she huffs, making me smile.

Lizzie's going into her fourth week of preschool and absolutely loves it. Each week she learns about a new letter and spends the week discussing animals, food, and other items that begin with that week's letter. She eats up everything while she's at school, and according to Miss Hanson, is thriving in her new environment. She's even made a few friends, which makes me very happy.

But her favorite part of school is when Walker picks her up. Not only do they discuss everything that happened during her school day, but they spend time finding her afternoon snack that starts with that week's letter. This week it's the letter P, and I was informed Walker has a big bag of pretzels waiting for her this afternoon.

"Are you excited for today?" I ask, as we reach the front doors.

Lizzie stops, her princess backpack almost as big as she is, and smiles up at me. "I'm the weader!"

"I know you are, and I'm sure you're going to be a great leader today," I reassure.

Miss Hanson opens the door. "Good morning, Lizzie. I see you have a bag of goodies for snack today."

"Yep! Peanut butter cwackers."

Her teacher smiles down, handing me the clipboard. "That sounds like a yummy snack today," Miss Hanson says, while I sign Lizzie in and note the name of her pickup. They will only release the students to the individual named on the sign-in sheet. Just another safety factor I love about this place.

"Bye, Mommy!" Lizzie says, hugging me around the waist.

"Have fun, baby girl. Love you."

"Wove you too!" she bellows, as she runs inside to hang up her bookbag.

"Thank you for the snacks," Miss Hanson adds, before turning her attention to another arriving student.

I jump into my vehicle with a smile on my face. It's amazing how relaxed and comfortable our new life in Stewart Grove is. I don't sense eyes on me wherever I go, nor do I hear their whispers. It's refreshing, and frankly, feels like I've found my purpose or my spot in this world.

Things are finally clicking into place.

I pull onto the road, heading to Walker's house. It's Thursday morning, and he worked last night to cover for someone. He doesn't always stay at my place, especially toward the end of the week, when he closes the bar and I have to get up early in the morning. I don't sleep as well those nights. I'd much rather be curled up beside him. Those are the best nights.

A car follows closely as I pass my apartment and head to the edge of town, but I don't pay it much attention. Instead, I focus on driving the speed limit and reaching Walker's house safely, yet quickly.

I park behind his Jeep, smiling as I slip from my own vehicle and make my way for the front door. Walker lives in a quiet area on the edge of town with minimal traffic. It's actually a great location, especially the big backyard. Lizzie loves to play back there, as long as the weather's decent. Now that we are in October, the temperatures are definitely starting to hover around the fifty-degree mark during the day and dipping down in the forties at night.

Great snuggling weather.

Before I can raise my hand to knock, the front door opens. There, standing in the middle of the doorway, is a shirtless Walker, wearing a pair of gray joggers low on his hips. My bottom jaw practically unhinges from the top, and I think I actually drool.

"Stop staring at me like I'm a slice of chocolate cake," he mumbles, reaching for my arm and dragging me into his house. As soon as the door's shut, he presses me firmly against it, kissing me hard.

Speaking of *hard*...

"You seem awfully happy to see me," I coo, rubbing against his erection.

"I'm always like this when you're around," he states, placing his lips on my neck.

"That must make things awkward at work," I tease, knowing full well he doesn't walk around the bar with a hard-on.

"You have no idea. Why are you late?" he asks, taking my hand and leading me toward his bedroom.

"I'm not late. I'm right on time. I just dropped Lizzie off," I tell him, toeing off my walking shoes once we reach his sleeping space.

"How's Lou? Was she excited to be class leader?" he asks through a yawn, crawling into bed and tugging me along. The moment I'm lying in his arms, he throws the comforter over us and settles in.

"Very excited. She couldn't wait to tell the teacher she brought peanut butter crackers for the letter P."

"Good," he mumbles into my hair before inhaling.

"Did you just whiff my hair?"

"Mmhmm. It's one of my favorite scents. Now that it's on my pillow, maybe I'll be able to sleep."

"You haven't slept?" I ask, turning in his arms and facing him.

He shrugs and closes his eyes. "A little. Busy night last night, and I got home late. Then, I couldn't sleep, so I turned on music, but even that didn't help. I missed you. I don't like sleeping without you," he whispers, his blue eyes locked on mine.

"What are you saying?" My throat feels suddenly too tight.

He shrugs. "Just that. I hate nights when you're not in my arms, Mal. That's a fact."

I swallow over the lump in my throat. "I don't sleep the best when you're not in my bed either," I confess.

"Hmmm," he murmurs, pulling me into his chest and kissing the crown of my head. "So, I sleep better when you're in my arms, and you sleep better when I'm there, so maybe we should sleep in the same bed more often."

Smiling, I reply, "More than about four nights a week?"

"More," he states.

I sweep my lips over his collarbone. "I like more."

"Mmm, don't I know it," he teases, flipping me onto my back and hovering over me. "You're sort of insatiable," he adds, nipping at my neck with his teeth and making me sigh.

"Me?" I argue with a giggle.

"You," he reiterates, sliding his hips between my legs and pressing his erection into the apex of my legs.

Hitching my ankles over his waist, I reply, "I have a feeling I'm not the only one."

"Oh, you're definitely right there, sweetheart," he says, claiming my lips in a possessive, bruising kiss.

That kiss is only the beginning...

"I had this girlfriend in college. It wasn't too serious, or at least it wasn't to me. We dated on and off. She was a great girl, but it felt more like a relationship of convenience than a relationship of passion, if you know what I mean," he says, my naked back pressed to his equally clothesless front.

"Senior year, she changed. Got all serious. Wanted a ring. I wasn't ready for that, so I broke it off for good." I can feel his breath against my ear as he holds me tightly against him.

"She accused me of leading her on, of using her," he adds, sighing. "Maybe I did, but that wasn't my intention. I thought we were both in the same place, but we clearly were not. I hurt her, and I hate that—still do, because she was a nice girl. That's why I don't get serious, Mal. That's why I keep women at a distance, refusing to let them get close. I've always thought it was because I didn't want that, but I think there's another reason."

I glance over my shoulder, meeting his eyes. "What's the reason?"

"You."

I can't help but smile.

"I wasn't sure what this was when it started, but I know now."

"Yeah? What is it?" I ask, my heart firmly lodged in my throat while I wait for his answer.

"It's love, Mal. I've fallen in love with you."

I wasn't prepared for his words, nor the tears leaking from my eyes.

"Why are you crying?" he asks, turning me so we're facing each other again. He slides his thumbs under my eyes, erasing the wetness.

"No one has ever said that to me before," I whisper, overcome with emotion. They're totally different than the ones I felt when Devon betrayed me. I thought I was in love with him, but maybe I wasn't. Because as badly as it hurt at the time, it was never as all-consuming and *right* as it feels right now.

But I can't help but recall how wrong I was when it came to my ex. What if I'm wrong now too? I know Devon and Walker are night and day different, but I can't stop wondering, what if…

"I didn't tell you that so you'd say it back, Mal. I said it because it felt right, but I don't want to pressure you."

I open my mouth to say the words I know he wants to hear, but nothing comes out.

He gives me a small smile and kisses my lips. "It's okay, Mal. You'll say it when you're ready." He tucks me against his chest and sighs in contentment.

"I want to say it."

"I know, beautiful. And you will. In your time."

I hug him tightly. I'm fully in love with him, yet something holds me back from making that declaration. I have a feeling it's because of fear. Not *of* him. I could never be afraid of Walker. His heart is too pure, too giving. He'd never hurt me, and I'm sure he'd rather physically injure himself than risk hurting Lizzie in any way. No, this fear is more about the deep feelings he evokes when I'm near, or even when I'm not.

I'm very much in love with Walker Meyer.

I just hope I'm brave enough to say it sooner, rather than later.

Walker

I pull up in front of the preschool entrance and get in line with all the other parents or guardians. This may actually be my favorite part of a Thursday. It used to be going to work, slinging drinks, hanging out with the regulars. You know, running my bar. Now, it's parking in the circular driveway and waiting for Lizzie to get out of school.

At eleven thirty, doors open and parents all step in front of their vehicles. I'm already smiling as I see the first little one fly out the door, wearing an orange pumpkin hat made of construction paper. "Mommy!" the little girl hollers, as she makes a beeline for a woman on the opposite side of the drive.

And so it continues over the next minute or so. The teacher verifies the individual picking up the child is the one on the list before sending the student outside. When there's only two students left, and I can see Lizzie inside talking to a young boy, a man walks up the sidewalk. He heads straight for the door and tries to open it, only to find it locked, since the doors can only be opened from the inside or with a key.

The teacher, Miss Hanson, steps outside to talk to the man. She smiles politely at first, but then something crosses her face. She glances through the glass door before turning and meeting my eyes. I can tell something's wrong by her body language, and before I know it, I'm walking up to where she stands.

"I'm sorry, sir, but I'm only allowed to release the child to the individual on the sheet," I hear her say as I approach.

"But I'm her father."

"Hey, Miss Hanson, is everything okay?" I ask politely, though I'm on high alert.

The man turns and looks at me, narrowing his dark eyes, but doesn't say a word.

"Good morning, Mr. Meyer," she says, stammering a little. "There seems to be a little confusion this morning on Lizzie's pickup."

"Confusion?" I ask the young woman, yet my eyes are locked on the man beside me.

"Yes, this gentleman says he's Lizzie's father."

My eyebrows arch into my hair as I give the man a more scrutinous once-over. He's wearing a white T-shirt under a black leather jacket and dark jeans. He looks freshly shaved, with a new haircut, and is wearing brand-new work boots on his feet. I can tell because there isn't a scratch or a scuff on them. All in all, the man claiming to be Lizzie's father looks normal. Like a regular guy I'd pass on the street.

I hate him.

"I was just explaining to…him, that I'm unable to release a child to someone not designated by the parent or guardian," Miss Hanson states, though clearly flustered by the situation.

"And I was just telling *her* that I'm Lizzie's dad."

Staring at the man who's trying to intimidate the young teacher, I ask, "Who's listed on the sign-in sheet as the individual you're to release Lizzie to today?" My tone is blunt and straight to the point. I'm done with this asshole's bullshit.

"Umm, you, Mr. Meyer."

"I'm her father," the man practically growls, clearly getting agitated to the fact he's not able to just stop by and claim his child.

"I'm going to have to call Miss Sargant," the teacher states.

"Is there a problem?" a woman asks, stepping up beside us.

"Oh, no, Mrs. Freeman. Dylan is ready to go," Miss Hanson says, her hands slightly shaking as she uses her key card to open the door.

The mom steps up to the door to wait for her son, while I remain on the sidewalk with the asshole. "You can't have my family," he states, his voice low as to not be overheard by the other parent nearby.

"That's not your decision," I reply, just as the teacher and the boy step out the door.

"Mommy!" he hollers, running into her arms. She gives us a quick glance before practically dragging her son away from the school, as if he were in danger. To tell you the truth, I'm not sure whether he is or not, but I'll be damned if this man is going to hurt anyone on my watch.

I look at the door and see Lizzie there. She waves, which makes me smile, and glances around in confusion.

"Umm," Miss Hanson says, as she rejoins us. "If you both will stay here, I'll run inside and call Miss Sargant."

"That won't be necessary. I understand you have rules to follow. I'll reach out to *Miss Sargant* myself," the man claiming to be Lizzie's dad says. There's no missing the disdain in his tone when he refers to Mallory. He looks at me before adding, "I'm sure I'll be added to the form as Lizzie's pickup real soon."

With that, he turns and walks away, heading down the sidewalk and away from the school. The man keeps going, not stopping to get into a vehicle, until he rounds the corner and disappears.

"I'm so sorry, Mr. Meyer," Miss Hanson states, clearly shaken by the ordeal.

"You did exactly what you were supposed to do," I assure her.

"I've never had a situation like that arise before."

"I hope it never happens again. I'll talk to Mallory later and make sure she's aware of what happened," I reply. "Can I take Lizzie now?" I'm suddenly incredibly anxious to get her in my arms and under my supervision.

"Oh, yes," she says with an uncomfortable chuckle.

Miss Hanson uses her key card to open the door. The moment she does, my Lou bolts through the doorway and runs straight into my arms. "Walk!"

"Hey, Lou. How was school?" I ask, positioning her on my hip.

"We made puntins!" she exclaims, pointing to the orange hat with lopsided black eyes.

"I love your pumpkin," I reply, kissing her forehead and carrying her to my Jeep.

When she's buckled in to her seat in my Jeep, I shut the door and glance around. I see no sign of the man claiming to be Lizzie's dad, but that doesn't mean anything. Something tells me we haven't seen the last of him.

Instead of driving to my place, like we normally do, I head for the bar. "How about a cheeseburger and fries for lunch today?"

"Yay! Mickey D's?"

"No, not today. Let's go see Mommy and get one of Jasper's big burgers."

"Woohoo! I can showded Isaac my puntin hat."

Smiling, I drive in the direction of where Mallory is. "He'll love it! I bet you can even get Isaac to wear it."

Lizzie giggles in the back seat. "It's too widdle for Isaac, silly," she states through fits of laughter.

"He does have a big head, huh," I reply.

First thing I notice when I hit Burgers and Brew is the full parking lot. It's not even noon, and we're busy. I pull around to the back lot and park in my usual spot. It only takes me a few seconds to get Lizzie out of the Jeep, adjust her pumpkin hat, and head for the back door.

"Can we dough see Mommy?" Lizzie asks, as we enter the building.

"Yep, in just a few minutes. Let's stop by and see Isaac first," I reply, picking her back up in my arms and moving toward the stairs. When we reach the landing, I can hear Isaac's voice, but I don't stop. I'm not sure who he's talking to, but this is important.

Stepping into Isaac's office, I see Jameson seated across the desk. "Hey, man," he says, instantly grinning when he sees Lizzie. "Lizzie!"

"Day! I dot a puntin hat!"

"Wow, look at that," he replies, jumping up from the chair and walking over to where we stand. "That's the best pumpkin hat I've ever seen."

Lizzie giggles in reply and points to the cabinet across the room. Isaac jumps up and retrieves the coloring book and crayons inside, setting them down on his desk. I place the little girl in his chair, remove her jacket, and help her get started with the crayons.

As soon as she's set, I nod to my friends to the back of the room, where they both move to meet me.

"What's up?" Jameson asks, already recognizing my agitation.

"Apparently, Lizzie's dad is here. He showed up at the school and tried to take her," I whisper so little ears don't hear.

"The fuck?" Jameson growls.

"Yeah, the teacher was all nervous because he just showed up and wanted her. I could tell something was wrong and walked up there. She wouldn't release her though, because my name was on the sheet."

"Well, that's good," Isaac replies, trying to wrap his head around what I told them. "What now?"

I sigh. "I'm going to have to talk to Mallory. She's never really given me the details about her ex and whatever happened back when she left. I figured she'd tell me when she was ready, but now, I might need to push her for facts sooner rather than later." I glance at my friend. "Did she ever say anything to you about him?" I hate that Isaac may know more about her past than I do, but I have to know.

Isaac shakes his head. "Not really. When she interviewed, she just said she was new in town and was a single mom. I told her we'd work with her, since I was raised by a single mom too. Hell, we all were," he says, pointing to our small group. In fact, Jasper is the only one of all of us whose parents are still together.

I sigh and glance over to where Lizzie is coloring. "I'm going to have to talk to her soon. I want her to know he's in town and what happened."

"Definitely, and we've got her back," Jameson states adamantly.

"Thanks, guys. I guess keep a watch out for a single guy. He's a little shorter than me and a lot skinnier. Dark hair and eyes. He was wearing a white shirt, jeans, and leather jacket."

Jameson nods. "I'm on it."

"All right, well, I guess Lizzie and I will head down for lunch. Any chance you can send Mal into the bar for a few minutes?"

"I'll make sure her tables are covered so you can talk," Isaac insists.

"Thanks, guys."

I carry Lizzie, while Jameson grabs the crayons and book, and head downstairs. I glance in the restaurant and spot Mallory right away. She's smiling as she delivers plates of burgers to a table, which makes me smile automatically. At least I know she's safe here.

We head for the small pub table in back, Jameson already retrieving the booster seat I keep in my office for Lizzie. Once it's secured to the chair, I set her down and help her fasten the buckle. Lizzie goes right back to coloring her masterpiece. I'm sure it'll hang on my office wall with the dozens of other pictures she's colored for me.

"Hey, what are you doing here?" Mallory asks as she approaches our table. I spot Isaac behind her, jumping in and taking care of helping her tables.

"Mommy!" Lizzie hollers. "See my puntin?"

"Wow, look at that hat. It's a fabulous pumpkin," she tells her daughter, kissing her on the crown of her head before glancing my way.

"Hi."

"Hey," I reply, pulling her into my arms and kissing her lips. I don't even care we're in the place we work. Up until this moment we've refrained from any sort of PDA in front of my employees, but today, I don't care. I need her in my arms. I need to feel her lips against mine. When I glance down at those green eyes, I can't help but recall my earlier proclamation. I had told her I loved her. I've never been in love before, but I know without a doubt, that's exactly what this is. The thought of something happening to her or Lizzie makes me want to crawl out of my skin. "Can we talk for a minute?" I ask, slipping my hand around hers.

"Now?" she asks, glancing over her shoulder to the restaurant. "We're pretty busy."

"I know, but this will only take a second. Isaac has your tables and Jameson will stay with Lizzie."

She seems hesitant, but nods. Mallory is quiet as I lead her to my office and close the door. "What's wrong?" she whispers.

I lean against my desk and pull her between my legs. With my hands resting on her lower back, I place a quick, chaste kiss on her lips and take a deep breath. "Something happened at pickup."

Mallory tenses against me. "What?"

"A man showed up, claiming to be Lizzie's father."

I watch as my words register. Surprise and fear flit through her eyes as they widen. "What?" she gasps, those green eyes I've fallen in love with filling with tears.

"Miss Hanson wouldn't let Lizzie come outside or release her to him, especially since I was there, and my name was on the sheet."

She opens her mouth, but nothing comes out right away. She swallows hard and blinks away the tears threatening to fall. I move my arms to her shoulders and pull her snuggly against my chest. Her fingers grip the back of my shirt as she tries to keep her breathing under control. "What did he do when he couldn't take her?"

"Well, he basically left. Miss Hanson said she was going to call you, but he didn't want that. He did tell me I couldn't have his family," I tell her, choking on the words.

The tears she was trying to fight fall now as she shakes her head. "I should have known he was getting out soon, but I wasn't expecting it yet. He was supposed to be in until closer to Christmas."

"In…"

"Jail. Prison. Whatever."

I bring her to my chest once more and just breathe her in. She's shaking and crying and fuck, do I hate that. I want to beat the shit out of the guy for making her cry. For scaring her. For breathing.

"About a year ago, he was arrested. Devon had been the primary target in a large drug sting operation back in Gibson," she whispers against my chest, her tears soaking into my shirt. "The problem was, he had Lizzie with him when they made the bust."

I tense. "What?"

"I was living with a drug dealer, and didn't even know it, Walker. He had our daughter with him that day. He was arrested and my baby was taken by Child Protective Services. I had to jump through all sorts of hoops and prove I wasn't part of it before they'd give her back to me," she weeps.

"Jesus," I mumble.

"I didn't know, I swear. We had been together for about three years when I got pregnant with Lizzie. Devon worked as an accountant. At least he did in the beginning. I learned after his arrest that he was the accountant for some questionable people, and at some point, started working for them. He quit his job and started selling drugs after Lizzie was born, and I had no clue. He went to work weekdays before eight and came home after five. So many nights I went to work and left her with him, Walker. I unknowingly endangered the life of my daughter."

"It wasn't your fault, Mal. None of that was. It was all on him, okay?"

She closes her eyes and exhales loudly. "I know that now. At the time, I blamed myself. Hell, everyone around me blamed me too. Devon was likeable and had tons of friends."

"They blamed you?" I ask, unable to believe what I'm hearing.

She shrugs. "Well, they didn't say it outright, but I could see it in their eyes. All of our friends just sort of disappeared when everything went down. Everywhere I went, I could hear their whispers and see them pointing. After Devon's trial and being sent away, I left town. I needed a fresh start."

I lean back and meet her eyes. "You are the bravest, strongest woman I know, Mallory Sargant. I don't want to ever hear you say one word to dispute that fact."

She gives me a slight grin. "It wasn't easy. When we moved, we had nothing. They froze all of our accounts. I sold a lot of our belongings so I had money for food and rent. Basically everything we had left fit into my vehicle."

I pull her against my chest once more and just hold her. "I'm sorry you went through that, Mal, but you're not alone now, okay? You've got me. And Isaac and the others. We're not going to let anyone take Lizzie from you."

"What do I do now? If he's here, he's going to want to see her."

"That's up to you, sweetheart. You don't have to let her see him before you're ready, if ever."

"He's her father," she counters, but I'm already shaking my head.

"He endangered her. You could have lost your daughter due to his negligence. *You* get to decide if and when he ever sees her again, Mal. Do you hear me? We'll get a lawyer."

She sighs and rests her chin against my chest. "I can't afford one."

"I'll help you. We all will."

"I can't ask you to do that."

"You didn't. I offered. No way is he going to take or endanger that girl ever again. I won't allow it."

She doesn't say anything for a few minutes, just lets me hold her. Finally, she pulls herself back, and reluctantly, I let her go. "I should get back out there."

I nod, but hate to let her go. "I want you to keep an eye out for Devon, okay? I don't know what his plan is, if any. Lizzie and I will hang around here today, so you know she's safe. When you leave here, I want you to go to my place," I insist, reaching into my jeans and pulling out my keys. I remove my house key and place it in her palm.

"I can go back to my apartment," she argues lamely.

"Not until we get a little more security there, okay? Please, Mal. I'm not trying to take over or tell you what to do, but I'm not sure I can work tonight knowing you're at your place and possibly exposed to him."

She looks down at the key before closing her hand around it. "Okay."

Sighing with relief, I pull her into my arms one last time. "Thank you. Now, let's go out there and see Lou. I bet she's getting hungry."

Mallory smiles, but it doesn't quite reach her eyes. "I'm sorry I'm pulling you into my mess."

I kiss her forehead. "No place I'd rather be, Mal. We'll get it figured out. Together."

Mallory

I feel like I'm constantly looking over my shoulder. As I finished my shift, when Walker helped me load Lizzie in my vehicle, and as I pulled from the parking lot to head to his house with the promise to text the moment we arrived. Lizzie's chatting animatedly in the back seat, completely oblivious to the turmoil surrounding us.

I glance in the rearview mirror and flip on my turn signal when I approach the apartment building. If we're going to stay with Walker, I should probably stop and grab some of our belongings for tonight and tomorrow. I also need to speak to Mrs. Fritz. After our talk in his office, Walker and Jameson got to thinking it might be better for Lizzie to stay with Walker, even on the days she doesn't have school. If Devon showed up, he'd have no problem overpowering Mrs. Fritz, and I'd never be able to live with myself if something happened to her because of me.

I stop in the first available parking spot and turn off the ignition. "Guess what, Lizzie?"

"What?"

"What do you think about having a sleepover at Walker's house for a night or two?"

"Wiff you too?" Her eyes light up with excitement.

"Yes, I'll be there too," I reply, giving her a reassuring smile. With my keys in my hand, I exit the vehicle and help Lizzie unbuckle from her harness. I take her hand in mine and head for the front entrance to the building. "We're going to grab a bag of clothes and go to Walker's house, okay?"

"Otay! Can I pway outside?"

Pulling open the door, I glance down at my daughter. "Probably not tonight, but I'm sure you can tomorrow."

We stop on the second floor, and I knock on Mrs. Fritz's door. She opens it with a smile. "Well, isn't this a surprise."

"I just wanted to stop in and let you know there's been a slight change in plans for a while. I'm going to stay with a friend for a bit," I tell her, careful to conceal the real reason we won't be in the building.

"Is it that handsome man who comes by at all hours of the night?" she asks, an ornery smirk on her aged face.

I can feel the blush move up my cheeks. "Oh, well, actually, yes."

"Good for you, dear. You deserve to be happy, and if that hunk of man does it for you, then don't walk toward him. Run." She sits back down in her easy chair and glances at the game show on the television.

"Well, it's just temporary. I'm still keeping my apartment, but while I'm staying there, he's going to let Lizzie hang out with him."

She waves a hand. "I'm here if you need me, dear. Just knock on the door and I'll watch her," she replies, her eyes now engrossed on the action on TV.

I give her a smile, even though she doesn't see it. "Thank you, Mrs. Fritz. I'll be in touch."

Again, she waves her hand. "Sounds good."

Lizzie says goodbye, and we exit the apartment. Once we reach the third floor, I pull out my key and unlock the door. The place feels the same, but I can't stop myself from glancing around, as if Devon will jump out from a closet or from behind the curtains.

My daughter pulls on my hand, clearly indicating she's ready to go to her room.

"I'll grab a bag, and we'll get it packed up," I tell her as she sprints off to her room.

I head into my closet in my bedroom and grab one of the two duffel bags I had taken in the move. Just as I'm pulling it out of the closet, I hear what sounds like the front door opening. My spine straightens, and it's suddenly hard to pull oxygen in my lungs. A floorboard creaks, and I realize instantly my mistake. I didn't lock the door behind us. In my hurry to get bags packed and go to Walker's, I completely forgot to lock the door.

Leaving the bag on my bed, I glance around for something—anything—that can be used as a weapon. I find a hair dryer on top of a box and grab it, praying it's heavy enough to at least distract whoever is in our apartment.

Creeping into the hallway, I spy Lizzie piling toys on her bed, completely oblivious to the intruder. I walk past the door, hair dryer raised behind my head. The moment I move to peek into the living room, hands grab at my shoulders, halting my movements. I try to swing, but he's too strong and easily stops my forward motion.

"Jesus."

I know that voice.

Glancing up, my eyes connect with Jameson's chocolate brown eyes. "Jameson?"

"Who did you think it was? And why do you have a blow-dryer?"

"I…" I stammer, unable to slow my racing heart. "I thought someone broke in."

"You left the door open, Mal. Walker would shit a brick, literally, if he was the one who showed up here." He takes the dryer from my shaking hands. "You were really going to whack me with this?"

"You…or whoever was in my apartment."

He tosses the dryer onto the couch and pulls me into his arms. The hug feels…different. It's not the one I'm used to, but I appreciate it nonetheless. "You're all right, Wonder Woman. Stupid, but all right."

I gape up at him and find him smiling. "I'm not stupid."

"You were coming at an intruder with a blow-dryer, Mal," he argues, as he laughs.

"Well, you shouldn't have broken into my apartment," I defend, pushing off his hard chest.

"First off, I was following you to Walker's place," he says, crossing his arms over his chest.

"That's not creepy much," I mumble, causing him to smirk.

"You took a detour, so I followed. My friend is a freaking basket case that he can't be with you right now, so I told him I'd hang back and make sure you got to his place okay."

"I told him I'd text."

He just smiles. "And he was still worried."

Sighing, I lean against the wall and close my eyes. "Thank you. I didn't realize I left the door open."

He steps forward and places a gentle hand on my forearm. "We don't want to scare you, Mal, but you're going to have to be extra vigilant until you figure out why the douche is here and what he wants."

Unable to formulate words, I nod.

"Day!" Lizzie exclaims, as she comes out of her room, her arms loaded with toys.

The moment Jameson sees my daughter, he smiles and drops to his knees. "Lizzie," he greets.

Just as she steps up to him, she shoves everything in her tiny arms against his chest. "Day, you gots my toys, otay?" she says, before turning back around and disappearing into her room.

I can't help but giggle. There is this giant man in my apartment, tattoos covering his arms, and he's holding every doll and Barbie my daughter owns. "I'll go get the bag. Apparently, the dolls are coming with."

Jameson stands up. "Go pack your bags, Mallory, and I'll help Lizzie. If we don't get you to his place soon, he's going to eventually come looking for you."

With a smile on my lips, I go back to my bedroom and retrieve the other duffel bag to pack my things. I don't know how long we'll be at Walker's place, but I know I'll feel safer while I'm there.

It's been a week with no sign of Devon.

He hasn't shown up at Lizzie's school, nor at the restaurant. Part of me wishes he'd just come here so I know what he wants. Is he looking to pick right back up again where we left off before he went to prison? Not happening with me, but he *is* Lizzie's father. I don't think I could keep her from him without a big legal battle.

The other part of me is hoping he just went back home to Indiana. Lizzie is thriving in school and loves spending time with Walker and his friends. The change in her, from a shy little girl to a more outgoing one, has been amazing.

It's midafternoon and the restaurant is practically empty. I've refilled salt and pepper shakers, wrapped silverware, and am now working on sanitizing the menus. It's the little mundane things that most may hate doing, but I enjoy. It's soothing and allows me a few minutes to just breathe.

"Hey, Mallory," Gigi says, coming up behind me at the servers' station.

"Hi, Gi." I offer her a smile. I notice she returns it, but her lips are tight.

"Listen, I'll finish that up. Jasper wants to speak with you in his office for a quick minute, okay?" The older woman reaches for the sanitizer spray and rag, taking it from my hand.

"Oh. Is everything okay?" I ask.

"Yep!" she states, a little too cheery. Something is definitely up.

And then it hits me.

Oh God.

Am I getting fired?

I give her a tight smile and make my way through the kitchen. Someone stands at the sink, rinsing a few dishes before loading them in the dishwasher, while a younger man flips a burger at the grill. I walk past them both to the back where Jasper's office sits.

When I approach, I knock on the doorjamb and smile. "Hey, you wanted to see me?"

Jasper stands up and grins. Of all the owners, Jasper's the one I've gotten to know the least. Sure, I know he's bossy and has a take-charge attitude, but on a personal level, I don't know him very well at all.

"Have a seat," he says, indicating one of the empty chairs in front of his desk. I notice the desk is full of papers and files, but in a way, it looks like organized chaos. What I don't see is anything with my name on it.

You know, like termination papers.

"Something has happened."

His words take a second to register. "Lizzie?" I whisper, that single word agony to speak.

"No, she's fine. She's with Jameson," he assures me, getting up from his chair and coming around to sit in the empty seat beside me. "I promise she's okay."

I meet his eyes. "Tell me."

"Walker was arrested."

"What?" I gasp, my mouth falling open in shock. "Why?"

"Drugs." He registers my disbelief and holds up his hands. "It's bullshit, Mallory. Walker doesn't do drugs, but they had a warrant to search his place."

I shake my head, trying to clear the images of me and my daughter playing in the living room. Putting her to bed in the guest room. Cooking dinner in the kitchen. We were there, and there were drugs?

"Don't go there, okay?" Jasper insists, grabbing my hand and giving it a squeeze. "Isaac called a lawyer. We're gonna get this shit taken care of."

I sigh as fear sweeps in. "I need to get Lizzie. Now."

He nods. "Okay. Jameson has her at his house. We'll go there first."

I'm already on the move. I untie my apron and make a beeline for the employee break room. I toss it in the locker, not even bothering to clear out my tips for the day. I grab my purse and turn back to the entrance. Jasper's there, keys in hand. "We'll take my car."

I probably should drive myself, but I'm sure it's safer with him behind the wheel. My legs move, but they appear to be on autopilot right now. Driving probably isn't in my best interest at the moment. Nodding, I follow him out the back door.

The late October afternoon is cool and dreary, and the breeze holds a bite. I ignore it though and follow my boss to his car. He drives some expensive number, a Mercedes, I think. I'm sure it's nice, but nothing registers as I buckle my seat belt and grip my purse as if it were a lifeline.

"It's going to be okay, Mallory. I promise," Jasper reassures, as he starts up his car.

He drives quickly, but safely, in the opposite direction of where I usually go. Within a few minutes, he pulls into a driveway of a small house with dingy siding and faded shutters. The landscaping is overgrown and the porch in need of a fresh coat of paint, but that's not what grabs my attention. At the end of the driveway sits the biggest garage I've ever seen. It has three large doors and is much newer than the house. In fact, the garage doesn't even look like it matches the house at all.

"Come on," Jasper says softly, placing his hand on my lower back and escorting me to the front door. The touch is jarring, but I don't pull away. The comfort he's offering is welcoming, especially in light of the circumstances.

"Mommy!" Lizzie proclaims, as she meets me at the front door.

I step inside and throw my arms around my little girl. "Are you okay?" I whisper, holding her so tight, I'm not sure either of us can breathe.

"Yep! Some powicemen came and took Walk for a wide! Can I dough for a wide too?" she asks, her eyes alive with excitement and energy.

Her innocent question brings sudden tears to my eyes. "Not today, sweetie."

"Hey, Lizard, why don't you go finish that picture you're coloring for Walker? This way, when he gets done with his meeting, it'll be ready for him."

She nods eagerly before taking off to the kitchen just around the corner.

Jameson helps me stand and guides me to the couch.

"I'm going to meet up with Newton and see what's going on," Jasper says, heading for the door. "You okay here?" I hear him ask the question, but know it's not directed at me. I'm grateful when Jameson replies in confirmation. "I got them. Keep me posted," he says right before the door shuts.

I glance up and watch as Jameson heads toward me. "You good, Mal?"

"What happened?" I ask, ignoring his question.

He sighs and drops onto the couch beside me. Jameson looks toward the kitchen, as if making sure little ears aren't nearby.

"Walker called me around noon, told me to get over to his place fast. Apparently, the county and city police showed up with a warrant to search the premises. They wouldn't tell him anything. He and Lizzie had to go out and stand on the front lawn while they executed their search."

He takes a deep breath and continues, "I just pulled up when officers walked out the front door with bags of shit. Drugs. Not a lot, but more than someone who used recreationally would have in their possession. They placed him under arrest right there, but I was able to walk away with Lizzie. We went down the sidewalk looking for grasshoppers, so she wouldn't see.

"Isaac pulled up then and sort of took over. He started making calls before they even had Walker in the back of the squad. I told Lizzie he was just going for a ride, so she wouldn't be scared, and Isaac talked to the lieutenant in charge about releasing her to me. He agreed, as long as I took her straight to you."

I suck in a deep breath, not realizing I wasn't even breathing. It's like history repeating itself.

My brain tries to process but is struggling to keep up. All I can focus on is the fact Walker had drugs in his possession and he was taking care of my daughter. Even after everything I told him about Devon, he still risked Lizzie. For what? A high? Money?

I jump up and start pacing the living room. "I need to go."

"Where?"

"Home. To my apartment," I state, turning and heading for the kitchen. "Come on, Lizzie. We're going to go back home."

"To Walk's?" she asks.

"No, to our apartment," I reply, gathering up the crayons and coloring books.

"But, I made dis for Walk," she says, holding up the hand-drawn photo. "It's me and Daddy Walk."

I freeze and gaze down at the drawing. It's a picture of a tall person with really long arms and legs and he's clearly holding the hand of a much smaller girl. They're both smiling with bright red lips and too-big teeth. The image blurs before my eyes as the tears fall fast.

"It's a beautiful picture, Lizard. I'm sure Walker will love it as much as the other ones in his office," Jameson says, squatting in front of her and taking the drawing.

"It's for his house. He can put it on duh fwidge."

My hands shake as I try to swipe away the tears, but it's no use. The moment I sweep them away, more fall in their place.

"It's going to be his favorite drawing ever," Jameson assures her. "We'll give it to him soon, okay?"

"Otay," she replies quickly. Then she turns to me and asks, "Mommy, can Walk be my daddy?"

My heart crawls up into my throat and lodges firmly in place. "I don't know, baby girl."

"Izzy says she has a daddy, and I want one too. I want Walk to be my daddy."

Realizing I can't speak, Jameson steps in. "Let's gather up your stuff, Lizard, and I'll drive you back to your apartment." He turns to me and adds, "I was able to get a car seat out of Walker's truck."

"But my dollies are at Walk's," she argues.

"I'll get them for you," he replies solemnly, but I know he's just appeasing her. There's no way he'll be allowed into Walker's house right now.

I stand by and let Walker's best friend take control. He helps gather up Lizzie's books and leads her to the front door. "Come on, Mal. It's going to be all right."

I want to believe him.

I just don't know if I can.

Twenty-Five

Walker

I'm climbing the fucking walls. I've been in this interrogation room for hours, or at least that's what it feels like. My mind is spinning. The knock on the door. The cops, most of whom I know from growing up in Stewart Grove. The warrant.

First thing I thought of was Lizzie. I had to get her out of the house as soon as fucking possible. As I stepped out onto the front lawn, I shot off a group text to the three people I knew would come running in the event of an emergency. I hadn't been wrong. Jameson was there in less than ten minutes, Isaac a little longer. Jasper stayed behind until he could get another chef to come in. Plus, he had the task of keeping an eye on Mal.

Mal.

Fuck.

She had to be worried out of her mind when she heard.

What a clusterfuck this is.

I have no clue where those drugs came from, and that's exactly what I told the investigators. And my attorney. And my friends. I don't do drugs, and I sure as fuck don't sell them, especially not the shit they found in my bedroom closet. Meth and pot. Cheap shit, on top of it.

Food was delivered about an hour ago, but I didn't touch it. No way can I even think about eating food, when all my mind can focus on is Mallory and Lizzie. My heart wants to climb out of my chest with fear. It's like history repeating itself for her, and I'll be damned if I let it affect her a second time. Even if that means I have to walk away, this bullshit won't touch her.

Not again.

Never again.

The door opens, revealing Jim Samson, the attorney Isaac brought to help, as well as Lieutenant Moyer, the lead investigator on the case. "Good news, Walker," the officer says, as he takes the seat across from me.

Jim sits, a smile on his face, as he listens to what the lieutenant has to say.

"What's up?"

"You're being released."

I take my first deep breath in hours. "Seriously?"

He cracks a smile. "Seriously. We checked the prints all over the bags of drugs. Know what we didn't find?" When I arch an eyebrow, he answers. "Yours. Know what we did find?"

"Someone else's?" I ask, though it's a stupid question.

"Someone else's," he confirms. "Sliding a sheet of paper across the table. This guy look familiar?"

I glance down, instantly recognizing the man in the mugshot. Devon Henderson. "Fuck."

"Yeah," the officer states, reaching for the printout and returning it to his folder. "What can you tell me about him?"

I go through what happened at the preschool that day when I arrived to pick Lizzie up, and how I told Mallory about it after we left. I shared what she told me of Devon and explained that I haven't seen him since that day. To be honest, I'd hoped he had left town, but clearly that's not the case.

"Mallory?" I ask, fear gripping my chest.

"She's here."

I swallow over the lump in my throat. "She is?"

He nods and smiles again. "Actually, she came in about thirty minutes ago, demanding we release you because we had the wrong guy."

The corner of my lip ticks upward. "She did?"

"Oh, she did. She told me she didn't know where those drugs came from, but she insisted they weren't yours."

Now I'm smiling. Fuck, I love that woman.

"The prints came back when she was here, and she's been cooperating and helping us build our case against Devon. The only problem is, we haven't located him yet. We issued the APB, and it's only a matter of time before he shows his face."

I sigh, leaning against the chair in relief. Before I can ask to see Mal, a knock sounds on the door and another officer steps inside the room. He whispers into the lieutenant's ear before handing him a folder and turning to exit the way he came.

"Well, it sounds like we have Mr. Henderson in custody," the lieutenant says, glancing over whatever report is in the folder.

"Really?" I ask. "Where'd ya find him?"

"Mallory Sargant's apartment."

My blood runs cold.

The first person to cross my mind, is Mal, but if she's here, then she's fine. It's the second person who makes my heart stop pounding and my knees weak. Thank fuck I'm already sitting, or fear would have no doubt taken me down. "Lizzie?" just saying that word terrifies me. If something happened to her, I'd never forgive myself. No, it wouldn't be my fault directly, but I'd still feel responsible.

"Is okay," he starts, reading over the report. "Apparently she was sleeping in her room, slept through the whole thing. Your friend, a Mr. Jameson Tankersley, might require some ice for his hand."

I bark out a laugh. "I'm sure he's fine."

"According to the report, Mr. Tankersley found Mr. Henderson slipping through the front door after jimmying the lock. He was able to subdue him until officers arrived."

A snort slips from my lips. "Oh, I bet he did."

"I believe there's a broken nose involved, but the statements don't exactly jive. Henderson claims your friend punched him in the face, while Tankersley is adamant the suspect tripped over a toy and landed on his fist." The lieutenant is grinning from ear to ear. "I'm sure the DA won't seek assault charges."

"I'd hope not," Jim says beside me. "Mr. Tankersley is a hero. Is my client released?"

The officer across from us nods. "He is."

I jump up and turn to my attorney. "Thank you, Jim, for coming down so quickly."

"I'm just glad it all worked out," he replies, shaking my hand.

The lieutenant opens the door and steps aside. "I believe the person you're looking for is to the right."

All I hear is his chuckle as I bolt from the small room and turn in the direction he indicated. There, at the end of the hall, is the most beautiful sight I've ever seen. Mallory is there, and she's moving my way the moment she sees me emerge.

I throw my arms around her and pick her up, holding her as tightly as I dare without cutting off her oxygen. "Fuck, you're even more beautiful than this morning," I mumble, inhaling the familiar scent of her shampoo.

"I had to come. I knew you didn't do it," she stammers quickly.

I set her down and just breathe her in. She's wearing cotton shorts and a hoodie and there's a pair of worn flip-flops on her feet. Her blonde hair is pulled up in a bun and her face is void of makeup. I just pray it's from that makeup remover she uses and not because she cried it all away.

"Lizzie?"

She gives me the slightest grin. "She's at the apartment with Jameson. They just told me *something* happened," she says, wringing her hands together.

"I heard. Thank God Jame was there."

She smiles. "He promised me he'd watch her and keep her safe. When I sat down and really started to think about the charges against you, I realized something was wrong. I *knew* those drugs weren't yours, Walker. I knew it."

I take her hands in mine and bring them to my lips. "How did you know?"

She gives me a watery smile. "Because I know *you,* and," she says, taking a deep breath, "because I love you."

A wide smile breaks out across my face as I pull her against my chest, threading my fingers into her hair. "Say it again," I whisper.

"I love you."

Then I claim her lips with my own, reveling in the feel of her against me. She's the balm to my soul, the reason I was put on this earth. "I love you, Mal. As much as I'd love to stand here in this hallway and hold you, how about we go home and get our girl?"

She smiles against my lips. "I'd like that."

"Come on." I place one last kiss on her lips, linking my fingers with hers, and heading for the exit. "How'd you get here?" I ask the moment we hit the concrete steps out front.

Mallory points to the car parked in the middle of the lot. My eyes widen as I glance her way. "He let you drive the Nova?"

The moment she's positioned in the passenger seat and is buckled in, I head for the driver's seat and do the same. She already has the keys out, so I quickly start up Jameson's car. The one he rarely lets anyone drive.

As I pull out of the police station lot, she says, "Well, I was in my room after putting Lizzie to sleep. I was lying there, and all I could smell was your pillow. I thought back to all the times you held me, and how when Lizzie was sick, you were there. I knew in my heart they had it wrong. I'm sorry it took me so long for my head to catch up."

I exhale, grab her hand, and bring her knuckles to my lips. "Don't apologize for anything that happened today, Mal. None of it was your fault. I'm just fucking relieved everything turned out the way it did."

"Me too." She sighs, sagging against the headrest. "I can't believe he broke into my apartment."

"I know he was arrested and hopefully going away for a hell of a lot longer than a handful of months, but I want to talk to you about your apartment. I know it's your place and I don't want to take away your independence or your decisions, but if you're going to stay there, I want to stay too. The thought of you and Lizzie being in that place all by yourself makes me crazy."

257

Mallory leans over and places her head on my shoulder. It's not easy, since she's belted in, but it's enough. "I'm not sure I want to stay there," she says. "The fact he was able to get in so easily, even with the locks engaged, is scary, Walker. I can't risk Lizzie like that."

I pull into the parking lot of the apartment building and glance up, spying the living room light on in Mallory's apartment. When the ignition is off and the keys are in my hand, I turn to her and ask, "What if I have a solution to both of our problems?"

"I'm listening," she replies, unfastening her belt and sliding a little closer.

"What if you moved in…with me?" My heart is tripping over itself, beating like a snare drum, and I think my palms turn sweaty as I wait for her to say something. She remains quiet for ten of the longest seconds of my life.

"You want to live together?" she asks, her green eyes so bright, even in the darkness of the car.

"Yes."

"We've only known each other two months."

I shrug, tossing my arm over her shoulder. "What does that matter?"

Now it's her turn to give me a little shrug. "It doesn't, I guess. Not really. What will your friends say?"

"They'll say I'm an idiot for waiting this long, that you're the best thing that's ever happened to me. I may have only known you for a couple months, but I knew the moment I met you that you were different. You were going to change my life."

Mallory grins and looks me square in the eye. "Lizzie and I are a package deal, Walker."

"I've never received a greater gift."

That's when she throws her arms over my shoulders and kisses me square on the lips. She tastes like mint and my Mallory.

My cell phone pinging with a text message has me pulling away from her sweet lips much sooner than I'd prefer. "That's probably one of the guys."

"Probably."

As we start to climb out of the car, she waits for me at the passenger door. I slip my hand around hers and lead her toward the apartment building. "You were already in your bedroom when you realized the drugs weren't mine. Is that why you're practically wearing pajamas?"

I see her blush under the dim security light by the entrance. "Yeah. I grabbed this hoodie out of the laundry, slipped on some shoes, and ran out to the living room to find Jameson."

A growl echoes through the night. "I know why he was there, but I can't help but want to punch my oldest friend in the face because he was here, at your place, protecting you when I couldn't."

"I thought you'd be happy he was here," she counters, a look of uncertainty filling her eyes.

"Oh, don't get me wrong, Mal, I am. More than you'll ever know, but at the same time I'm jealous there was a man here, in your apartment, because I couldn't be."

She reaches up and brushes her soft hands against my cheeks. "You have amazing friends, Walker. They stood up for you from the very beginning. Even when I wasn't there yet." I watch as her eyes turn misty and she works her throat to swallow.

"Hey, don't do that. We've already been over this. I don't blame you at all for being a little skeptical."

She nods but doesn't say a word.

"Why don't we go upstairs and see our girl?"

Mallory smiles an honest to goodness smile that reaches into my soul and gives it wings to fly. "Yes, please."

We walk up the stairs, hand in hand, and by the time we reach the third floor, she's yawning from exhaustion. Mal doesn't pull out her keys but knocks on the door instead. The locks are released, and a chain moved before the door opens, revealing Jameson. He looks relieved when he sees us both standing there.

"Fuck, thank God," he mumbles, opening the door widely for us to enter. Then he does something very un-Jameson like. He hugs me.

I find myself returning his hug, patting his back hard, and so fucking grateful he responded to my text as quickly as he did. He was able to get Lizzie away and out of there before she saw something no little girl should witness. She already watched her father be carted off in cuffs, and fortunately, she was too young to remember it. The last thing I'd want is for her to remember me that way.

"Thank you," I tell him, when he finally releases his hold.

"It was nothing," he downplays, but I'm already shaking my head in argument.

"It wasn't nothing, Jame. What you did," I start, but pause to collect my thoughts. "You saved my family."

I feel Mal brush by me and throw her arms around my friend's waist, hugging him tight. "Thank you for protecting Lizzie."

He looks uncomfortable as he awkwardly pats her on the back. It's like he doesn't want to get too close, which makes me grin. He's a damn good friend. "I'd do whatever is necessary to protect you and Lizard, Mal. Promise," he vows.

When she pulls back, she glances down at his hand. "Oh my God, your hand!" Mallory takes off for the kitchen, leaving us standing in the middle of the living room.

Jameson glances down and squeezes a fist. "It's fine," he hollers, but it falls on deaf ears.

Mallory returns a few seconds later with a frozen bag of peas and reaches for his hand. "Give me."

Reluctantly, he moves his swollen hand her way, placing his palm against hers. He stands there, while she nurses his hand with frozen vegetables to alleviate the swelling. With his left hand, he reaches into his pocket and pulls out a set of keys. "Here. All new locks on the door. You can give a set to the super, but we decided to change them after the police left and not wait for him to show up."

Mallory looks at him, a small smile on her lips. "Thank you."

Jameson shrugs. "We wanted you safe."

"I'm staying here tonight, but then she's moving into my place. I'm installing a security system as soon as possible and want those cameras where I can see the property on my phone."

Jameson nods and pulls his hand from Mallory's grasp, giving her back the thawing veggies. "Thanks," he says to her before turning his attention to me. "I've got a friend who can give you a recommendation."

"Appreciate it."

"Well, I'm going to head home. Call if you need anything," Jameson says, heading for the door.

I pass him his keys for his Nova and open the door. "Thanks again, man, for everything."

He grips my shoulder and squeezes. "We got your back, man." Jameson leans in and adds quietly, "So does she. She was all sorts of hysterical when she came out of her bedroom, adamant that you were set up."

I grin. "I know. I'm lucky to have her."

He nods and steps into the hallway. "You are. Don't forget it." My oldest friend throws a wave over his shoulder and heads for the stairs.

Once the door is locked, including the knob and a new deadbolt, as well as the chain engaged, I move to my girl. "How about we go lie down?"

Mallory yawns, as if on cue. "I'm ready."

I flip off the light switches and reach for her hand, leading her to the hallway. Our first stop is the small room across the hall. My intention is to merely peek in on her, but my feet carry me to her small bed. I crouch down and brush long blonde curls off her forehead. When my fingers connect with her soft skin, her sleepy green eyes open.

"Walk," she whispers, grinning up at me. "Did you have a fun wide?"

I snort a laugh. "I'm not sure I'd call it fun, but it was interesting, Lizzie."

"Can I snuggle wiff you, Walk?"

Smiling down at the little girl who owns my heart, I reply, "Absolutely."

She tosses off her princess blanket and reaches for me. I scoop her up and carry her across the hall, Mallory hot on my heels. "Wait! My pitcher!"

"Picture?" I ask as Mallory gasps, running out of the room.

Before I can ask what in the world is going on, she returns with a sheet of white paper. Lizzie takes it and holds it up so I can see it. At first, I'm not really sure what I'm looking at. There's a lot of scribbles and what looks like a whale with a shovel.

Then it hits me what I'm looking at.

The words written across the top help.

It says Me and Daddy Walk in blue crayon, too nice to be Lizzie's handwriting.

All the oxygen in the room is sucked out, and I find it hard to breathe. My vision blurs with tears. Tears of joy and pride and shock.

And love.

So much fucking love.

"Dat's you and me," she boasts proudly.

"This is the best picture anyone's ever given me, Lou." My voice doesn't even sound like my own.

With the drawing in one hand, she hugs me with the other, placing a kiss on my scruffy cheek. It tickles her lips and makes her giggle.

"Ready for bed?" Mallory asks, swiping tears from her own eyes.

Her daughter nods, handing over the drawing. When I set her down on the bed, she bounces to the middle and slips under the covers. I grab a pair of the shorts I keep in Mallory's new-to-her dresser and head for the bathroom to change.

Two minutes later, I'm back and dropping onto the bed. I'm exhausted, my body finally able to relax after the day. It's almost eleven o'clock, and I'm so fucking thankful to be here, in this bed with the two I love most in the world, than anywhere else. Mallory's wearing a T-shirt and shorts and facing me, a soft smile on her lips.

"Night, night, Walk," Lizzie whispers, curling into my chest and closing her eyes.

"Night, night, Lou. I love you."

"Wove you," she murmurs, as I bend down and kiss her forehead.

My eyes meet Mallory's over Lizzie's head, and we both smile. "I love you," I whisper, reaching my hand over and grazing my palm against her cheek.

"And I love you, Walker."

Mallory closes her eyes and falls into a deep slumber, and even though I'm tired, I just lie there, watching my girls sleep. Two months ago, I never pictured myself like this. A man who pushed away any sort of intimacy is now cradling it with both hands, as if it were the most important thing in the world.

In a short amount of time, I fell in love. Hard. It was confusing and scary, but I couldn't walk away from it—from *her*—if I tried. She's under my skin and embedded in my heart, right where she's supposed to be.

Finally allowing myself to close my eyes, I fall asleep, happier and freer than ever.

Epilogue

Mallory

"Twick or Tweat!" Lizzie hollers as she runs through the bar, making her way to Walker.

He's already moving, a huge grin on his face as he swoops her up in his arms. "There's my favorite princess witch."

"I weady for candy!" she bellows, making the later afternoon patrons laugh.

"How about you head up to Isaac's office and see what he has for you?" Walker says, setting her down on the ground and laughing as she takes off running. "Good afternoon," he whispers, before pulling me into his arms and kissing me soundly on the lips.

"Hi," I reply once I'm breathless from his kiss.

"Are my girls ready for trick-or-treating?" he asks, seeming to be just as excited to take Lizzie around the neighborhood as she is. He's talked of nothing all week, making sure to schedule extra Saturday help in the bar so he can accompany us. Even though Halloween is falling on the busiest night of the week at Burgers and Brew, Walker still put us first.

"Oh, we're very ready. I took her last year, but only to a few houses of people we knew, since she was only two."

"Well, come on. Let's go see how much sugar Isaac gave her," he states, taking my hand and guiding me to the stairs.

It's been a week since the incident with Devon. I've given my statement in cooperation of the investigation against my ex, as well as spoken to him. Walker wasn't thrilled with my request, but it needed to be done. The detectives working the case arranged to have Devon brought to an interrogation room, but insisted an officer be present during the conversation. I really only had one question, and that was why. Why did he choose drugs over his family? What did he think he'd accomplish by setting Walker up? Why did he break into my apartment that night?

Devon appeared remorseful over his actions, explaining they were merely that of a desperate man. He thought we had a future together, as if we'd just pick back up where we left off before his arrest. Of course, he needed to get Walker out of the way first, which didn't pan out the way he planned.

When I left that jail, I felt freer than I ever have. Even when he's released, which won't be for a few years, I made it clear he has no control over me and the only way he'd see his daughter is if he cleaned up his act. I guess we'll see what happens when we get to that part of the journey.

Walker also moved me into his house that very next day. He sent another SOS text to his friends, who all dropped what they were doing to lend a hand. It took less than an hour to clear out that old apartment of our things and take them to Walker's house. As I stood in that doorway, gazing at the lifeless space, I counted each and every blessing that transpired from our short time in that worn-down apartment.

Mrs. Fritz.

Burgers and Brew.

Walker.

His friends and family.

"Wook!" Lizzie bellows eagerly the moment we join her inside Isaac's office. She holds up a sack as big as she is.

"Holy cow!" I gasp, while she proudly displays her loot from Isaac. She's got king-sized candy bars and full bags of fun-sized ones too. "Isaac!" I chastise, unable to hold back a giggle.

He gives us a sheepish grin. "Sorry, I might have gone a little overboard."

"You think?" I ask.

Walker moves and glances in the bag. "You get any king-sized Snickers for me?" he asks, reaching into the bag.

"I share!" she insists.

"Let's get out of here before she goes into a sugar coma by osmosis," I say.

Isaac runs a hand through his hair. "Uhh, Lizzie's presence is requested in the kitchen."

I glance over in question, but then it hits me. "Seriously?"

He shrugs. "This is our first Halloween with Lizzie. We wanted to make it memorable," he informs us with a shrug.

After we stop in the kitchen to see Jasper—where Lizzie gets a new Halloween coloring book, crayons, and slime—we make one final pit stop to the stage, where Jameson is tuning his guitar for tonight's performance.

"Lizard!" he bellows, a rare grin on his lips as he sets his instrument down on the stand. "How's my favorite princess witch?"

"Dood! Am I a scare-wee pwincess?"

"The scariest princess I've ever seen," he informs, kissing her forehead. Ever since that night in my apartment last week, Lizzie and Jameson have developed a special bond. Jameson reaches behind his stool and hands over another bag of treats. There's enough in here to give her cavities every day for her rest of her life.

"All right, we're gonna head out and go see my mom and aunt. I'll be back at seven," Walker tells Jameson.

"Don't worry about this place. We've got it."

Walker takes my hand in one of his and Lizzie's much smaller one in his other and leads us toward the exit. "Let's do this."

Walker

It's almost eleven, and even though the bar is hopping busy, I take a few seconds to kiss the waiting lips at the end of the bar. Mallory grins as I press my mouth to hers and throws her arms over my shoulders.

"Hi," I whisper, stealing one more kiss before I need to get back to work.

"Hi yourself."

"Knock it off," Jasper grumbles, leaning against the bar beside the stool Mal occupies.

It's Halloween, one of our busiest nights of the year, and it just so happens to fall on a Saturday. The place is packed, at maximum occupancy, which doesn't make the people standing outside happy. A good chunk of our customers are in costumes, and that seems to make everyone a little rowdier than normal. Security has removed two guys already for fighting and warned a group of girls to keep their clothes on.

"You're just jealous," I tease my workaholic friend.

He scoffs, but I don't miss the look that crosses his features. Longing. He tries to hide it by looking away, but it was there, even for only a flash.

"It's almost eleven," Mallory acknowledges, excitement illuminating her green eyes.

"What do you want to hear?" I ask, leaning against the bar.

She shrugs and just grins.

I tap the bar. "All right, Mallory Sargant, I'll play something just for you."

The moment Jameson finishes his last song up on the small stage, I head for the jukebox. Even with patrons trying to give me space, it's still difficult to shuffle through the crowd. Damn, we're busy tonight.

The bar quiets down and waits as I slip the quarter into the machine. I find exactly the number I'm looking for and press for my song selection. The opening beat to "Kickstart My Heart" starts, and the bar goes wild. I haven't played this song since the last time Mallory was here on a Saturday night, which just so happens to be the night I realized she was different. The night I went to sleep with her in my arms and woke with her pressed against me on that lumpy old couch.

It was the start of something great.

Something beautiful and amazing.

The start of us.

I fight my way back to the bar and kiss her neck as I move behind her. Once I'm under the end of the bar and have more room to move, I prepare for tonight's performance. I find my old ballcap and shove it on my head and place my hands on the hardwood. Then, I jump, shifting myself up on the bar effortlessly and quickly.

When I gaze out at all the faces, I can't help but feel damn proud. My friends and I have worked our asses off these last few years, and our hard work shows. We have a successful bar and restaurant, and hopefully soon, a brewery too.

Everyone belts out the song around me, begging me to sing along. Sliding my hat on backward, I start with a little hip roll action, making the ladies go wild. A few dressed like slutty nurses and bunnies in the middle of the room and practically pushing and fighting their way up to the bar where I am. I'm seconds away from getting molested, if they make it up here, so I decide to move.

Besides, they're not the ones I'm dancing and singing for.

I walk toward the end of the bar where my girl is seated, moving to the beat of the song and singing along. When I get to where she sits, I rock my hips and do a little dip. Mallory's face is as a red as the devil costume just off to her left, but she's wearing a huge grin.

I dance and sing for my girl before dropping to my knees. I kick something behind me under the bar, but Jasper's there and catches it. I know she can't hear me singing, since the noise level in this place is deafening, but I do anyway, hoping she understands what I'm saying. She's the one who kickstarted my heart and opened it.

I rock back and thrust my hips upward in a move I saw on *Magic Mike* and laugh when she brings her hands to her face to cover her eyes. I grab her hands though, moving in to claim her lips right here in the middle of my bar, during the song. I'm making a statement.

To her and everyone around us.

The kiss is hard and intense, and if it weren't for all the people screaming and cheering around us, I'd probably get hard.

I finish out the song, singing and dancing for only Mallory. As soon as the song ends, I plaster one more kiss on her lips. "You're keeping your adoring fans waiting," she hollers over the noise.

I shrug. "Don't care. You're the one that matters."

"You know what I'm thinking?" she asks, leaning close and whispering in my ear. "Maybe you can show me that hip roll thrust move later tonight."

A burst of laughter spills from my lips. "You got it, Mal." With one last chaste kiss on her lips, I add, "Love you."

"Love you more."

"Not possible," I reply with a wink before turning and heading back to the middle of the bar. It's time to get back to work.

First, finish serving drinks to a bar full of patrons. Then, close down the bar for the night. Finally, take Mallory home and show my woman how much I love and adore her.

Sounds like one hell of a life to me.

Damn, I'm one lucky bastard. All it took was one woman and a tiny three-year-old to completely turn my world upside down, all for the better. To introduce me to love. To make me see how beautiful the world can be with a little color.

To kickstart my heart.

The End

Don't miss a single reveal, release, or sale! Sign up for my newsletter.

http://www.laceyblackbooks.com/newsletter

Books by Lacey Black

Rivers Edge series

Trust Me, Rivers Edge book 1 (Maddox and Avery) – FREE at all retailers

~ *#1 Bestseller in Contemporary Romance*

Fight Me, Rivers Edge book 2 (Jake and Erin)

Expect Me, Rivers Edge book 3 (Travis and Josselyn)

Promise Me: A Novella, Rivers Edge book 3.5 (Jase and Holly)

Protect Me, Rivers Edge book 4 (Nate and Lia)

Boss Me, Rivers Edge book 5 (Will and Carmen)

Trust Us: A Rivers Edge Christmas Novella (Maddox and Avery)

~ *This novella was originally part of the Christmas Miracles Anthology*

BOX SET – contains all 5 novels, 2 novellas, and a BONUS short story

With Me, A Rivers Edge Christmas Novella (Brooklyn and Becker)

Bound Together series

Submerged, Bound Together book 1 (Blake and Carly)
~ An International Bestseller
Profited, Bound Together book 2 (Reid and Dani)
~A Bestseller, reaching Top 100 on 2 e-retailers
Entwined, Bound Together book 3 (Luke and Sidney)

Summer Sisters series

My Kinda Kisses, Summer Sisters book 1 (Jaime and Ryan)
~A Bestseller, reaching Top 100 on 2 e-retailers
My Kinda Night, Summer Sisters book 2 (Payton and Dean)
My Kinda Song, Summer Sisters book 3 (Abby and Levi)
My Kinda Mess, Summer Sisters book 4 (Lexi and Linkin)
My Kinda Player, Summer Sisters book 5 (AJ and Sawyer)
My Kinda Player, Summer Sisters book 6 (Meghan and Nick)
My Kinda Wedding, A Summer Sisters Novella book 7 (Meghan and Nick)

Rockland Falls series

Love and Pancakes, Rockland Falls book 1
Love and Lingerie, Rockland Falls book 2
Love and Landscape, Rockland Falls book 3
Love and Neckties, Rockland Falls book 4

Standalone

Music Notes, a sexy contemporary romance standalone

A Place To Call Home, a Memorial Day novella

Exes and Ho Ho Ho's, a sexy contemporary romance standalone novella

Pants on Fire, a sexy contemporary romance standalone

Double Dog Dare You, a new standalone

Grip, A Driven World Novel

Co-Written with *NYT Bestselling* Author, Kaylee Ryan

It's Not Over, Fair Lakes book 1

Just Getting Started, Fair Lakes book 2

Can't Get Enough, Fair Lakes book 3

Fair Lakes Box Set

Boy Trouble, The All American Boy Series

Acknowledgments

A HUGE thank you to everyone who helped bring this book to life.

My editing team – Kara Hildebrand, Sandra Shipman, Joanne Thompson, and Karen Hrdlicka. You ladies are THE best!

The book team - Photographer, Wander Aguiar; Model, Pat Tanski; Cover Designer, Melissa Gill; Graphics Designer, Gel with Tempting Illustrations; formatting, Brenda with Formatting Done Wright; and promotions by Give Me Books. I couldn't do it with each of you!! You make it easy and fun.

Kaylee Ryan, Holly Collins, Lacey's Ladies, and my ARC team, thank you for listening, for your encouragements, and for your constant support.

To my husband and kids, thank you for always standing by my side and forgiving me when I submerge myself into my book world. It's not easy, but we make it work together.

To all the bloggers and readers, thank you, thank you, thank you. I hope you enjoy this story as much as I loved writing it.

About the Author

Lacey Black is a Midwestern girl with a passion for reading, writing, and shopping. She carries her e-reader with her everywhere she goes so she never misses an opportunity to read a few pages. Always looking for a happily ever after, Lacey is passionate about contemporary romance novels and enjoys it further when you mix in a little suspense. She resides in a small town in Illinois with her husband, two children, and three rowdy chickens. Lacey loves watching NASCAR races, shooting guns, and should only consume one mixed drink because she's a lightweight.

Made in the USA
Monee, IL
20 March 2021